JAMBACK ROAD

A Novel

Ron Miller

This book is a work of fiction.

Mayhaven Publishing, Inc.
P O Box 557
Mahomet, IL 61853
USA

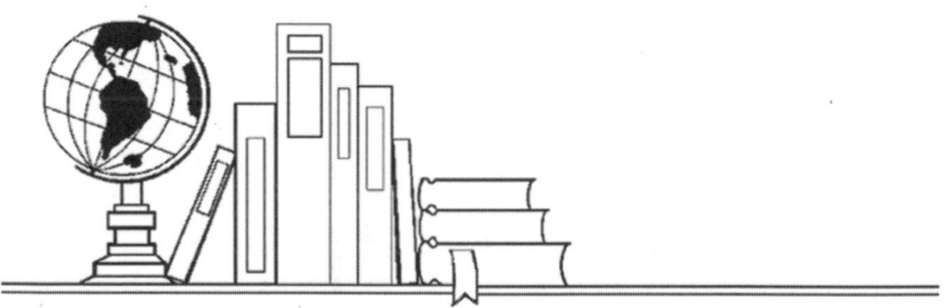

Cover Art: Dee Siegmund

First Edition—First Printing 2014
LOC: 2014949629
ISBN 13: 978 1939695017
ISBN 10: 1939695015

Dedicated To

Kathrine Kyle Clewis Miller

Winter 1960

From "Sweet Mary Asleep in the Snow"

Snow came to our valley today;
Covering all
Like a quilt upon a frame,
Soft, pure, and beautiful, it lay,
Concealing from all but God,
What rested upon the icy grass
Where winter's feet had trod.
Yes, Snow came to our valley today,
But had no plans to stay
And Sweet Mary lay beneath its shield,
And slept the night away.

—Ron Miller

1
Ollie

God made Jamback Road.

The Indians used it first, I guess, wandering down from the hunting trails to find the creek coming off Greenhazel Mountain. I often wondered if the trees were that deep back then, trees so full of themselves their branches nearly touched the ground.

The heavy spring rains must've dug the road out of a clearing, flooding off a rise and leaving the bare earth in its wake.

That's how we found it that autumn as we moved onto rented property again, filling one of the two houses that fronted Jamback. The other house was even further off the nefarious Highway 9, giving shelter to my irreducible uncle and his sweet Miss Jewel.

For some reason, Uncle Doug Thomas spent about as much time at our place as he did at his. His tenure with us, however, usually ended when Momma found his bootleg whiskey hidden under the bathtub, and he had to go stay with Grandad Wilston until Miss Jewel took him back.

On pleasant days, when Doug was feeling right, he'd come hauling up the dirt of Jamback like he was in a hurry to declare himself to the world. Of course we knew he wasn't. Uncle Doug didn't work. Momma said that when he came back from the war, some parts of him got left behind overseas.

I never questioned his world.

But it was that winter, when Jamback was loaded down with a heavy snow and Uncle Doug was put out of the house, more often than not, that he saved me from an odd evil that was chasing my life. He did it with the usual indifference of one smiling and easing his way through creation like he had nothing better to do. In my case, there was simply something in front of him needing doing and he did it.

God must've put Uncle Doug on Jamback Road for me. Seems like I needed him a lot.

One winter day, when school had let out and the remnants of the night's snow lay on the fields, I met my deep-country sidekick Sherman T. by the highway and we walked a few minutes down Highway 9, studying the easy patterns of the snow.

"My momma was talking 'bout you last night, 'O Chosen One'," he said after we'd made time in the cold, our faces red and chapped in the stirring wind. But our need to be outside and free was more important than the lashing from winter.

"I'm chosen all right," I said. "I choose not to see the twilight come because of what the night does to me."

"Bless his heart," Sherm said pathetically, mocking me. "Self-pity is a sin, Ollie. That's what my momma says. But she was lighting up the party line about you. You know how the women gossip.

"And I hope I hurt your feelings by mentioning the whole deal. I'm tired of you being the local hero. I'd like some worship-time at the altar myself."

"Yeah? What have you done worthy of worship?"

Sherm thought for a moment. "Other day I kissed Bonnie Bitt on the lips and ran like a cheap paint job."

I shook my head and bent over to find a nice-size rock to launch skyward. It traveled over a snowbank and disappeared into the darkening woods.

"Course," Sherm said, "it took some guts to go poking around a smelly cave where tar bats and rat intestines were scattered all over the place. Maybe no guts involved, come to think of it. You just got caught up in stupid."

We walked in silence, both reluctant to let the winter sun go away, even though it had been trying to put an end to our one annual snowfall.

"God's truth, Ollie. What's it like to kiss a God-graced beautiful woman? I know I'll never get past planting one on the innocent virgin Bonnie."

"You think I'm the kinda person'd kiss a pretty girl and tell a rank butt crack like you?"

Before Sherm could retort, we shifted our feet to the side of the road as a speeding car came spinning along through the slush, heading north toward Piedmont.

I didn't give the car any particular thought. But after a while I heard a gnashing of gears behind us and a motor raced as a car sped toward us through the icy remnants of the retreating snow.

"Some cowboy in a junker's heading toward our backside," Sherman warned. "We'd better move over and give 'im a place to pass."

Laughing, we stepped further to the shoulder of the road. I caught a side view as the dark form seemed to grow larger and louder as it approached us. I looked back to see a pointed hood coming toward us like a winged bat out of that provincial Nance Creek cave I'd stumbled over months before in my pursuit of the greatly-dismembered brothers. Now it was obvious that the driver was tracking straight for us with deadly intent, the menacing engine screaming in protest as the rear tires spun in a rage, trying to gain traction in the snow and ice of the gathering twilight.

Sherman T. saw the approaching death barge as quickly as I did, but he moved quicker, grabbing my jacket by the sleeve and pulling me out of the path of sudden death. We both fell sideways into the thawing mud of the ditch as the rugged sedan's front bumper passed through the space we had recently occupied. Then with a screaming of machinery and an ignorance of the laws of physics, the car disappeared around the next bend in the road.

I looked down at the sheet-white face of Sherman T., his body twisted and tangled under mine in the soft, clinging mud. I couldn't put a word into my mouth, couldn't think any thought except horror. Sherman got loose from me, and searched until he found a rock to throw—in futile retaliation—toward the car that had tried to end our day, disappeared in the dying of deepest twilight.

The wind was quiet that night, like it had been the night before when the gentle whiteness of winter fell, minding its own business, and proud of itself, I guess. I was feeling no pride at all.

My back was hurting from where Momma gave me a couple of lashes with the lamp cord. Ruining school clothes by sliding through a muddy ditch was reason enough to take a few shots. So I just took them and didn't say anything about why I dove into the ditch. And she didn't ask. She simply let that snake whistle through the air like its punishment would've kept the incident from happening.

I guess the other kids thought I was deserving because nobody came to my defense. They just watched as if Momma lined them up and made them. She rebuked me about my disregard for the family, but she seemed a little reluctant to punish me. There wasn't any contrition for my wounds.

"Slowly, Slowly Run, O Horses of the Night."

I read that line in a senior literature anthology today at school, and in study hall, my friend Genevieve underlined it with her pencil. Then she pushed it across the table for me to read again.

Evie was the Baptist preacher's daughter, so she was nice to everyone—even a soulful vagabond like me. She knew I loved literature, so she often gave me tidbits of her senior notes or poems. She wrote nice poetry about God and shared them with everyone. I tried to write a poem for her, but I had writer's block even before I wrote, "I get all sweaty when I think of you." Then I imagined what her adopted, but highly protective brother Raike would do when he saw that. I quickly scribbled it out. Raike was an all-right guy but he could handle a skinny guy like me without much effort.

At any rate, the phrase seemed to resonate in my head as I lay there thinking about the absolute possibilities of my imminent demise. I didn't want to walk the deadly blacktop of Highway 9 again. I didn't want to hear another car speeding toward me from behind, or feel the haunting reality of someone chasing Sherm and me toward a ruthless death. How much terror could my mind absorb?

I wanted to lay in bed and let those horses of the night run with me tied to them. All I could think of was where would they carry me?

Would it be a better place?

2

"Give every man thy ear, but few thy voice."

—William Shakespere

It was cold as a weasel's hammer the next morning.

But I got up like I always did, splashed cold water on my face to get rid of the night, and brushed my teeth. Breakfast was hot biscuits and sugar syrup. At least Momma called it syrup. It was actually boiled water laced with a little sugar to give it flavor.

The bus was waiting impatiently where Jamback connected to 9. Self-pity was all over me as I climbed on board and sat alone, hoping the older kids would ignore me as I tried to sort out my feelings from the previous day's events. The bus would creep and crawl its wavering path down the highway and eventually find the spot where Sherm and I had bailed out into the muddy ditch. My back felt raw and my face slightly feverish from the punishment.

I could guess how Sherm had handled the situation. He probably went home after the muddy slide, burst into the house where his parents would be sitting in the living room listening to the radio, show them his filthy clothes, and demand that his dad do something about the renegade that had tried to mow us down.

Mr. Monte would study the situation without saying much, but he would be fully alert, his calm exterior covering the anger that lurked beneath the surface. Something cowardly and senseless directed at his son—or someone else's son—usually drew Monte to the "stirrups." He'd be ready to ride like the vengeful Confederates of Plunkett's Hill, chasing the raiders that had come like the wind into our isolated valley.

After a while, the bus ground to a stop near Sherman's house, and he and his past-gorgeous sister got on board. Sherm looked as wrapped up in himself as I was when he sat down next to me like he did every morning.

I didn't say anything, just watched Sherm's older sister pass by my bashful brother Billy Rand, whose face got red just being in the proximity of such beauty. She smiled at brother Billy and I saw a thin, pleasing upturn in his usually sealed lips. How Sherm had such a beautiful sister was the greatest mystery of the universe. I'd heard other boys at school talk about how the Monte family was divided into two camps—those children that deserved to live and those that should have been euthanized at birth. Sherm fell into the latter category.

"You tell anybody about our great mudslide?" Sherm asked, looking straight ahead as the bus groaned and swayed like an old horse about to fall over exhausted.

I shook my head and turned my attention to a place on the ceiling so I wouldn't have to see the near-death scene as we rumbled past. The old bus would coast down the coming hill, round the infamous curve, and be right on the historic death-at-twilight ditch.

"I told my pop he should catch up to this toad and put a necktie on his redneck."

I looked at Sherm. "How we gonna identify anybody? All I saw was that hood coming right at us and a black jalopy disappearing 'round the curve. What other information do you have, Sherlock?"

"Don't go high ball on me, Ollie. I ain't got no crystal ball or nothin'. I just figured that weren't no accident. Remember—that cat stopped down the highway a while and thought about it before he got up a full head of steam and started after us. I reckon he'll head back toward us again one day and take another shot. Me? I plan to be ready for his sneaky butt."

"How?"

He pulled up the bottom of his coat, looked around to check for stray eyes, and grinned as he opened the flap of his jacket pocket. I saw the grey metal of some type of firearm concealed beneath a dirty rag.

My eyes got big. Even I was surprised at the stupidity of my friend.

"I hope you know that you're crazy, Sherman," I said in a whisper that had an edge to it. "What about Gorman? He'll be all over you."

"You gonna tell 'im?"

"Of course not."

We rode in silence, and I forgot about the upcoming twilight sight.

"Is that thing loaded?"

"Cat got a butt?"

I shook my head in amazement. "That rascal ain't likely to drive by the bus and try to pick us off as we disembark," I reasoned. "It's when we're out prowling the highway or off on the farm roads that the fool will try again. And you can't take that porkchop with you every where you go."

"Can't hurt to be ready. Besides, I know how to leave one cylinder empty so I won't shoot my toe off."

"Put that big momma in your locker and leave it there till no one's looking. You'll get expelled if Gorman finds out."

"Relax. I had it at school last year on a practice run. Never told nobody. Never got a flag."

"Well, don't try to impress Bonnie and whip it out. Sherm, you set new standards for stupid."

"You think Bonnie even speaks to me?"

"Thought you got some lip time on that sweetie."

"I lied. Just baiting you on that North reporter babe. Looking for any crumb of excitement in my dull and meaningless life."

"I won't even answer that."

Sherm pointed out the window. "I still see our skid marks in the snow," he said. "Look at that spot, Ollie."

I refused to look.

Sherm laughed. "Scared, ain'tcha?"

"Scared of how stupid you are. Don't come near me today."

"How do I manage that? We got all the dumb-butt classes together. Want me to go sit with the ones that really want to come to school?"

"Just hide that Civil War relic in your locker. Better yet, don't take it out of the jacket. Put the whole mess in there."

"You're kidding, right? Ain't no room for a jacket. 'Sides, I need the coat on me to ward off the cold of gym class."

"Then stay your silly butt away from me. I ain't taking a rap for your loss of appropriate mental functions."

Sherm muttered something inaudible and looked around for Bonnie Bitt. She was sitting two seats up on the bleachers with the junior high girls. She gave "Monte the Gunrunner" a dirty look and all her little friends giggled like Dixie.

Sherm smirked at her and carefully rearranged his gun holster pocket.

School went on without much regard for my steeped-in-the-blues soullessness. Sherman lugged that heavy pistol around in his coat pocket, surprising me to the edge of insanity that he got away without one of the teachers checking his awkward leaning to the gun side. In our school, however, the teachers sometimes ignored us more than they paid attention.

Whatever mischief the older boys got into—like putting an old car tire over the flag pole or tying a pair of girl's bloomers to the principal's office door—mainly went down in history as simplistic pranks as long as nobody got hurt in the process or thought much about why it shouldn't happen.

Sherman and I, being sophomores, and not exactly giants in the academic sense of things, laid out of the student spotlight and contented ourselves with watching the unobtainable, grandly-blessed senior girls as they dallied with the senior boys and looked past us like we were invisible.

It was while watching these female dolls rule the docile domain of underclassmen that a new player strut his "fine hour upon the stage." He came into our valley with the credentials of a crown prince, with the attitude of one of blue blood descent, and most importantly of all, driving a new Chevy that was rumored to have the highest performance engine that General Motors had ever developed. The mystery of the new car's engine laid more curiosity on my heart than my inquiring mind could withstand.

The day after the near-death-at-twilight incident, I got off the morning bus and saw the bright red Impala ease into the student parking area, a neglected piece of land within sight of the gym door and close to the vocational shop. Only students with cars, or their friends, were allowed on that sacred part of the campus.

Without regard for my own safety, I moved across the mud of the courtyard to the thin gravel of privileged parking. Subconsciously, I knew I was inviting danger. I was courting another near-death experience, but the pull of the that car, as it found its place, was more than I could resist.

I wasn't hesitant at all. I simply walked past the stunned group of senior slickers—their ducktail haircuts lathered with a greasy base of Brillo Cream, their worn leather jackets advertising their devotion to the shop class where they smoked, chewed gum, and whistled at the pretty girls—without fear of Mr. Luthin's disciplining their wanton activities.

As I started my inspection walk around the car, I was surprised to see a couple of layers of mud covered part of the rear quarter and the whitewall tires—like they'd been caught in an agrarian nightmare for city cars, venturing out where tractors and farm pickups roamed. But the fresh paint and the powerful exhaust of the high torque engine held my attention much as a nervous viper holds its prey hypnotized. While walking with my head down and my peripheral areas exposed, I bumped into one of the greasers that had about as much chance of graduating as God did finding peace on earth among all men.

"Whatcha doin' down here with the seniors, Jamback?" he asked with a snarl.

That brought me back to reality and a whispering from my better senses said my trip into automotive fantasy was over. I looked into the boy's pimpled complexion and got a whiff from his dirty breath.

"Brush those pearlies this morning?" I asked.

"You done wandered off the kiddie playground ain'tcha, boy?"

By now the other half dozen or so miscreants had taken note of my trespassing and they were eager to make my sin a federal case.

"Why you lookin' at this cool car, cellar dweller? Your daddy gonna buy you one, too?"

Much laughter erupted from the ones with the duck-tail haircuts.

"Wait a minute," a delinquent named Dirk said. "Don'tcha boys know who this here cat is? He's the one found them chopped up bodies in that cave up at Nance Creek. He's a hometown hero."

"Shore 'nuff," one of the other boys laughed. "That's Billy Rand's little brother. They live down on Jamback Road in one of them snappy, all-season tarpaper houses."

"What's 'at?" the first stupid asked. "What season?"

"Any season," Dirk jibed. "Weather don't matter to them boys. Holes in the wall so big you can throw a cat outside without opening the door."

They all laughed and hooted.

"Wait a minute. Wait a minute," came the next voice from the crowd. "We gotta be nice to this kid. Him and Eness Voit goin' steady now. They rode off in the night awhile back at Silver Run. Just the two of 'em in 'at black Ford. Ya gotta know this ain't only a local hero, but he rides shotgun on the fastest car in the county."

They all howled sarcastically.

"It's not the fastest anymore." Dirk's clear, strong voice could be heard over the raucous laughter, "Moorefield's got 'em all covered."

The boys whooped and hollered, and before I could head back to safe ground, I found myself face-to-face with the self-anointed crown prince—the new kid on the block.

He did not belong at our school.

We were mostly dirt poor kids from dirt poor families. Some had nice houses and decent cars, but not many. Mostly, we were just kids in a country school run by teachers doing the best they could with meager training.

I wondered why his family had decided to move into our neighborhood. His dad was a big-time lawyer and they belonged to the Bentonville Country Club. The Greek god was tall and lithe, wore light wool slacks that must have come from Birmingham or Atlanta. His hair was slightly curly, and it hung in sissy ringlets that covered his forehead—except they weren't really sissy looking. On him, they looked good. He looked so good, compared to our denim and home haircuts, the valley girls fell over in his wake as he strolled through the dim school hallways. He was the coolest thing in our valley since country radio.

"Tell you what, kid," Golden Boy was saying to me, "tell your buddy Voit that I'll be out looking for him this weekend. Tell 'im I got a wad of money that says my little Chevy will eat that black poot of a Ford for supper. Can you remember all that?"

I shrugged. "I have a question. Tell me, boy racer, why is your beautiful new car covered with a shellacking of cornfield debris? You boys in the Carolinas into that mud racing?"

His top lip curled up. "What's your name, boy?" he asked.

"Somerset Maugham."

He snarled and took a step toward me. I stood my ground.

"You boys catch that smell?" he asked without looking at his crew. He continued eyeing me. "That's the smell of cotton row, dressed in overalls. Don't be coming back over here, Maugham. You might get hurt next trip."

"Fortunately for you," I bluffed, "I was ready to head back over to where the normal kids are. The intellectual quotient of this group is somewhere between slow and slower."

I was ready to get back to my own side of town. And I wanted to bust that smiling face in the ordering mouth but I knew what our family rules were on fighting. Besides, he had Luthin's underachievers as his backup. I had no one watching my back.

Well, maybe one. One good one.

"Y'all leave Oliver alone," a strong, clear voice defended me from the direction I needed to travel.

I didn't have to look. I knew the voice. It was Raike Creed's, my friend Evie's brother. A senior, his presence on my side meant I was crossing out of enemy territory into a safe haven.

"Why you taking up for that pilgrim?" The new kid's voice whisked past me to where Raike was walking toward us.

"Oliver has lots of friends in this school, Moorefield. It would be best if you left off your bullying and got back with your delinquent crowd."

The delinquent crowd laughed, but not a single one stepped forward to challenge Raike.

"I'm just using that little snot to deliver a message for me, Raike. No harm in that. Matter of fact, I rescued this boy from a severe reproach from these guys. You gotta appreciate my good intentions."

"Your intentions won't be discussed, Moorefield. Just leave this kid alone."

"I'll cut you some slack this time, preacher boy. But don't make it a habit of crossing my path."

Raike laughed back at Moorefield as he stood even with me.

"You're right. We shouldn't travel in the same circles, but be clear, big man on a small campus, don't spread your big-time too far. Preachers' boys can take care of themselves, too."

There was a long silence. No more laughing. No more taunts or threats as Raike and I headed back to our side of the schoolyard.

"Don't associate with him, Ollie," Raike said. "He's just trash all dressed up."

I wasn't especially proud of myself for rebuking the shop boys—or Golden Boy. But securely beyond their reach, I covered myself in arrogance. I would go my way to class and they would linger in the shadows of the shop class, wisecracking and horse playing while the morning slipped along.

The day did not get any better.

Second period, I had Mrs. Finkle for American History. Our assignment had been to write a letter, or an original story, dealing with the American Civil War. I had jotted my work down hastily—had not proofread it—but at least I was ready to face the class and read my essay aloud.

Mrs. Finkle was as stern as teachers came. I usually found myself in the middle on most grades, never impressing her with my discussion questions. She had favorites. Those kids that were student government leaders, cheerleaders, or football players received her accolades and smiles. The kids from around Indian Rock and Jamback Road sat in the back of the class and kept quiet.

"Oliver," she said coldly, looking down her glasses toward me. "Did you complete your written assignment?"

"Yes, ma'am."

"Come to the front of the class and read your paper."

For all my shyness, when I walked to the front of the class, it was like another part of my brain kicked in gear. I had a role to play and I never feared speaking in front of a group. Even if the chosen ones were not my friends, they had to listen to me. I didn't hesitate to begin reading aloud:

> All day it had been rainy and cold, slicing through my body and into my soul. It was a coldness that was so encompassing that my entire spirit ached for relief, searched for any source of warmth or reassurance of hope. But it was not as cold or as penetrating as the notion of death that had marched beside me throughout the morning. I was sixteen years old, and for the first time in my life I knew what death, and war, and darkness of spirit was. I knew because I had witnessed...

"Wait a minute!" Mrs. Finkle interrupted me. "I wanted original essays or letters. Not something copied from a book."

I stood quietly in front of the class. My self-confidence ebbed away.

Mrs. Finkle came from behind her desk, reached for the paper, and snatched it abruptly from my hands.

"Young man, I should send you to Mr. Gorman for disciplinary action. Did you not know that it is morally and legally wrong to copy someone else's work and pass it off as your own?"

I was confused. I didn't know what to do.

"Sit down! You'll receive an *F* for this grade."

I went back to my seat with my head bowed, my face red.

Apparently, however, Mrs. Finkle was not through with my reprimand.

She followed me to my seat, admonishing me about plagiarism as the other students snickered all around me. I sat down and looked straight at the top of my desk.

"I should send you to see Mr. Gorman," she continued her tirade toward me, tapping my paper with her finger as she decided what else she could do to me. I was still confused and uncertain of my actions. I knew I could not represent myself, nor could I dispute a teacher's reprimand. She was the authority in the class.

When I thought the situation was coming to its close, and had decided I would accept an *F,* and not tell anybody when I got home, my not-so-bashful friend Sherman decided to wade into the confrontation. He sat next to me and out of the corner of my eye, I saw him raise a hand in objection to the teacher's accusations.

"Mrs. Finkle," he spoke clearly and strongly. Sherm had been to the office so many times for discipline matters that he'd gotten to the point of saying pretty much whatever he pleased at school.

I glanced sideways and tried to mouth "be quiet" to him, but he was on a mission to save me from further embarrassment.

"I guarantee Ollie wrote that there paper," he said firmly.

Mrs. Finkle was momentarily startled by Sherm's voice. Now she seemed uncertain what to do.

"And what business is it of yours, Sherman? Is this just a case of one Jamback person coming to save another?"

"No, ma'am, it's a case where you're wrong and the student is right."

"What!" Her face became livid.

I risked a peek at her, but quickly focused on my desktop. Sherman, though, was not afraid of Mrs. Finkle one notch.

"Ollie there's been writin' since he was about ten years old. I seen him start writin' a book one time and he got a lot of pages done, but he finally quit and hid it under his bed. You can talk to his momma about it. She encourages him a lot to do his writin'. So does Mrs. Murray, the English teacher down the hallway. Sometimes, in the summer, I go over to his house and he's writin' stuff and won't come outside to go fishing or nothin'. No, ma'am, I think you're wrong on this deal, and you need to apologize to my good buddy and let him finish readin' his paper."

Mrs. Finkle flared right up. "Sherman Monte," she said, "you cannot talk to a teacher as you just have. I ought to send you to the office with Oliver."

Sherman grinned. "It ain't nothin' to me to get sent to the office. Send me if you want to. But Ollie, there, ain't never been sent—on account his momma'll whip him with a cord off a old lamp when he gets home. Mrs. Holmes don't put up with no nonsense at school. Me? I don't care what you do to me. Talk's free as air. I just say my piece."

"That does it! Sherman. Go to the office."

Sherm shrugged. "Oh, I'll go down there if you tell me to, Mrs. Finkle. But what you're doin' to Ollie ain't right. And since he can't speak for himself, well, somebody has to see about justice being done."

Mrs. Finkle went back to her desk to get out a sheet of paper to write Sherman up for talking out, but just as she started writing the bell rang to end the period. She seemed further confused as to what to do.

"Class is dismissed—except for Holmes and Monte!" she finally screeched.

The other kids got up laughing and filed out the door, staring at Sherm and me. I figured life as I knew it was about to end. Monte was right. If I was sent to the office, Momma would destroy me when I got home.

"Oliver," Mrs. Finkle said acidly. "You sit back there every day so meek and mild and never contribute to the class. I try to include you people, with your muddy shoes and ragged clothes, and you make a show like you've done today. Oliver, I know you did not write this paper. Your test grades are mediocre and your intelligence is the same."

I looked at her red face and didn't say a word. Sherman wasn't through with his part, however.

"Lookie here, Mrs. Finkle," he said in protest. "You can say these things when the class is out of sight, but Oliver don't deserve none of your criticism. Sure, he's quiet in class, 'cause of what I told you. But you ain't got no right to lite in on him. Send me to Gorman and I'll take the licks. Ain't nothin' to me to get a whopping. But you ain't doin' my friend wrong."

Mrs. Finkle was almost out of control.

"Both of you get out of my sight! Oliver, you get an *F*! Sherman, I'll think about writing you up for the principal tomorrow. You'll hear from me."

I grabbed Sherm's arm and pushed him out the door ahead of me.

"Why did you let that old woman talk to you like that, Ollie?" he asked as we started down the hallway.

"She's the teacher, Sherm. She can do what she pleases."

"What's wrong's wrong. You just gonna take that *F*?"

"What choice do I have?"

"I'll give ole Gorman a earful tomorrow when I get called in."

"Don't take any licks for me, Sherm. Apologize to that old girl and let's drop it."

"Drop it? She'll be on our pink heinies the rest of the year. You just watch and see."

So time went on without me. And before Gorman could figure out who was involved in the parking lot face-off, or receive a disciplinary note on Sherman and me from Mrs. Finkle, the afternoon bell let school out and I rode the bus home thinking about an old joke I'd heard one time: "Dear Dorothy Dix, I am in the worse fix..."

It was no joke for me, however. I needed a high shot of sunshine to brighten up a failing winter day.

I'd been home about thirty minutes when big boy Sherman came flying down our dirt road like a truckload of Dixiecrats was after him.

"Ollie-ho," he sang out, his big Schwinn sliding in the loose gravel as he hit his brakes. "Apparently, you ain't heard."

"Heard what?"

"You know that old Cooper's farm near the dam? Old Goofy's place?"

"You mean the Dixie Flash? The bombed-out-bomber from the war?"

"Yeah, you know Goofy. You can throw a rock at him and he won't bat an eye."

"So, what's he done? Thrown his momma down the well?"

"Naw. He found a dead body down by the dam, covered over with snow."

My spirits came looking for me. My shoulders lifted. "Who says?"

"Old Miss Carpface, the Cooper's neighbor. They used her telephone to call the sheriff. She says the law's down there now pickin' up the body."

"Tell me who it was."

"I Will when I find out. Get yore bike. Hurry. We ain't got much time."

I ran for my rusty Western Flyer I usually kept up on the porch.

My sister Ryder came out the door as I started down the steps with it.

"Where you headed?" she barked.

"Tell Momma I've gone with Sherman."

"You tell her."

I gave her a disgusted look but didn't have time to argue. The soul-changing incident had found its way into my pathetic life.

"Diddly squat, Ollie," Sherman said. "That front tire's flat."

"It'll warm up," I replied as I stood on the pedals and cut grass for the world beyond Jamback.

After a few miles, I calmed down and stopped by old Evil-Eye Ford's filling station to put some air in the tire. She didn't come out the door to see who it was. Before her husband was shot and killed while doing duty as a full-fledged Ku Klux Klansman, she'd always come outside and dog-cuss us boys for using her air hose. Now she was kinda quiet and just kept the store. I almost felt sorry for her except Sherm's dad said Mr. Ford belonged to the West End Klan that liked to scare colored folks—and sometimes harm them. I didn't give much with folks out to hurt others. Somehow that didn't seem God-like. But here lately my sins had piled up one on another so I wasn't one to judge anybody.

I needed to get busy getting my own things seen about. For sure this body thing needed seeing about.

"Who was it he found?" I asked Sherman when we got a chance to coast a bit down Highway 9 before it gave off to the dam road.

"Carpface didn't know. Thought it was a girl."

"A girl? Lordy, Sherman, every girl we know was at school today."

"Sara Kate was out sick. I heard Bonnie tell another girl."

"Couldn't be her. You said the body was *under* snow. It had to be put there night before last."

"Way I heard it, old Goofy saw the girl's arm hanging out of the snow yesterday and told his momma one a' his war buddies was hid out dead in the snow. She didn't pay him no mind because he wanders off 'round the valley at night thinkin' he's still in the war. His brother Adam found the girl for sure today."

"What would any girl be doing at the Coopers? Everybody's scared of old Goofy."

"I don't do 'em, bud," he said. "I just report 'em."

Although there were not many telephones in the vast run of the valley, word of unusual occurrences traveled pretty fast through the farming community. And when we finally got to the dam road, we crossed our fingers past the old Confederate cemetery. And we hit high gear the last mile or so to the old farm 'cause we were starting to lather up like a horse in a Saturday matinee. The wind had died off considerably but that cold still hit our faces like it meant business, and we knew it did, so we just ducked our chins low and kept pedaling. It was heading toward four in the afternoon by then, and the retreating sun sneaked off behind the clouds, ready to give up the day.

There was a fair collection of cars and trucks there when we finally made Coopland. I recognized the sheriff's car and the state trooper's car. They were the ones who persuaded Billy Rand and me to help find that cave a few months back up at Nance Creek. All I had to do to recall that rainy evening was to close my eyes and the butt-naked images of those axed bodies ran over me like a spider web over the soul. But that was the other story. That other life.

A white sedan delivery wagon was there, backed up to the dam and Deputy Short and some other uniforms were holding people back a good piece. I saw Mr. Monte, Sherman's dad, standing in a group of farmers off down the dirt road. Several pickups and farm tractors were pulled in along the edge of that dismal played-out cotton field, the drivers craning to get a look at the latest death embodiment in our usually tranquil valley.

I wanted to angle in where I could maybe see the body, it being covered by that morgue wagon and crowd of uniforms near it. I threw my bike into a bush and motioned for Sherman to follow me up the face of the dam. We scampered through the undergrowth until we ridged out on top of the piled earth, then we walked to the backside of where the authorities were. It was a brilliant plan except the dam curved off toward the woods right quick-like, and we had to go tree-to-tree straight down to approach the spot where we could see.

But we got there too late.

Just as we broke foliage, and could pick up a perfect look at the site where the body was, the door to the county morgue sedan slammed shut and there was nothing to see except a lot of lawmen shaking their heads, talking and pointing, all looking grim.

I was particularly surprised to see Mr. Gorman there, talking to Highway Patrolman Bishop. They couldn't see us, squatted down in the bushes, looking for air like we were breathing through a soda straw.

"What's Gorman up to?" Sherman asked. "Maybe it was Sara Kate."

"Naw," I gasped back. "I bet they wanted him to identify the girl too, if it was one of his students. He knows every sinner in the valley."

"Oh, yeah. Reckon he'll tell us tomorrow?"

"Your dad's over there," I said pointing to a group of overalled men under a far tree. "He'll find out."

"You know that big patrolman," Sherm said. "Go ask him who it was."

"You kidding me? He'd bite my head off and spit it over the dam into the lake."

So we didn't find out who the body under the sheet was.

I was too freaked by the law officers to go winging up to them and blurt out a silly question that would elicit a look of scorn, so we just wandered close to where the body had apparently been, receiving some deadly looks from a young state trooper. Then we slithered over to the group of men that included Sherm's dad.

I liked Mr. Monte. If he liked you, he was kind and smiling. If he didn't like you, he'd just as soon throw a rope around your Adam's apple and squeeze until your lungs jumped outta your chest. That's what Sherm and I decided, anyway. We figured out he was the leader of the Valley Troop— not to be confused with the Ku Klux Klan—but I understood their uniforms were identical, and if you were on the receiving end of their attention, I don't reckon you'd much care if they were from one side of Cottaquilla Mountain or the other. One fat rope was same as the next when it was your neck getting stretched.

Mr. Monte was the Grand Wizard of the Troop.

I'd read in a discarded college textbook, one of my older brother's brought home, that Bedford Forrest was called the "Wizard of the Saddle." That was because of his Civil War Cavalry encounters with the damn Yankees. After the war, when Forrest was asked to help guide the beginning startup of the Invisible Empire—a name Robert E. Lee had used when he had kindly refused the offer of directing that carpetbag-hating group—it seemed natural that he be given the title of Grand Wizard of the Klan. At least that's what the book said, so I believed it.

I always wanted to question Mr. Monte about the goings on of his bunch. Sometimes he'd lay out a few crumbs of thought for me to ponder, and sometimes he dismissed me with a wave of his heavy, calloused hand as he headed for a seat on his porch swing.

We caught up with him just before he started back toward his mud-covered farm truck. "How'd you boys get this far over?" he asked, yanking the door handle on his truck that looked like a refuge from a Russian winter.

"Got our bikes over yonder," Sherman replied, motioning toward the bushes where we'd left our wheels. "Who was that got themselves a ride in the meat wagon, Pop?"

"Wasn't anybody we'd know, son. Y'all get on back to the house before it gets dark."

"Was it boy or girl?" Sherm persisted.

" 'Best I heard it was a girl, but she weren't one that went to school with you boys. Mr. Gorman couldn't recognize her."

"Was she about our ages?"

"Mite older—maybe seventeen, eighteen," he said.

"Was she naked?"

"Hush that talk, Sherman. This here is serious business. You know all you need to know. Get that bicycle working and get on home."

"How 'bout we throw our bicycles in back of the truck and ride home, Pop? Mighty cold out here."

"Seems I recall you rode them wheels over here. I suggest you ride 'em back. I didn't invite you to come."

Mr. Monte cranked the truck, leaving us in a cloud of blue smoke that did the best it could to dissipate in the afternoon cold. But mainly, it just clogged our nostrils as the ugly truck moved slowly up the dirt road.

Sherman swore considerably at being left behind, then followed me back toward the bikes. The crowd was beginning to break up and night was nibbling at our heels. We went slower up the road than we'd come down. Even thoughts of a fresh ghost joining those already prowling through the Confederate Cemetery wasn't enough to urge our tired legs on the pedals. But the cold was getting itself set for a long night's run so I forgot Sherm and rode for home.

In the twilight of Jamback, I pondered the day's happenings and slowed my pace, gathering my courage before I looked for the cold doorknob that would pass me into the house.

The day had been a challenge. I thought back on the run-in with Moorefield, Mrs. Finkle's tirade, and the dead body in the shadow of the dam. I liked to dwell on the intrigue, not the reality, of the girl that had been left to the elements. The great mystery of the body in the snow was a cause of concern.

"Somebody told me about some trouble at school today," Momma said, sitting in the big chair near the kitchen, her Bible open on her lap. Throughout the house I could smell the overwhelming call of supper, but my stomach would have to wait.

"Nothing big." I sat down on the coarse couch. Stuffing oozed out the arm and the cushions sagged under me.

"What were you doing buddying up with those greasy-haired boys from King's Farm Road?"

"I was only looking at a car," I defended.

"Always a car, Ollie."

"And the other thing worked out okay."

"What other thing?"

I knew little sister Ryder liked to gloat as she tattled to Momma about my sins of the day. Had Ryder heard about what happened in Ms. Finkle's class? I was sure she'd leave no tale untold.

"I got up to read my paper on the Civil War," I said. "I wrote it last night, but when I got through only a couple of sentences, Mrs. Finkle interrupted me and accused me of plagiarism in front of the class."

"What did you say?"

I shrugged.

"Did you not defend yourself?" she asked.

"No, ma'am."

She looked down at her Bible. "Not a word?" she asked.

"No, ma'am."

"She send you to the office?"

"No, ma'am."

She studied her Bible, holding the cheap reading glasses to her face because a part of the frame was missing.

"You did the right thing."

I took a long breath.

"What did Sherman T. say?"

I was startled.

"Ma'am?"

"Sherman T. I know he couldn't stay quiet."

"No, ma'am. He tried to argue with the teacher that I was right and she was wrong."

"The teacher's always right."

I nodded.

"Sherman go to the office?"

"No ma'am. Not yet anyway."

She finished her Bible reading and started toward the kitchen to see about supper. "What did you learn about the dead body?" she asked.

I walked behind her, feeling relieved now that I'd short-circuited Ryder's condemning testimony at supper.

"We got there too late. They were closing her up in the morgue truck when we arrived."

"A girl? Anybody we know?"

"No, just a stranger."

"Why would a strange girl be caught up in that big snow 'other night?"

"I don't know. Sherman'll talk to his dad tonight and maybe we'll learn something tomorrow."

"All the girls at school today? Ones you know?"

"Yes. Gorman was there checking her out."

"*Mr.* Gorman," she corrected.

"He didn't know her, either."

"That patrol captain there?"

"Yes, but I was afraid to ask him anything."

"Probably wise not to approach him."

She was nearly finished preparing the potatoes. "Get your sisters to set the table and wash your hands."

I started to back out of the kitchen.

"Oliver," she said looking at me with those grey, penetrating eyes. "You did right obeying the teacher."

I nodded and hurried out to find Ryder.

"You know what, though?" she called.

I stopped again and looked back at her.

"Don't let one unknowing person discourage you. There'll be others to reject you, but God gave you a gift. Make sure you use it wisely and fully."

I was especially joyful as I ran to confront Ryder. My appetite suddenly returned and I realized I'd not eaten since breakfast.

3

"Stars over snow,
And in the West a planet
Swinging below a star."

—Sara Teasdale

Sherman came over after school the next day.

He was in an all-fire hurry to get back over to the Coopers to see if we could find out any more about the dead girl.

He'd talked to his dad, and it seemed whoever had dumped the body had taken great care to place her gently on her last bed of rest and covered her with a coat to ward off the snow. Only the snow had deposited itself heavily in that part of the valley, completely covering the girl. Goofy's finding hadn't amounted to anything. It took his brother Lyle's uncovering of her body to get the attention of the local folks.

Maybe I should have been bolder and asked Captain Bishop about the situation, but being the way he was, I knew he wouldn't reveal any mysteries to me that he wouldn't tell anybody else, so I had to read about the case in the paper at the Ford store—until old Evil-Eye came out the door. She pulled the paper from my hands and put it back in the rack. She knew I was the only one really interested in the murder, and she figured I didn't plan on making payment.

I didn't have a nickel, so I just got on my bike and lazily circled the lot waiting for Sherman to arrive so we could get out of range of those eyes that could melt steel. Evil-Eye Ford should have hunted up Time and killed it. She got uglier by the minute.

I didn't have the paper long enough to see two new bylines. I'd started noticing such things since the last murder that took place in our valley. I'd been close to that fellow Winston from the newspaper, and to the reporter Miss North. I was still hoping to hear from her one day. She was prettier than Lauren Bacall and smarter than a college professor. If she'd told me the world was ending in forty-eight hours, I'd go kiss the prettiest girl in school, tell Mrs. Finkle to suck a persimmon, and hide Momma's whipping snake so the other kids could live happily for the last few hours of their Creation.

The new female reporter's last name was Lane, but I didn't reckon I'd have a call to meet up with her. Her story seemed a bit more objective and less biting than her co-worker's.

Wintertime was itself and I wore Billy Rand's old jacket and a World War II aviator cap that had come down through the family from somebody. When Sherman showed up, we went off by the Chink Road, kinda looking as we went along, because the article had alerted me to the possibility that the Snow Girl was missing part of her clothing. But I hadn't gotten to what it was before the newspaper was repossessed.

Of course when you look your hardest is when you see the least. So Sherm and I cruised past the resting Confederacy, made our way through the pine thicket over the marshy ground, and finally to the dirt road that led off to the Coopers.

"Here we are, Dixie Detective," Sherman said. "What in a holy hog's butt are we looking for?"

"Just feel the atmosphere, Sherm," I replied. "Just think of that beautiful young girl hidden by some bushes and all covered over, dying away in the quietness of the deep snow. And we're able to be near this spot. Don't you have a sense of local history?"

"I have a sense of what Ms. Cooper's cookin' for supper. Smells like pokesally. Hate that smell."

"I'm appealing to that sense beyond the obvious, Sherm. Imagine you were the killer putting that lovely down over there in the cold night. What wicked heart could do such a thing to such a beautiful face?"

"I heard she was beautiful, well dressed, had on expensive jewelry. Must've come from a wealthy family."

"None of those around here. Maybe on the other side of the mountain, in Bentonville, there is."

"How would you know?"

"Billy Rand told me."

"How's he know?"

"He almost dated one of their girls one time—him being handsome and athletic and all."

"Why didn't he?"

"Hard to date when you ain't got a car to ride in or a telephone to talk on."

"So, where'd he meet her?"

"His buddy's dad is an architect in town so his boy had a new '59 Chevy convertible—bright red. I rode in it one night when they were hitting the drive-ins. The boy was popular because of his car, and this one doll of a girl moved right in on Rand. Thought he had money, I guess, but when he never could contact her, well..."

"Can I hold my tears for another time, Ollie? This crap is too much for a boy from Indian Rock."

By this time we were approaching the old cotton patch, being careful to avoid the mud and gimpy spots where the melting snow had puddled up. Spots of ice still lingered in the shade of gaunt trees and we were no longer sure where we were headed, so we rode as slowly as possible. A few yards away, I could hear a clear voice calling to us. We saw a figure on the porch of the Cooper's house.

"Uh, oh," Sherman said. "Pretend you don't hear. It's Old Goofy."

I looked toward the house. "We'd better get outta here," I said. "That ain't Goofy. That's his brother Lyle. I hear he's meaner'n old Evil-Eye Ford."

"Can't be," Sherm replied. "She's got blood lines of the devil himself. That's what my dad said."

So we turned, 'best we could on the narrow road, and headed away from the wasted trip to the Coopers. Approaching the Confederate Cemetery, I chained in and sat across my bar looking at a strange sight.

Sherman passed me, then realized I'd stopped. He turned and gave me a questioning look. I pointed toward the cemetery as it lay quietly up the side of the forlorn hillside, bramble bushes and pieces of wild grass sprouting out of a few leaning headstones and sunken mounds of earth. No one ever went there anymore except in the spring when Methodists got up a Saturday crew and came up the hill to tend to the overgrown grounds.

Someone had backed their car up beside the last row of headstones, and it sat there quietly in the late afternoon shadows. We couldn't figure out its make or model, it being far enough away that it was almost a part of the line of overgrown bushes and broken trees that swayed easily in the dying wind of the winter day. There was, however, a quality to the car that brought to mind the vehicle that had tried to run over Sherm and me as we walked Highway 9 the first day of the snow.

Was it my imagination? Was I still traumatized over finding the two torsos in that old coupe near the cave months back? Would I ever see shadows and darkness as consoling things again? Or would I forever feel pursued, as if I was a ghost that could never rest or be free of evil?

"What's wrong?" Sherm's voice called to me through a fog that covered my brain and held it captive.

I rode my bicycle ahead as fast as possible, never looking back, listening for the sound of black tires eating up the road as they sought my soul.

When I reached the split in the road that took me away from Sherman, I didn't pause or say a word. I simply continued my flight into the coal-black shadows that were gathering around me. I flew through them with the wind as my friend, pushing me into darkness.

I had to examine this thing when the house was quiet and the night was deep. I knew I couldn't go on being scared of every shadow that shifted or every tree branch that clattered against the house. Not to mention the winter wind that could raise the hair on the back of your neck. At least that's how it affected me. Tie it together with two bloody torsos, two rotten killers, the emerging threat of some boogie man hiding in a blacked-out car that seemed to flow along the edge of night, and I was getting as loose boweled as the dude sitting on top of the first Russian rocket.

What I needed to do was approach that old black car with the dark innards and scream in the driver's face, "What do you want with me? What have I done to you?"

Maybe the driver was the headless Clayton Adams or Henry Black, come back in ghost form to mock me for disturbing their rest in that deep, dark sepulcher by the cave. As if they liked it there where the north wind couldn't find them and their spirits could pass time as easy as water in a winter creek.

Clayton and Henry. Pictured in the paper, dressed like they were human beings, didn't reflect what they did to that retarded woman. The more I thought about it, the more I considered the killers' point of view.

Man, I had to stop that thinking. They were long gone. Buried up at Spruster's Hill in the Church of Christ Cemetery, way back under the low branches of an oak, partially hidden by the wild grass and bushes. Buried under the red clay like ragweed of the fall that browned itself for winter and spread ugly over the mounds. Mounds that spoke of a fresh violation of the soil, and tiny slabs of granite that told their names and dates of life. Two old indigents taken by the Christians and given space to rest though I knew their secret restlessness and their long nights of wicked searching and moaning.

Was it my troubled thinking that made every dark car and every dark afternoon my personal pit of hell? Miss North had been a strong pillar for me to lean on, but now that she was gone all I could do was trust my own faith. I kept reciting the 23rd Psalm that I'd learned in Sunday school.

From the window I looked into the night and shook my head at its evils, at its attempts to take me from sanity, at its baiting of my imagination of things ghoulish and death-wrapped, and of its cave-black steeds shrouded in the invincibility of...

I sucked my breath in quickly. It was past midnight and the house was as dark and quiet as a morgue. It was not my imagination. A figure stood in the blackness near the barn in the faint light of a million stars. He was a real person, not a vapor that trailed about on the arms of the wind. He stood without moving, watching the house. He drew on a cigarette, but all I saw was the tiny glow of a red dot from the upstairs window. I pulled at the old curtain to cover me from his view, though I knew his eyes could not find mine in the blackness of midnight.

When I looked again he was gone. And stayed gone as I watched full into the edges of morning. The stars watched with me, quiet companions in a black heaven that took my thoughts and made the fear within me real.

4

"What joy is the seeking of manhood; a manhood that is well hidden."

—Ron Miller

Weldon surprised us all when he lurched ahead into a parking slot.

It was on the dark side of the drive in, near the hedges and too far for a curb hop to respond. It was a coveted parking space, and though we were restricted to looking over our shoulders at the passing cruisers, at least we were stable on the lot and no one could repudiate our Saturday night follies in Bentonville. Weldon knew the ideal position was butt-backed up to the hedge, but his character was not dominant enough to stand up to the abuse if he halted traffic and made all the cool cruisers meditate while he angled the shoebox Ford into the space.

Sherman and I squawked at the nose-first approach but since it was Weldon's ride, Rand reminded us of our manners so we zipped up and watched the beat go on behind us.

I looked out the starboard side to see who our neighbors were and was sorry I did. Cigarettes glowing in a closely-closed dark Chevy coupe betrayed the faces of the Mill Village Gang. It was the Hacketts we'd heard about over the past year. Their idea of a rousing night on the town was drinking beer and shouting insults at the cute East-side girls that braved a venture through our lower domain in their daddies' cars. Naturally, the girls ignored the dirty car and its vulgar occupants, leaving the greasers of the Goal Post for the more appropriate hangout way north on McClellan Boulevard.

The younger brother, Don, cranked the window down on the ugly car next to us and leaned out to holler at Billy Rand. "Hey, Valley boy," he shouted over the hum of the radio. "How many people died in that wreck?"

He pounded on the door at his great joke and was posturing his lips to take another slug from his longneck beer when an angry Weldon shouted across Billy Rand toward him, "Nobody died in the wreck, good buddy." Then he hollered back spitefully, "But we got your sister in the back seat with us."

That was enough.

I saw it coming and cranked my window as fast as I could. The beer bottle ricocheted off my door and landed back on the dirt. Weldon took action immediately. He didn't wait for the Hacketts to come after us. He fired the engine to life and clutched us straight across the front of the ruined Chevy coupe. Hostile horns behind us lit up the atmosphere as another bottle bounced off our trunk.

Weldon was right to leave.

Somewhat of a coward, he was especially leery of the Mill Village Gang. I didn't blame him. I was uncomfortable myself as we burned the back tires getting out of the path of the next beer bottle and narrowly missed the approaching chain of cruisers that expressed their anger with their horns.

Weldon hopped the exit curb with the energy of the fearful one, reminding himself to steer clear of the splotched Chevy in the future. He broke through another wave of horn-blaring as he nosed the Ford through traffic and set himself free, heading north on Noble Street.

"Big Donnie will knock my teeth out next time he sees me," Weldon said fearfully as he banged the gears, asking the little flathead motor for all the power it could manage.

"Y'all keep an eye out the back and see if he follows us. That was his brother Harold driving. That greaser just got outta prison on parole. I don't wanta be the reason he gets sent back."

"Maybe you need to be quieter sometimes," Rand suggested.

"I can't let him mock my car. You heard what he said."

"But look what they're riding in. I've seen dirt-track cars in better shape."

"Yeah," Weldon agreed, "and they just looking for a fight, anyway. They don't belong at the Goal Post. They just wanta insult somebody and get up a ruckus. Throw their weight around and take their meanness out on some innocent kid."

Rand was exasperated. "If you knew what they were doing, wise-cracker, why'd you challenge them by insulting their sister?"

"You ever seen their sister?" Weldon asked, still nervous, looking in the rear view as he drove.

When Rand shook his head, Weldon trembled slightly.

"That girl'd scare the rattlers off a diamond back."

"Aw, she can't be that ugly."

"You remember Judus Britt in the third grade?"

"Sure."

"Remember how she was so ugly they only let her come to school three days a week?"

"I don't remember that," Rand said. "She got caught in a fire or a truck crash or something. Not nice to make fun of her."

"I ain't making fun. She freaked me out, man."

Weldon was a wimp's wimp. His hands shook on the steering wheel and Sherm and I laughed at his cowardly shaking.

"Hope they ain't following us up to Urby's. Y'all got your doors locked? Keep 'em locked while we're cruising. Can't never tell when some Westside hood'll try to break in on us. Lordy, I'm as scared of Harold as if he was a nightmare on wheels. They say he killed a dude out at the race track for taking one of his wrenches. I wouldn't fart in his presence without asking permission. He's meaner'n old man Fortune who used to run us off his property for stealing plums."

"You still mad at Mr. Fortune?" Rand asked.

"Why not? Them plums was on public property. We had a right to take what we wanted."

"Public property? How come we had to climb over two fences to get to 'em?"

"Well, he weren't going to miss a handful of plums. They belonged to God, anyway."

Rand wouldn't start up on the "God argument" 'cause Weldon could be harder to talk to than a pissed-off lion tamer.

"Calm down," Rand suggested. "They're not following us, and we gotta get something to eat somewhere. I say let's get something at Urby's. It won't be as crowded as the Goal Post, and we can park near the back and look out for that old Chevy to come in the lot."

"I vote for that," Sherman said. "I'm so hungry you could put a weenie on top of my head and my tongue'd beat my brains out trying to get to it."

I felt like I needed to remind Sherman again of his social behavior.

"Now, don't be waving and hollerin' at every girl we see. Some of their boyfriends might get upset and take out after us. Be cool."

"Aw, Ollie," Sherm said, anticipating the party girls that came by throughout the night so he could put his usual junior high level hits on them. "You know how smooth I am. It's just that these chickadees are so top heavy and flat-out good lookin'."

Weldon looked over the seat at me. He couldn't see Sherman sitting directly behind him. "Where'd you find him, little Holmes? He another one of them afterbirth things your crazy dog dragged in?"

"He's harmless," I assured the front seat. "First night on the town and he thinks he's James Dean."

Weldon let the topic drop as he looked down at his gas gauge. "All right, boys," he said, slowing the car as it approached a short line of traffic backed up where the two lanes converged. "I'm gonna need some gas money. Down to a quarter tank. Everybody pitch in a quarter."

We all did as told, buying nearly four gallons of fuel at the Direct Station, a two-pump operation with a pay shack the size of an English telephone booth. Cheapest gas in town, though, so we lined up behind several other cruisers waiting their turn at the pump.

"Regular or Ethyl?" Weldon questioned out loud. "Cost more for Ethyl but we might need some extra power to get away from them Mill Village boys. Think I'll go with the lady Ethylene."

Rand just shook his head in the dark.

We were pulling back onto Noble Street and heading north toward Urby's when a red flash powered past us going in the opposite direction. The car made so much racket from its exhaust cutouts that the noise rattled around inside our little car.

"Horseshavings!" Sherman let out. "What was that?"

"Moorefield," Billy Rand said. "He's out prowling tonight. Guzzling and muzzling the women. That cat's got it all. New car, gorgeous girls, money to burn..."

"A jailhouse record," Weldon put in.

"You sure?" Rand questioned.

"Word 'round school is that he's been locked up a couple of times. Drinkin' and speedin' 'round town. The cops lock 'im up and his daddy gets him out. Boy's got it made. He could get away with murder."

"Reckon that's why they moved to our poor little valley?" I asked. "They could live on the mountain in Bentonville and be closer to the East-side people."

"You seen their house?" Weldon asked. "I'll take y'all by there sometime. It's that huge, two-story country place with a duck pond beside it and little hills glidin' down to the road. Upper part 'a Nance Creek. Built by one a them big shots owned the pipe shop. They got maids and everything."

"Reckon they like country livin'," Sherm put in.

"Why does Golden Boy hang out with the greasers at school?" I asked. "Dirk and him are thick down at the shop class. I hear they get girls to go back with them and smoke 'n spark while Mr. L. ain't lookin'."

"Mr. L. ain't never lookin'," Weldon said. "I got shop with them boys. All they do is chase skirts. I think Gorman's scared of their parents. 'Fraid he'll get sued or something. Old Goldie's daddy's suppose to be a hotshot lawyer outta Carolina. And they say his momma's a drop-dead looker."

"How's that?" Rand asked. "She must be forty years old."

Weldon shrugged. "I ain't seen 'er, Mac. But if she's got money and good looks, I don't see why she don't move into town."

"Maybe Goldilocks couldn't get in them schools," Sherm said.

"What do you mean?" I asked.

"My pop's one of the trustees for our school," Sherm bragged. "He told me when the Golden Boy come to this area, there was a big powwow and some fierce arguing before he was allowed to register."

"You don't know nothin'," Weldon objected. "Money moves mountains, boys. Them folks can settle anywhere they like."

"Well," Rand said, "he won't be with us long, this being his senior year. He can spark all the girls and graduate to big-time sparkin' at some hot university."

"You're right there," Weldon agreed. "He ain't no concern of mine."

"He might get after all your pretty girls, Wellie," I said sarcastically.

Weldon had none. We all knew it, so he shot me a quick bird as he hooked a right into Urby's.

Urby's, on North Noble, was my favorite, next-level drive-in. Although the lights were dimmer and the curb hops less attractive, there were never any fights or ruckuses. Best of all, the burgers were only nineteen cents. That fit my budget just fine.

We got a prime site on the back row, flashed our lights, and waited for service. From our perch, we could see the cars approach from Main Street and start through the yard. Weldon shut off the engine and my feet got cold immediately.

"I'm shiverin'," I complained before we placed an order.

"You wanta buy more gas?" Weldon asked.

"All I got left is food money," I said. "What'd my quarter buy?"

"Almost one gallon. That'll get you home. Maybe! 'Cording to where we go from here."

"Let's go out to the Sandwich Shop," Sherm blurted out.

"What in the world for?" Weldon turned to look at him. "You'll get yourself killed out there. I was out there one night with a hot chick..."

"Margie the Largie," Billy Rand laughed.

"Yeah, well, she mighta got serious that night but two cats got to fightin,' and the cops came and shootin' started up. I was so scared I couldn't coax my love life back to normal for three days."

"Just the sight of Margie does that to me," Billy Rand quipped.

"Yeah, well, Billy Rand, you can get some cool numbers to talk to you. Best I can do is pick up a few crumbs here and there. Margie ain't too bad in the dark—if it's real dark—and if she don't breathe that garlic breath directly on you. 'Course she is a little rough on the edges. Kept callin' all the boys 'Ace' and told the curb hop to kiss her broadside for lookin' up her dress. She was on me like I was glue on back 'a her stamp. I don't know if I coulda marched in the parade for her or not. She kinda scared me before the bullets started knockin' the lights out. Handcuffs and hot moments don't go hand in hand."

"How about Rock Castle?" Sherman asked next.

"Where you gettin' all this stuff?" Weldon asked.

Sherman shrugged. "I hear names. I don't know locations."

"That's another hangout," Billy Rand enlightened him. "Knives down there aren't part of the silverware—they're weapons of choice."

"Where's the coolest place then?"

"We can't go there," Weldon said.

"Why not?"

The front seat shared a mutual look.

"You'll find out later," Billy Rand said.

The curb hop knew Weldon so they talked while my feet were changing into chunks of ice. I ordered and made the usual jokes while we waited.

Traffic was slow coming through Urby's. The winter weather was one reason, but that other "cool" place was the hot spot. I longed to go there but knew Weldon never would. He'd been before and it wasn't a pleasant thing. The Eastside kids that hung out there were downright cruel to the valley boys. I wondered where Moorefield fit in.

We were finishing up our burgers and fries when a black steed, with a monster lick to it, eased over the ditch leading into the lot. I didn't need to see the driver to know who it was.

"Sonofaditchdigger," Weldon muttered.

"What is it?" Sherman asked.

"Eness Voit," I said quietly.

"What's that?" Sherman craned his neck to see through the windshield.

"Black Magic in person," Billy Rand said. "The baddest Ford on God's earth."

The full bodied Galaxie knifed over our hood with the grace of a long distance runner. Its sinewy muscles were in the throaty roar of its exhaust. It carefully picked its way through the potholes of the lot, seeming to sniff each vehicle with a curiosity that left it fuller of itself as it rejected each lead sled as so much paint and chrome. It knew its way through the night. It knew it had no equal in the collection of scattered machinery at Urby's. This was King Richard in the flesh. Pure royalty.

"Sounds evil," Sherman observed in awe.

"It is," Weldon agreed. "It is."

Black Magic eased its way through the drive-in like a skiff finding its watery path through the darkest sea. Except there was a boldness and a confidence that told others of its fierce runs under deep country skies, lit by starlight on a moonless night, its flight unequaled by meeker souls.

"That's Ollie's kinfolk," Weldon said. "Him and Voit outrun the valley boys down at Silver Run. Ain't that right, squirrel?"

I came back to the cold car at Urby's, but my mind was warm in the thoughts of past races and times spent.

"You rode in that bad Ford, Oliver?" Sherman T. wanted to know.

I nodded and looked off into the night. It was a private time I didn't want Sherm to mock or low rate.

"What'd you have to pay 'im to letcha ride?"

I shrugged and watched Black Magic leave the lot. Voit's girl was sitting close to him, so close it was hard to tell which one was the driver. I wondered who she was and where he'd met her. I could ask at the next drag. Only this time the ultimate drag race would be Voit and the inexorable Moorefield in his crimson phantom, the loud bruiser that had blasted its way down Noble Street earlier that night with open disdain for the law.

"Wonder if Moorefield can take him," Weldon said as the orbs of red blinked out of sight heading north on Noble.

Probably off to circle the Tavern, I thought.

Big Don never came North to Urby's, so we sat there while the night got deeper and the car got colder.

Finally Billy Rand spoke up, "We'd better crank up and get moving or they'll find us here dead in the morning."

Weldon laughed and fired the little engine to life, but it had set so long the heater couldn't do any good until we were way down toward the middle of town. He decided to turn west to visit the Sandwich Shop. Out of deference to Sherm, I thought, then reconsidered. He was looking for Margie. "Ace of a girl," as they say.

We crossed the tracks gingerly and then hit the gas to build up momentum for the uphill run of the darkened viaduct. We were getting deeper into the lower order of things.

Margie lived dead center of where the bootleggers set up trade and commerce, making her as hard living and abrasive as the ducktails and leather jackets that bossed the rear recesses of the Sandwich Shop. I was praying Weldon wouldn't stop and back into a rear parking space. The hoods hanging outside theft-battered, wrecked cars were as caustic looking and as evil leaning as the delinquent term implied. There was a sinister pallor that bespoke their attitude and made us look like choir boys in search of light on a cold January night. Even Weldon's anemic Ford took on fresh qualities of character as it cruised past the cars with their front guts torn out and fenders that were mangled and corrugated.

I felt boxed in as we eased by the first turn. When the traffic nudged to a halt, Weldon rolled his window up tight and checked the door lock. We were already locked tight in the back.

The reticent curb hop pulled at his short cigarette and leaned back against the corner of the building. He appeared to be younger than us—maybe thirteen or fourteen, shivering in the cold as his undersized sweater lost its battle with the nipping wind. I felt for him but he glared at us like we were alien invaders, and flipped his cigarette butt so it caught the slickness of the hood and skittered off the side. Weldon grimaced, then smiled and half-waved at the boy as he tried to inch forward.

A thick girl with a huge bosom, more like an older woman than a teenage girl, was causing the traffic problem. She was leaning in the driver's window of an unidentifiable mechanical beast in front of us, laughing and slapping at the boy's hands as he tried to touch her upper body parts. It was a game the cardinals played in the spring in our back yard by the pond. Flittering and dipping over the airwaves, they sparked in the way that nature intended.

I don't know what nature intended with Margie the Largie.

I ascertained, from front seat whispers, that this was the chosen one. Only it looked like anyone could choose Margie. She was the type of girl you heard about, wished to meet, then were disappointed when her broad features and crude manners became the reality.

After several minutes of waiting patiently, the two cars behind us began cutting loose with their horns. The indignant driver flirting with Margie leaned out and cussed at us like we were at fault, flipping us a vile gesture that said, in a thrusting motion, he meant it. Weldon shrugged, palms up, like he was cool, but I doubt the delinquent could see us through the glare of the corner light. Margie gave a final tease, shook her ample rump at the smoking beast, and stepped back to the curb.

When the hood realized that his number had not appeared on Margie's datebook, he smoked his way out of the lot, leaving room for us to roll forward and meet the sweet promise of the night.

Weldon couldn't get his window down fast enough as he saw those huge boobs floating toward him. Billy Rand leaned away from the nocturnal attraction and hid his grin with his hand.

"Ace," Margie leaned forward and peered into the depths of the car, smiling with yellowed teeth, and sporting a fresh attack of acne that had pitched camp on both puffy cheeks. I moved closer to my door panel and prayed that Sherman knew enough to keep his flapper still in her domineering presence. "It's colder 'n a snowman's genitals," Margie said as she leaned over next to Weldon. "Who the hell you haulin' 'round tonight, Wellie?"

Weldon laughed nervously and tried to be clever. "Ain't nobody much, Margie. Got me some boys from the valley. We just kinda lookin' 'round tonight. Too cold for the drags."

"Y'all need some hot dates to keep y'all warm." She spoke in a throaty way that reminded me of a smoker's voice. "Don't reckon y'all on the queer side, are you?"

"Nothin' funny here, Marg," Wellie replied, laughing haltingly. "Just out pokin' around. Fixin' to head on to the house."

"Night's still young, Wellie. Why don't you dump these Baptist Home children at their momma's door and come on back here for a little free fall in the back seat."

Weldon didn't know what to say.

"Know what I really need tonight, Wellie?" she asked when he couldn't form an answer.

"What's that, Margie?"

"I need me some good liquor and a bad man."

"Well, now, that's funny..."

"How's it funny?"

"Well... I thought you were gonna say some bad liquor and a good man."

"You qualify either way?"

"Huh? Well, sure, I got it covered, Marg. You know me—smooth as ice and rough as sandpaper. I fit the bill like a sack of groceries."

Margie raised up off the door molding to let out a monster scream at a cat behind us, reminding them to be patient by using finger signals. "Some looters ain't got no consideration of others," she said, leaning back over toward Weldon as the horns continued to sound throughout the rear parking area. We were blocking the road to Tenth Street, and cars behind us wanted to leave the parking lot but we had all traffic tied up.

"Let them frog stickers wait. I wanta hear something hot and handy from you, Wellie Boy. What you say? You, me, out behind the sewing factory. You get these grammar school kids on home and you come on back with a full bottle of Jackie D."

"Jackie D.?"

"Hell, boy, you know I don't drink nothing 'cept that Jack Daniels old-age whiskey. Clears out my throat and makes my sex motor hum. You'll see what I mean."

"Yeah, well... Let me..."

"You ain't chicken-winging out, are you, boy?"

"Lordy, no, girl... I... I just gotta get these kids... er... boys home."

"You comin' straight back, ain'tcha?"

"Sure am, girl. I sure am. You just sit down inside there and I'll be back before you can say Jackie D."

"You ain't lying, are you? Last boy stood me up can't pee straight no more. I fixed him like a gelding."

Weldon squirmed in his seat and tried to laugh off the threat. "Now, Marg, we been friends a long time... I shore wouldn't be standing you up."

"Keep what I said in mind, lover. Me, you, and a bottle. You got a big back seat."

"Well, yeah, I reckon I do... Say, hold off 'bout twenty minutes and I'll be right back."

"Jackie D."

"Right. Jackson Delight... ha... Jack Danny... ah... full bottle... new cork..."

He was easing out on the clutch, rolling us forward just as a mean looking character came up alongside the car and banged his fist against the metal door frame. Sherm and I jumped as the boy cussed us in a steady stream of vulgarisms. Weldon accelerated to the entrance and nearly pulled into the path of oncoming traffic. He was shaking worse than when Big Don Hatchett threw beer bottles at us. Now he was mumbling under his breath. Rand was doubled over, laughing.

"Quit laughing, y'all," Weldon said as we started back toward town. He laughed nervously. "That ol' girl never heard of Doublemint gum."

"Where you gettin' the whiskey?" Sherm wanted to know.

"What!" Weldon exclaimed, resuming the big-man role now that he was clear of the huge-boobed woman. "I ain't gettin' nowhere near that girl. You see the size of that body? I couldn't work on that if I was Charles Atlas."

Rand continued to laugh. "You ever go back out to Shop, Weldon, you better be ready to perform or you'll be sitting down to pee!"

Weldon gave us all a collective bird finger and concentrated on his next turn from uptown. He hooked a right and we motored a few blocks south before he pulled into the lot of the Rock Castle. He parked among sparse cars and flashed his lights for service.

"You hungry?" Rand asked.

"Naw, man," Weldon replied, showing him his shaking hands. "I need somethin' to drink to settle my nerves."

A bundled up woman in heavy gloves came over to take our order. She snarled contemptuously when Wellie ordered a cherry Coke.

It was a topic nobody wanted to talk about—especially late at night.

We had missed connections on the drag races, had spent time circling the Oxanna hangout called "Buck's." So as the night wore on we escaped town trappings and motored quietly into the valley of our youth.

I was both relieved and disappointed.

Sooner or later I'd see Eness Voit again, and I'd tell him that Moorefield was looking for him. And if Eness even recalled me as a "brother," he'd smile that grin that was meant to say all's well with him, but it was crooked and not a full grin so you couldn't really tell if he was fixing to ride off in his black steed in pursuit of history, or if he was going to lean on its flanks and examine the night and make them guess and wait.

We went near the Cooper's place by two miles when we were back in the valley and gutting it toward our house.

Sherman T. brought it up. “I seen that girl’s ghost last night,” he said in a low convincing voice.

“What girl?” Billy Rand asked, but he already knew.

“The Snow Girl. Her ghost was lookin’ ’round our barn last night ’bout midnight. I seen her from my winder. She was lookin’ for something. Like she was lost and didn’t know nobody or which way was home.” He paused. “It was serious stuff.”

I waited for the attacks to come on his good name but silence filled the car. Sherman’s eloquence had reflected our own souls.

“I know who killed her,” Weldon finally said.

No one spoke, waiting for his answer.

“It was them mountain people out White Gap Road.”

“Why?” Billy Rand asked.

“She was too pretty to live,” he said matter of factly. “Made them already ugly creatures look like alien mutants.”

“She made us all look hicky,” I said. “Why would we kill her for that?”

“That’s my theory, okay?”

“Your theory sucks the big one,” Sherman put in. “I think she committed suicide.”

“Why?”

“Same reason. Too pretty to live. Couldn’t find nobody pretty ’nough to marry. All her kids’d be ugly slugs and she’d have to smother them, so she just died early and left a beautiful corpse.”

We didn’t bother to refute that line of thought.

The lights picked up the lonely highway, guiding us through a darkness broken only by an occasional farmhouse light.

“I think this friggin’ valley is jinxed,” Weldon said. “God’s truth. Look what all’s happened here the last few years. Ain’t no other place ’round had such shootings and killings and such. We must be the garden spot of the world for criminals. Think how we could promote that for tourist trade. Maybe signs on trees or take-out ads in *Life* magazine. Spooks and ghost hunters be flocking in here by the droves."

"By the what?"

"Droves, you know. Like bumper to bumper stationwagons. Kids with their faces pasted to the car winders lookin' for a deranged killer or for a wayward ghost. Like that one Sherman T. seen last night."

"Bull. He didn't see no ghost."

"I did, too."

"I saw somebody at our barn the other night," I pitched in quietly. "He was leaning by the corner, smoking a cigarette."

"Aw, heck, Oliver," Billy Rand objected. "Don't start that stuff again."

"You're a morbid liar," Weldon agreed.

"What kind of liar, Wellie?"

"Bite my buns, Ollie. You didn't see no ghost!"

"I didn't say a ghost. I said I saw *somebody*, meaning a living body that walked and smoked and disappeared when my heart slowed down long enough to look again. I ain't lying."

"Your little brother's a nut case," Weldon said to Rand.

"We all know that. Mainly, we ignore him."

"Well, I'm going to find out who killed the Snow Girl," I blurted out without thinking.

"Oh, Lord," Rand said, exasperated. "Look what we've created—'Sherlock' Holmes. Ollie, we ain't related to that Sherlock fellow. He's not in our family line. Your investigative curiosity will ultimately get you killed. You won't always have Captain Courageous to get you outta tight spots. One day your luck will run out. Besides, Momma will put the brakes on your crime-fighter's career."

"Say what you want," I mumbled, looking off into a darkness so thick I was blind in it. "There must be a simple solution to all this mysterious stuff. You watch. It'll come around, and I'll be a part of the discovery."

Sherman T. had to chip in his part. "Go for it, Ollie. I'll be way over the other side supporting you."

"Other side where?"

"Other side of the lake, I hope. Whoever put that pretty one face-up in the snow won't catch me anywhere near his business."

We got closer to home and our curfew.

Weldon lived about a mile from us with his grandmother. I don't know why he didn't live with his parents. He'd just always been with his grandmother and called her "Momma" just like we called the iron woman who ruled our humble home.

I would ask Billy Rand a little later about Weldon. He seemed an alright guy. Nothing to write an essay about, but a cool enough fellow. Besides, he had wheels and we were always between them with him when they were rolling. Best kind of friend to have.

Weldon looked at his watch and grinned. "Hold up," he said. "We got time for a little bushwhacking?"

"Nope," Rand objected. "I'm tired, cold, and we got church tomorrow."

"Won't take but a minute to see who's gettin' the chick-a-dee-wrap tonight."

"We're gonna get shot one day. I'm hitting the floorboard when you start throwing that spot around."

"Chicken droppings, Rand. You're chicken-house fodder."

"Take me by the house. And let these uninitiated go with you. I'm out of this deal."

"Where we headed?" Sherm asked.

"Spam heaven," Weldon called out. "Going to see who's rockin' and who's blockin'. Might pick up a stray."

"Pick up some hot lead," Rand warned again. "One of those village boys won't take kindly to you lighting up their world."

"I'll let you out at Jamback. You can walk home."

"Too cold. Take me to the house."

"Nope. Hold your horses. We'll be up there in about two minutes."

We *were* up there in about two minutes.

Across an icy stream that was not a deterrent to the secret pleasures of the night, the old Ford nearly slipped a tire. But our back seat weight helped, so we pulled out of the creek and went about a hundred yards to a clearing in the woods. Weldon doused the lights.

There were only two cars there, parked a short way from us. We edged closer, but the windows were fogged up by the couples' breathing so we couldn't see squat—as much fun as watching ice melt. And my feet were chunked up again. I was like Rand, I wanted to head home and pull the quilts over my head. One dull Saturday night except for the beer that ran down the outside of my window and made a smell that I was glad I didn't have to explain to Momma. She'd be checking that mantel clock in just a few ticks.

Weldon couldn't stand it, though. He got as close to one car as he could, flipped on his spotlight, and aimed it straight into the front seat, as if he was the law come to break up the party. We still couldn't see anything, the occupants obviously hunkered down in the seat where the light couldn't find them. I was kinda glad.

The next car, for just a flash, had two silhouettes on the back window. So Weldon sent a ray into the back of that car, too, laughing and calling out "look-ee-see-me" in a sing-song chatter as he raked the interior the best he could.

"Watch it!" Billy Rand yelled suddenly and hit the seatcovers.

Weldon laughed. "Chicken droppings," he said. "He's just rolling the winder down. He ain't gonna do nothing."

The shotgun blast caught Weldon by total surprise.

He doused the spotlight and rammed the gas pedal to the floor. The little Ford did its best to respond, but the ground was grassy slick and the car veered to the side and attacked a thicket of bushes.

Hitting reverse, Weldon backed us up until we were near the area where we came in. I was leaning over out of the line of fire of the windshield but I could still see the person we had disturbed. He was a tall, dark man with his shorts around his knees as he stood butt naked by his opened door reloading his shotgun.

"He's loading up again," I shouted to Weldon. "Get us outta here."

Weldon was trying to do that, but he missed the slight opening to the field and took half a small tree with him. He swung wildly over the dirt path, barely a walking trail, until we hit the creek. Water went all over the windshield and the engine sputtered like the distributor was wet, but it righted itself and pulled us away as the next shotgun blast peppered through the trees around us.

In a few minutes we were back at Jamback Road and idling toward our house. Nobody said a word until we opened the doors to get out.

"Billy Rand," Weldon asked as we got out of the car. He was still shaking as he spoke, "You recognize that car? That rascal shooting at us?"

"Sure," Billy Rand said. "That was Harold 'Hootie' Hackett."

Weldon sucked in his breath and about fainted.

5
Sunday Blues

Sunday afternoon was simply the day after.

But now the sun came back and the road out of our valley had Rand, Butch Cox, and me on it.

I was like the thirsty man crawling into a desert oasis—just glad to be there—so I was as quiet as a mouse eating crackers and catching the crumbs so they wouldn't be heard. The back seat was my domain, and I was content to let the whistling of the convertible top be music played by the wind at 75 miles per hour.

Not that our roads could sustain that kind of speed for any period. Once we drew closer to town, the traffic picked up and we moved westward, retracing the night-before route that had featured big Margie and the decadence of the West End. As I understood, we were heading for a local racing legend's garage. The man's name was Blue.

"Where'd this fellow get his name?" Rand asked as we slowed our speed to cross several sets of railroad tracks in the industrial area that sported two or three soil-pipe foundries. The closely-built, shotgun houses ran up to the sides of the tracks and stood their ground under the harshest of conditions. Their occupants endured those harshest conditions as well: low paying jobs in the foundries, limited social opportunities, and a toughness of spirit that found its external expression in the coarse and unsympathetic character of the people. I'd heard rumors that many of these bluecollar working class were active members of the Ku Klux Klan. But that was dad speaking and I wasn't sure if he based that observation on fact or suspicion. Dad claimed that the only class lower than the Westside dwellers was the colored and it was the Klan's job to see that the colored kept their spot as the lowest rung of society.

I wasn't too sure about that bit of home-spun reason, but I was interested in the man's unusual nickname.

Cox laughed. "Remember in grade school how all the boys had nicknames?"

Rand nodded.

"Way I heard it, was this cat's name was Eugene. 'Course that got shortened to Gene and then one day somebody said, 'Call him Bluejeans.' After a while, they dropped the jeans part altogether and he was just 'Blue'."

"Everybody call him that?"

Cox nodded and grinned. "It's in the phone book that way."

After a mile or so, we pulled away from the fetid smell of the pipe shops and the scenery improved. The houses were nicer, had large, well-kept yards, with a hint of small domestic gardens in the back. I had been up the Pike once or twice, so I knew there were some decent folks around, once you got past the segregated gas stations that had the Jim Crow signs out front—"We Serve White People Only!"—and the auto salvage yards.

I was doubly quiet as we neared Blue's garage because I'd heard that if he didn't care for you, he'd tell you to "get the hell off his lot and not come back." I wasn't sure where Butch stood in relation to the temperamental mechanic so I had adopted a vow of silence.

We passed the dormant high school, a freshly painted building that caught the afternoon sun in a bath of brilliance. We took a dip and a sharp curve as Blue's alley was off the road to the right. Butch had to watch the ditch and a tight-setting of a pole, but we squared out, and when I looked again, we were beside a block garage that had more clutter and car parts in front of it than God has names in the *Book of Life*.

But it was cool stuff.

A Chevrolet engine with individual exhaust headers pointing skyward. A fuel injection system I'd only seen in California magazines—their long throats spreading at the top to draw in air to the formidable racing engine. Race-slick tires were in a jumble near the open garage door and the race car, looking like an early '40s Willy's body, was setting on jack stands at all four corners, its innards torn away, and its interior spartan saved by the roll bar that strengthened the area over the driver's seat. My first upclose look at a professional race car.

I was drawn into my own moment in time.

I was my solitary self and the race car was by itself. It let me look upon its nakedness with impunity. I felt a quirk in my stomach similar to what I'd felt a few years earlier when I accidentally walked up on Millie Cleghorn in the woods while she was taking a leak. I didn't know girls' butts could be so soft and mesmerizing.

The car was like Millie. It didn't say anything, it just let me enjoy the sight. Small miracles bring huge rewards in the learning cycle.

"How'd you do?"

The man must've been Blue.

He was shorter than Billy Rand but solid-built, like the veins that traced his forearms and defined his biceps under the rolled-up mechanic's shirt had got there the old-fashioned way. He earned them.

He was surprisingly mature looking though I'd heard he was only a few years older than Butch. His eyes were the telling mark. They met yours, cold and steady, and stayed with you as you tried to look away. His strength was in the face that had already seen the Gasser wars. His hair was dark and combed straight back—short after it left the widow's peak. His hands were large and dirty with the trademark of his work. He didn't smile or acknowledge our presence except for a simple question to Butch. I knew Butch would not introduce us or explain. We were simply hangers on and they both knew it.

I moved cautiously near the old Gasser race car and tried to see inside it, but I felt Blue's eyes on me so I stood back and examined the engine from ten feet away. This was one day that my smart mouth would not dredge up trouble.

Blue's cool determination and steady eyes brought the son of Lucifer to mind. It was Sunday and, contrary to our upbringing, it was not a day of rest for him. Apparently, he was knee-deep in a racing experiment. The local drag strip would open by mid-February, so he was using this time to prepare his own equipment for the next season.

"Not good." Butch was saying in reply to the question.

"Didn't think so," Blue said. "I heard you comin' up. Vacuum leak."

"Can you fix it?"

"Not today. I got the rear end tore outta my race car, and it'll be a week or more getting parts run down."

"That your engine yonder?"

Blue nodded. "I tore it down the day after the season ended. I'll be ready in a few weeks."

"You running Gas again this year?"

"Yeah. Me and Mayer. That Mad Dog's always gonna be there. Wish

I had his money and equipment."

"You still the best," Butch complimented shyly. "First time I been beat."

"Black Magic, wasn't it?"

Butch looked down and nodded.

"Don't worry 'bout him. I heard he was going to Chevrolets come Spring. Gonna run Lassiter Mountain or Sand Mountain. Ford's up for sell."

"Naw!" Butch was surprised.

"What Harp told me last night. I saw him uptown at the Rock Castle. Claims that Voit kid is more interested in somebody else now that you ain't no threat."

"I want another shot," Butch said, embarrassed that he was taking a back seat. "Who's he after?"

"Blue Mountain boys. Got 'em up a nasty homemade outfit that's suppose to be bad. They ain't cranked it yet. Still beatin' on the firewall and welding junk everywhere. I heard it looks like a plane crash."

Butch didn't bite on the Blue Mountain boys. He was more interested in the incorrigible gravel-slinger from our side of the mountain. "There's a new kid in town in a stock Impala with the big motor. Claims he's the fastest car in the valley now."

"Rich boy?" Blue asked. "Fancy pants?"

"That's him. You seen 'im?"

"Heard about 'im. Don't need to bother to come by here. I ain't workin' on his stuff."

A casual look around and Butch was ready to leave. Blue, however, wanted to talk on another topic. "How come you boys gettin' so many folks killed out your way?"

Butch laughed and shuffled his feet like he was trying to think of something clever to say.

"Bodies just keep turning up," he finally said, grinning. "Little

Holmes, there, is the one in the paper. He found the torsos in that old cave. He don't look like much, but they say the bloodhounds come over to his house for lessons."

Blue smiled for the first time, and I was glad that part of the ice cap had melted—even at my expense. "He's too skinny to be out chasing bad boys," he said.

"He may be thin but he loves drag racing," Butch pitched in on my behalf. I hoped he wouldn't mention my connection to Voit.

" 'Course he's a traitor piss-ant, too," he said.

Here it comes, I thought.

"He saddled up with Voit that night Eness run me at Silver Run."

"No."

Blue winked at me like that was cool, so now I figured he was, too. "You like old cars, little Holmes, you get your momma to let you ride to Green Valley with me one night in the spring. I'll look out for you."

"Thanks, Blue," I mumbled.

"I need me a good helper," Blue explained.

"Thought your new wife liked racing, Blue," Cox said.

Blue laughed. "You know how them women are, boys. She got a little mad when I was building carburetors there on the coffee table, and she didn't like me washin' my grease rags with her house towels, but what really cooked her goose was when I rebuilt that transmission in the bathtub."

We all laughed.

"She didn't leave, did she?" Cox asked.

"She weren't none too happy. But it was the racing got her. I told her I raced at Lassiter Mountain on Friday, Green Valley on Saturday, and Huntsville on Sunday. After a while she figured she could beat that schedule. She does Eastabooga—seven days a week."

Chuckles all around again.

"I been racin' every season since I was sixteen years old," Blue said proudly. “Other night I was hanging out at Dallas Drag Strip down south of here. Sunday night, it musta been, ’cause it was raining off and on all afternoon. But some of the boys waited out the rain hopin’ to win that fifty dollars for Top Eliminator. Weren’t but a few drag cars left, but one that everybody was scared of was an old boy from Georgia that had a Oldsmobile motor in a forty Ford body. When the rain let up and the Foggy Hollow boys took their brooms and swept off the strip, that ol’ Oldsmobile motor was too hot for anybody to handle.

“Well, it got on toward dark and old man Patch, the track owner, got on the speaker and said he was gonna give the fifty dollars to the Georgia boy ’cause the track was too wet to run. My buddy Gravy Biscuit was there in his ’57 Chevy that was running good, but it couldn’t do nothin’ with that Oldsmobile motor.

“I went up to old Gravy and told him to take his racing slick tires off the back and put on his street tires. He didn’t want to do it but I talked him into it. Then I got old man Patch to let the Chevy and the Olds motorcar run for the fifty bucks. ’Course, old Patch was in thick with the Georgia boy, but he wanted to keep people comin’ back to race so he ’llowed it. ’Cause it’d be good for the run and the Olds’d win anyway.

“They got up the line and that big Oldsmobile motor was screaming, but with them racing slicks on the back he weren’t goin’ nowhere on that wet track. Old Gravy eased out the clutch on his street tires and they hook up and carry him down the quarter mile before the Georgia boy can get that Ford to launch.

“Old Patch was mad as thunder but he had to pay up. Gravy told me to stop by the Rainbow Inn on the way home and *he’d* buy me breakfast.”

We all smiled, enjoying Blue’s exploits.

As for myself, I simply loved drag racing. I loved the race cars, loved looking at them, being near them. Even if I had not a chance of ever owning one, I still could hang on the fence at the strip, or walk through the dirt pits and listen as a small-block Chevy motor hit its absolute peak in rpm’s.

Keats said, "A thing of beauty is a joy forever."

Race cars were beautiful. And they were a joy to me.

Blue must have shared my obsession.

Racing was his everything. Cox said he'd been married four or five times, and that he didn't drink, or play cards, or chase wild women. He raced. Sooner than later, the wives raced out of his life. Yet he seemed perfectly content.

Our whole visit changed, however, when a dark car with a cracked windshield and a wrecked front fender roared down the gravel of the alley and skidded its tires until it stopped inches from Butch's Chevy. A pair of greasers took their time getting out of the abysmal vehicle, acting like they were the coolest humans around. They both wore dirty T-shirts and cheap leather jackets. Their hair was wrapped around their heads with grease the viscosity of some farm-equipment product. The driver sneered around the acne of his slick-skinned face and flipped a cigarette butt that landed at Rand's feet.

I looked at Blue. His face muscles tensed and the brief smile of a moment before was a memory beyond recall.

"Uncle Blue," the greaser grinned through his sneer. "I got a skip you need to see about."

Blue was angry. "I got a bill you need to see about, Fly. I ain't lookin' at nothing you got. Matter of fact, that junkyard refuge makes my eyes hurt to look at it."

"Help a nephew out, Unc. Mom'll love you."

"She only loves you, greaser, but I ain't sure why."

The greaser surveyed the crowd as if seeing us for the first time. His eyes became hard and his sneer reappeared. Another greaser, stockier, but almost a match, appeared behind him.

"You that Holmes kid, ain'tcha?" he said, looking directly at me.

I didn't move or say a word. My face felt flush, though, and I admit it. I was scared.

"My best buddy's in jail on account of you. Seth was my cousin and best friend. Now he ain't nothing but a number. Thanks to you, you little prissy fart."

Billy Rand and Butch both took a step forward to defend me. The two greasers got close enough to breathe their bad air in our faces. I didn't know what to do.

"Hold up!" Blue's voice covered the situation quickly. "I ain't havin' no bad blood at my place. This here's my business and my home. If'n you wanta threaten people, Fly, you get off my property and go elsewhere."

"You ain't sidin' with blood?" Fly sneered at him.

"Blood ain't got nothin' to do with it. Get outta here and leave my customers alone."

"I'm a customer and family, Blue."

"You ain't nothing but worthless. I'm ashamed to claim you."

Swearing, Fly and his sidekick started toward the car. He turned to point back at me.

"I ain't forgetting that face. You better stick close to Momma, Holmes. We got folks to take care of rats like you. You'll see 'em comin' but you won't know who they are. Keep an eye out. We got plans for you."

That was one ride I wish I'd missed. One Sunday I wished I'd stayed in the valley. Blue wasn't Lucifer, but his nasty nephew was.

When we were back in the car, waiting for the dust from Fly's high speed exit to clear before we nimbly sought our escape from the West End speed shop, Blue looked at us with a sorrowful expression—almost as if he wanted to apologize for his nephew's behavior and overt threat. But Blue was not the type to apologize to anyone.

It was simply a retreat back up the Pike as Blue returned to the stark skeleton of his race car.

The Sunday blues crept into my spirit. And though they had been near me many times in my life, they never lessened in their intensity or consequences.

Butch was sympathetic.

As the convertible moved carefully over the thin asphalt we'd conquered before with deliberate speed, he looked over the front seat and said, "Don't pay any attention to that fool, sport. He's just one of these West End punks that likes to scare kids. He's the kind that hangs out with that bunch of greasers at the Sandwich Shop—all mouth and no action."

Rand agreed with Butch, "We've been in worse fixes than this, Ollie."

I looked out the window and tried to resurrect my fallen spirit. Someone had once told me that when we could not change our circumstances, we should change ourselves. I guessed I was due for a major makeover.

6
"Now in the dark of February..."

—George Macdonald

Time got on busy without revealing much about the girl in the snow.

And we went back to doing the usual business of getting to school on the grey days and working our way through the weekends.

Dad got hurt at work in the cotton mill and got laid off without pay. So Billy Rand worked afternoons at the Monte farm, and I helped Mr. Moon on his paper route and tried to round up other odd jobs for some extra money. The girls wanted to work, too, but Momma wouldn't let them waitress at the two country cafés, saying decent folks didn't go in service to others in that way.

I didn't know what she meant, but I never questioned her ways. It was finding enough work to buy groceries and keep the electricity on that kept throwing stumbling blocks in front of us. Momma didn't let on that she was discouraged, having gone through tough times before with the older brothers and sisters that lived away now with their families. She kept saying the supper prayers with the passion that always edged her words, and we kids tried not to agitate each other or aggravate the situation for Dad. He was mostly quiet and limped from the bedroom to the kitchen on his daily attempts at staying busy and healing enough to go back to work.

Mr. Moon tried to help with additional work, but the worst gig he got up for me was at the curious Miss Frema's farm. He came around the car that bore his newspapers like king's gold and laughed at me. "Ollie," he said in a jovial mood, "I ain't quick to tell you this, but Miss Frema, down Shakeymehead Road, needs a boy to do some work for her Saturday morning. Reckon your momma'd let ya ride yore wheel down thar?"

"Sure, Mr. Moon. What she want done?"

He grinned like his fox dogs were about to overtake Mr. Buster's hounds on a summer night in valley history.

"Now I aim to tell ya." He paused and rubbed the back of his neck. "She's a mite curious."

I shrugged. "You know we need the money. I ain't a bit afraid of hard work. 'Long as she pays me."

"Oh, she'll pay you alright. How much is the main thing."

"Momma says it ain't polite to ask how much before a job starts."

"Well, yore momma's a good woman, but she ain't never worked for Miss Frema."

I shrugged again. "Reckon one morning won't kill me."

This time Mr. Moon laughed, almost admiringly. "I knowed ya'd say that so I told 'er ya'd better be thar in the mornin'."

"Thanks, Mr. Moon."

"Don't thank me yet, boy." He started back to his car. "Some lessons in life come mighty hard. Yes, sir. Mighty hard."

Miss Frema was kinda like valley royalty. Her family owned the biggest farm back in the old days, but when her parents died and there was only Miss Frema to see about the many acres, she was unable to keep the farm going. Her field help left her and what was a beautiful house and rolling farmland became simply idle acres. The fields grew into primitive undergrowth and the stately house, once aristocratic and proud, became a place that passing kids mocked as being ghost-laden and evil. Now it was my turn to vanquish the devils from my mind and ride my wheel up the rutted dirt road and knock on the door.

First light wasn't too far gone when I parked near the decaying front steps and looked about the shadows of the winter morning. I didn't know what to expect. Having never seen a glimpse of Miss Frema, I looked with anticipation as I waited for her to answer my knock. And waited. Mr. Moon said she wanted me to come early. Now she wasn't there to receive my offer of labor.

I knocked again, almost timidly, as if my presence, my noise, would interrupt years of her perpetual reclusiveness. How was I suppose to respond? It was a long ride back over the dirt road to home, and the wind under the February sky was crossing the rampant growth of the fields and snapping at me on the exposed front porch.

I was about to try one final time before leaving the neglected farm house and its unkept acres, when the front door opened a sliver, very slowly. I couldn't see anyone, but I knew the curious heir to the Shakeymehead Road fortune was watching me.

I removed my tattered hat and tried to remain courteous in posture as one eye examined my presence.

"I'm Oliver Holmes, ma'am," I said with as much courage as I could manage. "Mr. Moon sent me over to work for you today. Did... Did I come too early?"

The door closed quickly, leaving me holding my hat and wondering what my next move should be. If I went home empty-handed, Momma would chastise me for wasting my free time on a Saturday morning. Although I still had my paper route to deliver at mid-afternoon, she would want a more productive day from me.

Should I stay or go?

Maybe Miss Frema hadn't heard me when I spoke. Perhaps she thought I was one of those railroad tramps that had wandered by her place these few miles from the tracks. I approached the blistered and paint-peeling frame of the door and rapped a little harder.

A long silence. Then I heard a scraping within and the curtain near the door was brushed briefly. I caught a fleeting glimpse of a dark face against the window. Very brief and very deliberate, I thought.

"Miss Frema," I said in a respectful voice. "I've come to work for you this morning."

A long silence, again. Then the door creaked open on its rusty hinges. As slowly as dusk falls on a winter day, the concealing and weather-beaten door opened, to my fascination, on the rotten, neglected porch.

This time the little round face came slowly out of the shadows of the house into the grey of the winter morning. There was no expression to her bloated and puffy features. Small eyes had some wart-like growths on the eyelids. Full lips bore a purplish mole on the lower part of the mouth. A nearly flat nose, and no neck visible under a high lace collar—probably in vogue decades ago—distinguished her from anyone I had ever seen. A Sunday church hat, with a torn net, covered thinning grey hair, but I guessed she hadn't been to church services in quite a while.

In spite of her shocking appearance, I managed a secret amusement. My mind went almost immediately to William Faulkner's story, "A Rose for Miss Emily."

I smiled to assuage the obvious fears of this reclusive woman from another era and spoke softly, "Good morning, ma'am. I'm Oliver Holmes from Jamback Road. Your paper carrier, Mr. Moon, said you might have some work for me this morning."

She looked at me tersely and made a step back toward the door. Her hesitant venture onto the porch was about to end.

"I can do any work that you might need," I said.

She paused as if gauging the sincerity of my voice. Apparently my appearance had not impressed her. Or, perhaps she couldn't see very well. I couldn't tell her age. "I did *not* send for you," she said. "Why can't I live in peace in my quiet eloquence?"

Her voice was soft, but had a condescending tone that gave me a quick evaluation of my worth to her. I decided I'd done enough to force the job interview. "Well, I'm sorry to have disturbed your peace, ma'am. I guess I've made a mistake."

As I made a turn to go, her voice lifted itself to a different level, and she announced to my retreating profile, "I'll commission you to eradicate the weeds from my front yard."

I looked back at her with an inquiring face. I gestured toward the front of the house where a mixture of weeds and dormant grass had given no appearance of civilized care in quite a spell. "What part of the property are you referring to?"

"Don't be insolent. Start to work or leave my property."

"Yes, ma'am. Any sling blades or shovels around here to work with?"

"No!" she said emphatically and slammed the door.

I guess I stood there confused for a long while, wondering if she was slightly mad. Her appearance, her voice, and her directions suggested a separation from reality.

"Commissioned to eradicate the weeds..." I mumbled weakly and went out to the yard. "Might as well attempt to clear out a rain forest with my bare hands."

The wind came up behind me and found every exposed skin area. I either had to get busy clearing the yard or hit the trail for home. I decided to start on the yard. I wasn't sure Reclusive Reonda would ever appear again to pay me, but she'd commissioned me so I guess that meant some contract existed.

The yard was a challenge to my bare hands and young back. The big clumps of Johnson grass came out fairly easy, but vines and nasty renegade shrubs resisted, armed with briars and sharp bark that had my hands cut and bleeding. My fingernails were soon encrusted with the dark soil of her former flower beds, and my muscles grew weary in the slow passage of the morning hours.

Once, when I returned from carrying a load of brush and gangling roots to the pasture beyond the yard, I saw sweet Frema's moon-shaped face scrutinizing my work from the security of her front room window. I pretended not to notice her and bent back to the task of weeding and tearing away the undergrowth of the path around her front porch.

I took no breaks and asked for nothing as the morning climbed out of its grey dome and the day lengthened toward evening. My hands were bloody claws of dirt and grime and my clothes were an equal match. I realized Miss Frema was not going to offer lunch or any respite from the cold, bloody ordeal. After several hours, even my stubborn pride had enough and I hauled off the last bunch of rubbish. The front yard was plucked clean on both sides of the dirt walk, but it was no more appealing to me than it had been as it appeared in the morning's hesitant light.

I went slowly up the steps and knocked on the door, my energy allowing only a meek sound that may not have been heard inside. I leaned against the porch column and waited for Miss Frema.

It seemed an eternity before the door creaked partially open, and a boney, ivory hand extended out toward me. I looked down and saw that the hand held dollar bills. As I reached for the money, the hand dropped its reward and withdrew into the house. I moved as quickly as I could to capture the money before the wind took it from my grasp. I stuffed it, crumpled, into my pants pocket and staggered weakly down the steps.

I was too worn out to pedal my bike up the intervening hills. I pushed it alongside the highway and coasted down the other sides, allowing gravity to pull me half the way home.

When I finally rode the backside of the last hill to our front steps, I entered the house, thankful for the relative warmth, forgetting the cut of the day's bluster. Momma was in the kitchen, so I went there first and handed her the two dollars that Miss Frema had paid me for the day's work. She didn't say a word as she took the money and glanced at my bloody and gnarled hands. I went quietly to the bathroom, soaked my hands in warm water, treated them with a mercurochrome Dad used for his mill injuries, changed out of my dirty clothes, and lay down for a feverish nap.

Momma woke me in time to eat before I rode my bike out to meet Mr. Moon and deliver my paper route. Although she never said a word about my efforts for the strange Miss Frema or my meager pay, she gave me an extra ration of beans, and my hot cornbread had a covetous dab of butter on it. I ate it gratefully and headed back out into the wind of the February day.

Times were difficult while Dad got himself in shape enough to work. Food was scarce and work after school and on weekends took up most of our time. Sundays we still made the long walk to church and Brother Creed laid out his thoughts on how the Bible related to us on a daily basis. I listened and understood the best I could, but mainly I looked down the pews to where Genevieve was sitting with her mother.

I don't even have a stray thought about why, but she had picked me out as her friend but had asked that I call her Evie, and her special smile seemed to be just for me. I liked to hang back after church and talk to her a minute before Rand gave me a look and I had to meet up with Momma and the other kids and head home.

It wasn't really too much of a conversation, but it was more than we had at school because she was older than me, so we didn't often see each other.

I don't know where I found the time, but I'd written some poetry and had pressed it into her hand at school one day in the hallway. She knew what my writing meant to me, so she took the work without speaking and read it over the weekend and gave it back to me at church with encouraging words on the tattered paper. They weren't love poems. They were simply along the lines of whatever poet we were studying in Mrs. Murray's class.

But Evie never faltered in sending a sweet note or speaking a word of praise. It elevated my spirits during the grey winter days.

"What's that pretty girl see in you?" Sherm had asked me one day during gym class.

"Don't know. Don't care," I answered.

"I always thought she was smart," he countered. "But she can't be sharp if she considers you worth pulling out of the river."

"We meet on a higher level than your mind can understand," I said.

"Only level I know is how nature 'tended boys and girls to be. You don't know it, Ollie, but the sexes are different for a reason."

"Go think small thoughts, little brain," I said. "And leave me and my relationship alone."

"Relationship? What's that?"

I ignored him, and he went off to spy on Bonnie Bitt.

7
God's Chosen Soldiers

You'd think enough struggle went on in daylight hours.

But one night, a few weeks into dead winter, a new challenge surfaced. It was nearly midnight and we were all asleep in a house nearly as cold as the great outdoors when some of God's lowest creatures came to see us, theft their aim, vengeance their goal.

They approached our rest with silent feet, bringing evil to our doorstep. They came down off the mountain, I guess, crossed the creek, and started for the front yard when Billy Rand saw them. I say "I guess" because I was asleep. Rand saw them first and woke me and then went off to wake up Momma. He shook me on the way out and I heard something about "the Good Lord" from his mouth. By then I was wide awake because of the light flickering its way through a moonless night and reflecting off the window glass. I thought the barn was on fire. You know how your mind grabs at things quick to give you some understanding of what's happening around you when your senses can't take in the real thing until you run it past the situation a couple of times—and then it makes some sense.

What I saw out the window did not make any sense, however. And the Good Lord's name, in those exact words, came to my lips as I looked out into the pit of night. It was the scum of the human race, come to call in the deepest part of the night when Dad was off at work in the cotton mill and we kids were bundled up in the cold house in cotton quilts and separate dreams. But the cold had a new ally this night, with the lowest level of cowardice. They had to cover their faces for anonymity and to bolster their strength. They had the lynch mob mentality of whatever driving cause they were pushing at the time. And, of course, they were soldiers of God, come to do his work.

It wouldn't take Momma long to dispel that myth.

Momma and Billy Rand went out on the porch after Rand told me to hang back and stay out of sight. He told Momma that they were probably trying to scare me because I'd had a hand in turning in that Seth "Black Angel" fellow to the law. Momma looked at me in the dark like she was disappointed in me, but she pulled on her only sweater and told Rand to stand beside her and she'd do the talking. I had to hand it to her. She didn't appear scared one inch. She was like the Lord's angels were marshaled up there in the darkness to undergird her strength and she wasn't about to be scared of piss-ant types that came in the night and brought fear and threats to children. I pressed myself against the wall and almost felt sorry for them as they stepped out into light cast by the sea of torches.

Momma didn't wait for anyone to speak. She raised her voice in defiance. "Get off our property!" she shouted. "I got children sleeping in here and I ain't having you scare a one of them."

The group stopped and a couple of the Klansmen stepped forward to reply to her words. "We got word that wickedness and such is goin' on down in this hollow, and we come to chastise those that live in the devil's ways."

I heard Momma laugh.

"You chicken-feathered bastards think for one minute I'm gonna allow such riffraff as you to come up to my house at midnight and make judgments against my family's name and character?"

I meant to tell you about Momma. She was a woman whose soul belonged to Jesus, but her mouth sometimes "picked up" when it came to her children.

I looked around the opened door, through the screen, and could see a front of white robes, each one holding his own burning torch. They were back a piece off the porch in the chert of the farm road.

So this was the Invisible Empire.

This was the same group Grandma had lauded for their work against the scalawags and carpetbaggers. This was General Nathan B. Forrest's finest troops reincarnated. And we were their cause on this cold winter's night.

"We got our duty to do right by the Good Book. Those that live outside the pages are exposed to the flame of cleansing. We got our sworn duty to do," the closest robe was saying.

"Let me get this straight—you got a name? Or do I just call you the son-of-a-buck that gets to talk? Those other chicken-feathered varmints with you, they ain't got sense enough to talk? They just follow you and do whatever hateful thing you can come up with?"

"We're here to bring light and righteousness to this dark hollow."

"Light? What do you call light? You got maybe eight, ten hoods out there carrying a kerosene torch. That ain't the light you're talking about? I hope not. You don't know the light or you wouldn't be covering your faces and sneaking through the dark to scare a family that ain't done nothing to bring God's wrath up."

"We are God's chosen soldiers."

"If you're God's chosen ones, then I need to pray for each one of you."

"We heard you was testy. We ain't holding with women that mock the Lord."

"Mock? You talking mockery? Show me in the Bible where God's followers had to put on robes over their bodies and hoods over their heads to hide their faces and bring judgment to the 'wicked.'

"In the first place, you don't know me or my children. But I know you. You're the cowards that hide behind each other and bring trouble in your proud talk and judgment in your harsh work. Well, your harshness and dark spirits ain't doin' nothing tonight. You ain't got no mandate to chastise me or mine. My man's off working nights at the only job he can hold so he can feed these five children in this old house. He ain't never give a minute's thought to looking out for somebody else's sins such as you say. We tell our children to be strong in God and hard in the books.

"What are you telling *your* children 'bout where you are tonight?"

"Don't be testing us, woman—you Jezebel. We ain't past dragging you off that porch and flogging that back."

Momma laughed again.

"Take the first step. You want to set somebody right, you gotta come through me. But when you step, you better be sure the devil's right there behind you because I got the Good Lord and all His angels on this porch with me. You take one step, and try to harm one hair on one head, and you won't live to see morning come up over that mountain."

There was dissention in the ranks as Momma's strong voice challenged them. A few stepped back toward the barn while the spokesman and a shorter one tried to wave them forward. Momma didn't waiver in her message. "Only sin we carry with us is the original sin from the Garden. Me and my children don't lay out with harlots, or steal from the merchants, or bring trouble to the table. We work for every penny we spend and we praise God for every penny he gives us.

"What praises are you giving tonight? Is anybody off at your house trying to terrify your children or whip somebody's back? The biggest thing wrong with you bunch of cowards tonight is you got the wrong house to come up on and the wrong God to serve. You can move on to another house, but you better get the right God in your heart. But if you want to carry out your mandate, come on up here and meet God's angels."

I chose that moment to walk out onto the porch. I figured somebody in the crowd would recognize me.

There was a murmuring and some confusion so I guess they did.

I stood on the side of Momma that Rand wasn't on, and she was solid as Gibraltar. We all faced the burning torches and the fear dressed in robes that now seemed perplexed and void of a mission.

"That's the one," I heard one of the shorter ones say. I could've sworn it was the pock-faced Fly we'd met at Blue's on that Sunday.

"We come this far," Fly's voice started up, urging the others who were hanging back at Momma's words. "Let's pull 'im off that porch and get on with it. That on'ry woman can't stop us from doin' what we should."

"Wait a minute," another voice said over the emphatic Fly. "You done told us a story, boy. These here ain't no sorry white trash folk... That there's a momma and her school kids. I didn't sign up for hurting no kids."

Fly turned to address the Klan members with obvious desperation. "I told you boys the truth. This boy here's the one turned in Seth and 'em to the po'lice. We gotta teach him a lesson!"

"Seth got what he deserved," another voice hollered back. "I thought we was going after some kinda mixed family that lived like black hollow folks. These here folks ain't nothing but poor workin' people. We ain't got no call to go scarin' 'em out here in the middle of the night. I say we git on back across that creek and go home."

Other voices joined in unison to that idea and several of the torches began to turn back toward the creek.

"Wait! Wait!" Fly called out hoarsely, trying to rally the troops to his cause. "We done come a right smart way and I ain't for leavin' till we get some even justice on this here boy. Next thing you know he'll be pointin' a finger at you boys and tellin' the law secret stuff."

"Better git yore stories straight next time, Fly. We ain't lookin' to be hard ass on a family mindin' its own business. Them kids gotta go to school in the morning' and we done them a bad turn. Come on here, let's go before we do more damage. We done took a misstep here and I ain't so proud of it. Y'all come on with me and let's go."

The ranks were thinning out. A couple of the robes were headed back down the chert road that led past the barn. Others turned to follow, not hastily, but at a definite retreat now that their night had been exposed as a personal vendetta by one of the lowest-ranked members. Not that any one of them enjoyed any esteem in my book. Anybody that had to hide his identity to go do his devil deeds was a mighty poor witness of a man, anyway. Besides, I truly believed that God would stand with a woman protecting her family in the face of evil. He would send His angels to stand before her. He always sent someone.

"Who's that comin' down the road?" Billy Rand spoke, gesturing up the hill where a white form seemed to be floating on the night air, much as those Confederate ghosts of our youth would prowl the graveyard while we lay on a far hill and watched them outfitting for one last battle with the Yankee raiders.

The West End Klan had seen enough. First, God's strong, defiant woman and now a ghost floating through the night like Gabriel come to stand with the woman and her boys on a dark porch at the clock knelling midnight.

I watched as Fly joined his brothers in an ignoble retreat toward the creek. They had barely cleared the barn when the form in the white shirt came to the edge of the yard and stood there like it was not understanding the fuss that had preceded its appearance. We could barely make out his face and form. He just stood there looking at us like he was standing in a field waiting for sunrise or waiting for someone to take a hand and guide him home. He was obviously lost.

Finally, I recognized the man from our sojourn into the lair where the Snow Girl had lain. Sherm and I had thought that he was the one calling to us that afternoon at the Coopers. Now, he was standing at the gate waiting for his mind to catch up with his body. “That’s old Cooper,” I whispered in the dark. “He’s nuttier than squirrel do-do.”

“Watch your mouth,” Momma said.

8
"Home is where, when you go there, they have to take you in."

—Robert Frost

It turned out to be one of those indescribable nights. I noticed that I was having a lot of those lately.

It started without interest as Rand and Weldon decided to scare up some Blue Branch girls over near the old Christian Church. We called them Blue Branch because they lived near a creek by that name that ran mountain water year 'round to a lake that gathered up the valley's water. The old joke was that you had to carry an ax with you to pick up these girls because you'd have to stop and clear the fallen trees off the dirt road that lead to their shack.

Old Man Hamrist was all we knew their father by. His daughters we knew from school. They were sample models. You know, as if the Good Lord said, "I'll make a few samples and send them out in the world and see if they're acceptable."

They were acceptable. Let me tell you. Even as little as I knew, these samples had all the right equipment and the right portions of each. Few boys ventured over the branch to pick up a Friday night date, but their loss was Weldon's determined gain. Except it was Sunday night and the girls from Pinetuck Hollow needed a ride home from that old church. Weldon had set it up to be there when the doors let out the sparse Sunday night crowd. Of course, dallying down the steps was Lexie and her twin sister Lydia.

I asked Rand how they got such names, but he just grinned and said something like, "Call 'em Jack 'n Jill, I don't care. They're born lookers."

And lookers they were.

How did I get saddled with the two biggest puberty-wrangling cowboys in the valley? The same story. Sweet Momma sent me along to catch the out-of-bounds passes and to keep the morality of one Holmes kid intact. What she didn't realize was that Lexie and Lydia had such a charm about them that she sent the wrong interloper. I was beginning to understand that there was a lot of learning available outside of school.

The girls were matching bookends.

I don't know if Lexie or Lydia sat down in the back between Rand and me. All I knew was she made my face run hot, flush-like, and her smell was sweet and pure, like angel dewdrops had settled in her hair and gave it that sheen like a Kansas wheat field. She had some freckles that dared stretch over her nose like they were proud homesteaders, but they were so naturally aligned that she didn't try to cover them with makeup. She just left them be and they were cute as puppies looking out from under a protective mother's pouch.

It wasn't my place to talk, but when Weldon had eased out of the gravel and dirt church yard, and brother Rand played dead silence in the presence of the Pinetuck beauty, I had to open my mouth and begin to question. Much to Rand's chagrin. "Are you Lydia or Lexie?" I asked quietly.

She laughed, as did her sister in the front seat who was helping Weldon shift gears on the column-shift lever.

"Who are you, little blonde-haired boy? Or is that red, an auburnish color in the moonlight?"

Her question came back playfully, but sweet. She ran a hand through my hair and caused a storm of reaction inside me. Outside I tried to keep myself cool.

"I'm Oliver Wendell Holmes," I said. "Self-appointed keeper of Leopold and Alphonse."

She laughed again. "Do I look like a Lydia or a Lexie?" she asked.

"I can't tell you apart at school," I replied. "Out here in the dark where there's only the moon, mostly blocked out by those dark clouds, I'm completely lost."

"Momma just liked those names. Lydia is a family name and Lexie is short for Alexander. They call me Lexie at home. At school, too, I guess."

I nodded in agreement, accepting her explanation, but still not sure if I could separate them at school. Looking to the front, I noticed that Lydia had relinquished the gear shift chores and was busy running a pink tongue into Weldon's ear. How he kept the car on the two-lane blacktop with "Susan Hayward" tantalizing his ear gave me new respect for his driving ability.

Back seat girl was following the lead of the front seat. Billy Rand was locked down by the door panel, his arms around the pretty girl and their lips locked in an undeniable warming of the heart. She seemed to be positioned more over his body than she was on the seat so while I was quietly learning, as the naked plum trees shot past on the narrow road, I was also as out of the scene as a Baptist preacher at a college fraternity party. Plenty of lascivious action was taking place, and I might as well have been standing outside the power building on Noble Street watching the show-window television set. A right smart bit of fondling was going on, and I was more the voyeur than the keeper.

After several minutes of windshield-fogging breathing, Weldon pointed the nose of the little Ford toward a familiar point and I knew my censorship services were about to be negated. I recognized the territory even in the depths of the now moonless night. And when the yellow glow of the filling station lights lit up the windshield, I knew this buster was about to be parked too far from home to walk there easily. And too far from home training to bring about a moral consciousness to the situation. Just the way the two couples required it. I wondered if they were actually going to park up the hill from where the shotgun lover had sprayed our public scrutiny in his private anger. What did I care?

The car eased to a brief halt at the edge of Evil-Eye Ford's station so I breathed my last fond breath in the presence of the Blue Branch twins and got out without a word.

"We'll be gone 'bout an hour," Weldon said, as he eased out the clutch. "Sit down over there and we'll come back for you."

I waved him off and got out into the biting cold.

Young love on seatcovers. Cold wind on my young butt.

Somehow I got the worst of this deal.

Evil-Eye Ford was manning the cash register as I entered. She was drawing on a cigarette like her lungs were two giant jugs unable to be saturated with the defiling smoke. She gave me a painful look like I was the next-to-last person she wanted to walk through that door. I ignored her silent stare and wandered over to the battered drink box and looked into its dark depths for a Royal Crown Cola.

"Your daddy know you're ticketing stuff here?" she asked, acting like God wanting to know what Moses had done with the Ten Commandments.

"I got money," I replied, quietly opening the RC on the corner opener and listening as the metal cap plummeted to the existing pile in the receptacle.

She blew smoke toward me and reached a hand through its fog as I imparted my last quarter. “Whatcha doin’ out so late on Sunday night?” she wanted to know.

“I just came from church,” I said truthfully, thinking of the twins’ Christian indoctrination for the evening.

“Why ain’tcha home?”

“I’m waiting for my friends,” I said.

She made a show of depositing my quarter in the register and returned my fifteen cents change like they were forty pieces of silver.

“I’m closin’ up here directly,” she warned. “Ain’t good to be open too late with all the crazy going-ons here in the valley.”

I nodded my agreement and thought I’d pass time in the relative warmth of the store by leaning against the Coca-Cola box like I’d seen adults do countless times in the past. The wind whistled down off Cottaquilla Mountain and found the country store, pulling at the old wooden door that couldn’t seal itself properly against the elements. A splattering of icy rain hit the dirty windows and oozed slowly down the panes like sleet.

“God awful weather,” she mumbled under her breath and looked off into the night.

“Happens every year about this time,” I said to her, smart aleck-like—not caring if I offended her.

I did and she glared. I wimped out, looking away from her, turning my attention to a single yellow bulb over the counter swaying as if the wind had found it there and was playing with it as it would a swing in the park that glided under Nature’s hands.

“Who them friends you waitin’ on? That storm’s settlin’ in. I reckon I’ll cut off the gas pumps and get to the house.”

“ ’Said they’d be back in a few minutes.”

She was quiet, looking at me like I was holding her from a warm fire. “Ain’t much business this time a night. Not in this here weather, noways.”

I didn’t reply.

What were my options? I really didn't want to finish off the RC, but I hated to waste the dime. I was hungry, but I wanted to save the change for later in the week. All she had to eat for that kind of money was the infamous marshmallow Moon Pie and a Royal Flush candy bar. We had missed supper in order to hitch up with Weldon and make the Blue Branch connection. Now I was out of the circle, anyway, and my stomach wrapped up on my backbone and asked for filling.

I considered making a dash for Jamback, but facing the icy rain and that north wind didn't appeal to me. I wasn't sure how long Evil-Eye, facing me across the dirty concrete floor, would be happy with my company. I quietly prayed that a few customers would drop down off 9 and self-pump their gas out there in the uncovered island.

What else could I do except pray?

I could build character and pull my thin, tattered jacket about me and go out bareheaded into the teeth of a winter storm that was getting itself together for a night of spite and fitfulness. Calculating that I was facing the wind rather than getting pushed along by it, it would take an hour or so to walk to the nefarious Jamback and then Pig Trail Road to our house. Then to Momma who'd be there ready to flail the hell out of me for being out on such a night. It'd surely be my fault for not staying with Pistol Billy Rand and Wet-Ear Weldon. Mission failure, in her eyes.

What was I to do?

Nothing. Part of my prayer was answered as a noise rose over nature's winter howling. I turned, startled, and looked into the dim light of the pumps as a dark phantom rode to a halt, shaking the ground in its impatience, rattling the wooden door of the store entrance until it slipped its meager latch.

Evil-Eye used words I figured were obscene as I'd never before heard them. She came out from behind the high glass counter that fronted the door, struggled to pull it closed, and leaned over to see who or what was vibrating the window panes.

I wanted to cuss, myself, as I saw Golden Boy kill the beast and get out and run for the store. One of his riders got out, too, but began pumping gasoline into the phantom of the night. Moorefield stood quietly for a moment just inside the door, shivering in his cool sweater and expensive slacks. He looked like a magazine model, stepping out of a clothing ad. He had blonde hair, now blown and damp, and his hooded eyes took in the dirty country store innards quickly. A confident smile rode over his lips and stayed there. "The great Voit disciple." He winked at me.

I figured I didn't have anything to lose to him. We were off school grounds and he wouldn't start up anything in Evil-Eye's place.

"So," I said, "they let you out of jail for the weekend?"

His smile continued. He took a step toward me, but it didn't seem threatening. It was more like he didn't understand this punk who was always thorning his side.

"Why is it you try to rile me up, Holmes?" he asked.

"Just natural curiosity. How does a big shot like you end up in a dead-end school like ours? What's the intrigue with the agrarian lifestyle? Tired of the sophisticated Charleston society?"

"What do you know about my background?"

I smiled casually. "Not much. Word out in Choccolocco is that you got tossed out of a couple of private schools and had to come graduate with our country scholars."

"Scholars?" He laughed. "I passed through that curriculum in elementary school. I'm just waiting for spring to come so I can get on to a real school. Be careful what you seek, little trash boy. You might not like what you find."

"If I'm suppose to be so trashy, Golden Boy, why is it I've never been arrested for breaking the law? I've never been tossed out of school. Never been chastised by the church. Explain the duplicity to me."

"Look in the mirror more often, sweet boy. You need a close haircut and a dermatologist."

"Better than a thick folder on daddy's desk."

"Did I miss something here? Why are you talking to me this way? Where's your backup? Where's your posse? Dirk and I could crush you like a roach and wipe you off our shoes on the doormat. Just keep running that sassy mouth of yours."

"I don't hide anything," I said. "What're you hiding?"

"I'll give you my opinion when the time's right. When I have time to deal with a zero like you, you'll know my boiling point. Don't push my patience tonight."

His shadow and boy servant came bristling through the door like the wild was about to destroy him. Dirk stomped his feet and made a production of throwing his wet, dark hair back out of his face. He looked at Moorefield, then snarled as he recognized me. He brushed past Golden Boy and grabbed my jacket in his thick fist.

"Look, Duncan," he sneered. "It's shit for brains."

Before he could hit me, Moorefield placed a hand on Dirk's shoulder.

"Easy, Dirk," he calmed his sidekick. "We'll take care of 'Run-off-at-the-Mouth' at a later date. We got things to do tonight. Pay the lady."

Dirk-the-Jerk released me and patted my twisted jacket. "Sorry if I messed up your cover." He grinned. "Where'd you get that weave—at the Salvation Army?"

He and Moorefield erupted into laughter.

"No," I responded. "Your momma left it."

Dirk was back on me again, only this time his hand was around my throat. I knew I was in trouble because Moorefield was simply standing by enjoying my struggle for air. Dirk was strong and his fingernails were digging into my windpipe.

Then a strange thing happened.

One minute Dirk had bad intentions written all over his face. The next there was a short grunt and he loosened his hold. It was an awkward moment for me, standing there, my breath ebbing away while an external force was challenging his. He didn't fully let go but the pressure slackened and I quickly drew in air as I saw a strong dark hand gripping Dirk's wrist, twisting it slowly down and away from my throat. Dirk seemed a frightened animal, reduced from the stalker to the prey. His snarling mouth lost its dominance as a greater strength took away his physical advantage. I strained, in the deep shadows of the country store, to make out my rescuer. He was only a silhouette inserted into the space where evil was darkest and my personal demise had been imminent.

As if by a spell, Dirk and Golden Boy drew back away from me, their eyes locked on the man who stood calmly, yet firmly, between me and them. They began a voluntary retreat that was almost indetectable. They were no longer interested in me. They were forced into a threatening situation themselves, and their courage shrank as they realized the futility of further struggle, a struggle that had fallen from their favor to the one commanding the situation.

"How you boys doin' tonight?"

The voice was low, familiar, and, to my ears, pleasant. He looked at me and I could see the perpetual grin that covered Uncle Doug's yellow-stained teeth, caused by smoking roll-your-own cigarettes and drinking any intoxicating liquid. This rainy night I was positive he'd had a drink or two. But no matter to me. He was usually drunk and I was always glad to see him.

"What you doin' out on this cold, wet night, Ollie?" he asked innocently, like we were downtown on a Saturday night and he was questioning my curfew, not caring at all about the abusive youngsters that had recently imposed their strength on me. He had looked away from Moorefield and Dirk as if they were conquered entities and were nothing else to be concerned about. The boys themselves seemed unsure whether to slink away or wait for their official release. Either way, the door seemed to be attracting them as they watched Uncle Doug out of the corners of their eyes.

Evil-Eye Ford interrupted the stalemate, speaking as if her insertion into the taunt atmosphere were as routine as being the late night cashier. “You owe me a dollar for gas,” she said.

I looked at Dirk. His eyes were still wider than usual. Moorefield no longer seemed as frightened, but was definitely wary of the man in the shadows wearing the military field jacket. Dirk paid the dollar from his front pocket, and he and Moorefield went out the door into the harsh rain, letting the screen slam on the doorframe.

Evil-Eye started a laugh that ended in a cigarette-smoke cough. “Doug Thomas,” she snorted as her wind returned. “There you go scarin’ off my customers. They was about to forget to pay me. Why you wanta do that?”

Uncle Doug looked at her and laughed. His face was wet from the rain but I could make out the dark skin and the deep widows peak of his coal black hair. His face was not particularly handsome, but it was not unpleasant to look at, either. I had never seen it in a grimace of any sort. He laughed a lot and hugged Momma with affection, calling her “Sis.” She loved her baby brother in return, regardless of his affinity for the alcoholic’s nip.

“You’re a lost soul, Doug Thomas,” Evil-Eye said as she deposited the dollar bill in her cash drawer.

“I ain’t lost my soul, Louise,” Uncle Doug replied. “It just wandered off somewhere and ain’t come home in a while.”

They both enjoyed the moment, sharing a knowing glance over the shadows. I suddenly realized Uncle Doug had a whole different outlook on Old Evil-Eye. Maybe I should, too.

The rain made itself known again against the frailty of the store’s windows. “What you doin’ out on a nasty night like this, Doug?” she asked.

He sighed as if he could explain easily enough, but there was no concern in his voice. “Miss Jewel put me out in the storm.”

“What’d you do now, you crazy man?”

Doug looked at the floor, shuffled a couple of steps to the drink box and leaned against it for support. “ ’Guess I forgot the two rules of the house.”

"Just two?"

"Well, two that turned out important tonight."

"What was 'at?"

He laughed. "No cards and no drinkin'."

Ford hooted again and looked for a smokeable butt in the ash tray. "You picked a good night to buck 'gainst the house. Where you plan on beddin' down?"

"Aw, I got me an old buddy down on 78's got a barn that's warm and dry. Smell ain't much, but the animals don't complain none."

Doug looked back at me, having laid out the events of his evening. "How come you ain't home, boy?"

I looked down at the floor, not sure how to respond. "Billy Rand and Weldon went off sparkin' the Blue Branch twins. I got left off here."

Doug grinned. "That Billie Rand's too bashful to be courtin'. Ya shoulda joined 'im, Ollie."

I shrugged. "I'm not very sociable."

He laughed. "You ain't gotta be sociable—just somebody special. You're special, Ollie. I'd bet on you in a bear fight."

Evil-Eye was back on her business side. "I hate to tell you boys this, but I gotta close up and get to bed. Gotta open early in the morning for them pipe-shop guys."

Doug mockingly objected, "Ya puttin' us out in the storm, Louise? I can't catch a break. What say I come over and lay on your floor tonight?"

"Better head out for that barn. If'n I was to take ya in, Miss Jewel'd be over here tomorrow to scratch my eyes out."

"Nary a misdeed or a misstep from me, fair lady," he said lightly. "The juice flows through my veins and deadens my brain."

"Sober up out there in that wet stuff, Doug Thomas. This old girl's too tired to be concerned over a drunk like you."

"Cruel woman," he said, still lightly, still with humor in his voice. "A vagabond in the wind. But what of this child? My blood-kin that lacks safe transport to his abode. Must he face the outrageous fury of the winter storm? Where, woman, is your sense of decency?"

"Decency went home 'while ago and I'm right behind it. I'm lockin' up and cuttin' the juice. Out, out, riffraff."

Doug still grinned as he drew his collar up and staggered toward the door that was rattling in the gusts of wind that drove the rain.

"Sorry, sport," he told me. "Yonder is the highway and yonder further is a haven from the storm. You go your way and I mine. That barn loft will house me sufficiently until dawn. You try to catch up with that brother of yourn. Say, if I get back in good with my Miss Jewel, I'll come back by the house Sunday and let you drive her new Chevy."

"Thanks, Uncle Doug, but I don't have a driver's license."

"That's all right," he said and patted me on the back. "I don't either."

I nodded and frowned as we stepped out into the rain. I knew my direction was north into the wind. I also knew Doug Thomas had no destination at all. If Miss Jewel had cast him out into the weather, then he would stagger blindly until he found a tree to sit under in the cold, wet forest of someone's unfenced land, or he would sleep in the first ditch that captured his final stumble in the pitch darkness of homelessness.

"Come with me, Uncle Doug," I urged, taking his arm as we stood outside the now dark country store. "It's about two miles, but we'll be there in an hour or so. You'll die out here in this cold and wet."

He stood up straight as if awaiting military inspection of the ranks. "Doug Thomas sleeps in the bed he makes for himself."

With a half salute to his forehead, he headed off south toward Highway 78, many miles down the valley.

These elements were extreme for our forgotten valley. The rain came in sideways like the wind was catching it high up and bending it so it traveled parallel to the ground until it hit something. When it hit my face, it was like ice pellets fired out of a gun. Character building? More like suicide in the cold, dark country. Let that wind and sleet gang up on you and nature'd win every time.

I gritted my teeth and tried walking backwards out of the lot as Ford cut the lights and I had the darkness to fight along with the elements. The ditches were filling up fast so I walked the shoulder of the road and thought of Billy Rand and Weldon. Whatever beating I got at home was nothing compared to the one I was facing now. What was the old sermon that the preacher used on the suffering servant? I couldn't compare myself to anything divine, but it was a wretched existence as the night closed in on me.

Further up the road, I got to thinking there was no way I could hasten my step, or make the road home shorter, or bring the shelter closer to me.

The rain got worse. I was in the total void of darkness, and my goal of reaching the house seemed almost unobtainable. I walked with my back to the wind for a while, but I nearly fell over on the uneven surface. I took it on the chin again, thinking of the warm place up ahead through the trees that were swaying in the wind, and beyond the low hills that still had to be climbed and conquered, tittering over their crest to meet the wind at its highest point—and then to descend toward the homefire.

I heard the rumbling of the beast before I saw its fiery eyes come over the hill ahead. I didn't have to question who it was. No other car had descended the rolling hills that lead into the valley, and I'd heard that great growl before, the almost ethereal sound now that it rode the wind solemnly and covered the blackness of the night. I tried to move out of its trail and hide myself down the grassy side of the hill because I felt danger growing as it hurtled faster and faster down the icy road. Its beacons of light were the eyes of the dragon, its ear-splitting exhaust its inexorable breath—as it roared toward me. And then it was upon me. I continued my slow walking, head bowed, rain running off my face onto my drenched jacket, cold feet moving at will, eyes ahead toward the next step in the darkness.

I ignored the beast's hot breath as it settled beside me, dominating my world. The door swung open and lights came on. I refused to look at the car or to acknowledge the voices calling to me. I stumbled ahead, determined to die in the night before succumbing to any threats or deeds of evil that would befall me in the dragon's lair.

"Get in here, Ollie," a familiar voice beckoned, and I realized suddenly that I was mistaken. It couldn't be. It was Billy Rand's voice and the phantom snorting at the reins was Weldon's green Ford, one of its four doors beckoning to me like a shelter from the storm that I thought was beyond my grasp. I ran the few feet to the car and slid into the warmth of the backseat, burying my face in the softness of the cushions, content to let a few tears form in my eyes, knowing that no one would notice in the wasteland of my beaten face.

The door slammed and the Ford rolled ahead in the storm, its tailend protecting me now, like the skin of the ship that harbors and cradles its mates from the death and blackness of a demanding sea.

"You idiot," Billie Rand said to me over the seat. "We said we'd be back for you. Walking in this weather. Ain't he the stupidest brother you can have, Weldon?"

Weldon never looked but he defended me. "Leave him alone. He's got spunk, walking home like this. Lookee there, big 'un, the station's closed. Ain't a light showing down yonder about a mile."

I didn't have to look to see the night. It was there with me in the soaked clothes and shoes. It was there in my heart and soul where I feared the worst had befallen me. And yet I had been rescued.

"Another time," both Dirk and Moorefield had warned. But I'd worry about them after this night was conquered by the purging light of dawn.

"Keep goin' south, Weldon," I said. "Our Uncle Doug's homeless tonight. Miss Jewel put him out again."

They both grunted disapprovingly.

"Fine night," Billy Rand said. "Fine night."

Weldon continued south of Evil-Eye Ford's place. He and Rand both keeping watch for the stumbling image of our adventurous uncle in the winter downpour. We were almost to Highway 78 when they decided we had missed Doug Thomas and that he was probably lodged down for the night in a ditch alongside 9. We began a slow crawl back up the road, all of us now searching the darkness for any dark form that would indicate our kin. There was no traffic so we moved back and forth across the road, checking every clump of grass, every strand of bushes that might conceal his trembling body. The storm didn't bother to move away over the fields toward Georgia. 'Just sat over the valley, pouring its cursed rain out in full measures, taunting the wind to do its part in the hammering of anything frail or castaway in the forgotten vestue of the night.

We were nearly back to Evil-Eye's place when Weldon spotted a dark form halfway in a ditch near a thick forest. Perhaps Doug Thomas had tried to make it into the woods seeking shelter, but had not made his way without harm. And then we spotted a lump just off the road. He was not moving. Faced downward, his uncovered head catching the brunt of the rain.

I opened my back door quickly. "I got 'im," I said, stepping out into the storm as Weldon drove as close to the edge of the road as he could without getting the little Ford stuck in the mud.

When I got to our uncle, I didn't bother to check him for life. I'd prayed already that he would survive until we could find him, so I left that part of the equation to God. However, because of his battered form and the shifting mud of the ditch, I was unable to lift him by myself. The water was halfway to my knees and Doug's legs were completely underwater. I could barely see his waterlogged body in the blackness.

Stronger hands assisted me in the dark. With all three of us straining to dislodge Doug from his resting place, we managed to drag him from where he'd collapsed and toward the back seat of the car.

I maneuvered his body in a semi-upright position so I could manage to wedge myself inside. And just as I caught a long, deep breath of success,

Weldon had the green Ford pointed into the wind and Highway 9 became our watery pathway toward home.

"He still alive?" Rand asked, looking over the front seat, his own hair, face, and clothes as thoroughly soaked and out of whack as mine.

" 'Best I can tell," I replied, "If we had a beer, we could pop the top next to him and he'd open an eye to see who had the brew."

"That ain't funny," Rand said seriously.

"Definitely not," I said, "but thanks for hunting him down. When he left me at the store, I figured he'd cash it in tonight. He had nowhere to go, except out to Evil-Eye's barn, and he wouldn't go out there."

Rand looked back into the thin vortex of light cut in the darkness. "Some days," he said, "I feel sorry for him and some days I figure he don't try too hard to be normal."

"He can't be normal," I defended. "How'd you feel if a horde of German tanks was running up on you in the dark? Ain't like you can shake that reality out of your head."

Rand didn't say anything.

Weldon concentrated on his driving, trying to find a high spot in the road where the rain was not accumulating. By and by, he swore about the weather and wiped the windshield furiously—like he couldn't see where he was headed. Doug Thomas moved on my shoulder that was holding him upright and a noise came out of him like he was trying to return from a deep sleep.

"He's stone drunk," Weldon said. "I got a uncle lives in Rabbittown that was shot up in the war. He works on his farm all the time, but at night he don't sleep much and Aunt Mildred has to leave the light on for him."

Rand was still skeptical.

"Even if he's messed up, he can hold a job. Try to wake him up, Ollie. Momma's gonna be all over us getting our clothes wet and muddy."

"Yeah," I agreed. "Tomorrow being school."

"She'll be up all night again," Rand said.

"Whatcha mean?" I asked.

"Other day when you and Sherman T. went mudsliding, Momma stayed up all night washing your clothes in the sink and drying 'em by the fire." He looked over the seat at me. "How you think they got cleaned for school? We don't have a clothes fairy."

Doug Thomas' eyes came up slowly. When he could make out that he was safe in a moving car and that the rain was not pelting him into unconsciousness, he put on his infamous grin and hummed a line or two of some strange ditty.

We traveled on into the night, listening to Weldon cussing the weather and Doug acting like he was asleep on a park bench on a Sunday afternoon in June. Just before we reached Jamback, he roused up briefly and whispered toward me. I could barely hear him. "Let's get in out of the rain, Ollie..." His eyes closed peacefully. "The night's cold and the storm's furious with us."

"What's he mumblin'?" Rand asked.

I shook my head in the dark. "Nothing."

9

"The mills of the Gods grind late, but they grind fine."

—Greek Poet

"Stay away from Moorefield."

Billy Rand gave me good advice as he left the porch.

He and Weldon had managed to line up dates with Lexie and Lydia, and I was not needed this night. Not that I was ever needed when the sweet flower of youth needed plucking by two country Romeos who couldn't tell a sonnet from a critical essay.

Darkness had not found us yet. The sky was cold and clear, the woods of evening were catching the light and stealing it away for morning. A winged creature found itself in a solitary sky as it traced its path homeward.

I pitied myself as I sat on the porch steps and threw rocks across the yard, but without much spirit. After a while I figured I'd travel on over to Sherm's house and see what new jokes he had for me. Might find a magazine I hadn't seen before, or maybe ask Mr. Monte about his winter farm work, or what he'd heard about the Snow Girl. Nobody had mentioned the beauty in the snow, lately, but that tragedy was foremost in most people's minds.

Momma finally acknowledged my request to leave the yard for Sherm's, but not until she reminded me again of the evils that had recently chased our dreams into nightmares and had preyed upon our family with a relentlessness that had all of us on edge.

Of course her warnings were dead on target, and even Rand's thoughts on the Moorefield possibility had me skeptical about venturing past Jamback for any reason. I shouldn't have gone, but I suppose I allowed our dog, Harry S. Truman, to persuade me to give Highway 9 a quick shot on a dull Friday night. Truman repeatedly came over and pulled at my pants leg like he needed a trot. I relented and halfheartedly started up the road on my Western Flyer, away from our safe base.

I took up a good head of gravity-induced speed once I started south on 9, and Truman broke into a hard trot in his efforts to be my sidekick. But he soon lost ground to my speedy wheels. When I was about a mile from the house, I looked back to check the dog's location, and instead of seeing his shadow as he chased me in the twilight, I saw a set of headlights moving at such a deliberate speed that my heart bumped up against my chest and my brain gathered up anxiety and held it close.

Not again. I was dumbfounded.

Not taking any chances, I eased my bike to the far side of the road. How many lowlife characters would I face this time? More than one. The West End boys never traveled alone.

As I slowed my bike, the car seemed to slow its pace as well. Of course, looking back into the remnants of twilight, I could not discern if it was another reenactment of *Sleepy Hollow*, or if Weldon had decided to creep up on me and laugh like crazy when I wimped out.

Harry S. didn't wimp out. He caught up with me in a final burst of energy and paced along beside me, happy to be back in the race. I called to him encouragingly and continued to let the wheels ferry me on into the darkness.

What if it was Weldon?

I ought to pick up a rock and bounce it off his windshield. That'd put his sausage in the grinder. He'd be madder than old man Wilts was that Halloween we let all his goats and cows out of their nocturnal places and he spent two days rounding them up. Naturally, we were kinda getting back at him because he liked to fire off his shotgun in our direction every time we cut across his pasture heading for the Cheaha foothills to hunt.

Weldon should have been halfway to Blue Branch by now. It couldn't be him. He wouldn't waste time scaring me if he had Lydia's sweet-smelling hair on his brain.

What if it was the West End boys or the Mill Village gang?

They were like pillaging Vikings on an angry sea. Took whatever they wanted. Intimidated folks. If I bounced a roadside rock off of their windshield, it'd be paramount to declaring war on a sovereign nation. Alone on 9, with only my bike and my dog, I'd put myself in a bad spot. Momma said there'd be nights like this. She didn't know exactly how right she was.

The car kept coming, its lights on low, its engine making a threatening sound. They seemed in no hurry to reach me, although I must have been the focus of their attention. If I sped up to reach the Monte's, would they speed up as well? Would this thrust of meanness cause me to hit the ditches to evade their efforts, much as Sherm and I had given ground before to save our lives? Whatever happened to that world we used to know where we prowled the hollows and farms of Choccolocco without imminent fear stalking us? Did we grow this new awareness, or did that old human nature of pure meanness grow beyond us—then turn on us like we were the weaker race?

A voice in the car called out to me. I didn't recognize it, so unless Weldon was trying to pull a fast one, it wasn't his jalopy that idled, closing in on me. A silhouette against the blackness of the car, the glow of the cigarette, and the smell of heavy tobacco moving through the still air told me this was not someone I knew.

"Been studying that bicycle, boy. Why don't you get off it and I'll put it in my trunk and take it home to my little cousin."

Laughter from the car. More than two in there. I'd heard Mill Village idiots liked to steal stuff. But out from under me?

I stopped my bike and straddled the bar. The car eased up even with me and stopped. The driver flipped his cigarette in my general direction. Low laughter again from the dark hulk.

"Hey, fuzzy face, what you doin' out here alone on this highway? I almost didn't see ya. Coulda run you down and not know..."

"Where ya live?" called a second voice.

I considered if I wanted to answer their questions, or if I should ignore them and hope they'd evaporate in the dark like some awful odor.

"You one a them funny boys ain't got no tongue?" the driver asked. This brought more chuckles.

You're just laughing fools, I wanted to say, but I was in a fix. I knew it and my dog knew it. Harry S. Truman growled at the car like he was protecting the king's entourage.

The driver took note. "You ain't gonna sic that mad dog on us, are ya, Ace? Sounds mighty mean. Wouldn't bite a poor boy like me, would he?"

"I wouldn't if I was him," the other voice said. "Might die from poison."

Some laugher followed, but this time the driver got ticked off at the comment and turned back to the darkness of the interior. "Shut up, Arlin, or I'll put my foot up your butt."

"Why don't you try that, big boy? See where it gets you."

The horn blurted out abruptly, as the two struggled momentarily. Then they laughed again and the attention came back to me.

"Look, boy," the driver said. "We ain't got all night. We lookin' for a light green Ford automobile that gets itself drove by a tall, skinny boy with slicked back hair. Name's Wellborn or somethin' like that. Tall and ugly—like a duck with its neck too long."

I was shocked! Weldon! They wanted Weldon.

"I...ah... I don't think I know that boy," I lied, stuttering slightly. I hoped my voice didn't betray me.

It did.

"Look here, twinkle toes," the driver's voice returned. "We want this here boy bad. Me and my girl was out sparkin' in Lovers Lane 'other night and this nasty green car pulls up beside us and starts throwin' its spotlight inside the car. Well, that 'bout lit my fuse. I swore I'd get back even with 'im but I can't find 'im. He just disappeared. Now, I need yore lyin' face to point out which one a these shacks is his so I can thank him properly fer ruinin' my night in the bushes."

I guess I had to say something. "I'm new around here," I lied. "I don't know many folks."

"You go ta school here, don't 'cha?"

I nodded half way in the dark.

"Well, how come ya don't know this cat? Can't be many green cars and duck necks in this Podunk community. Ya jest lyin', boy. I hate it when people lie to me."

Arlin came back to the conversation. "Come on, Hootie," he said. "Let's leave this here kid alone. He don't know poot 'bout no boy you describe. That coulda been ten people. They all skinny ugly out here. Look jest like their mommas and daddys."

"That's right, honeymuffin," a female voice from the back seat intervened. "I ain't fer spendin' no Friday night ridin' 'round these backwoods lookin' for somebody we don't even know. I'd rather be back at Lovers Lane or back uptown gettin' somthin' to eat."

The driver's voice prevailed. "Both ya whiners shut ya faces. I said what I'll do and I'll find 'at flashlight boy and 'im gonna cut 'im good. He'll 'member me after tonite."

Cut 'im good? This couldn't be Harold Hackett, better known as "Hootie," the convicted killer. The one that preferred to knife people that stole from him? What had Weldon stolen? His loving time? And now here I was being made into a Judas so Weldon could get his comeuppance.

This night was way off my charts. All I wanted to do was shake this crew and get back to the house. Brother, talk about a tough Friday night. How was I gonna separate myself from this bunch?

"There's a gas station about a mile down the road," I said, trying to think if I could postpone their discovery of Weldon and save my young butt at the same time. "I hear that lady runs the place knows everybody 'round here. She stays open late every night. She could probably help you out."

"Which way's 'at?" Hootie asked.

"I know where he means," Arlin said. "Old Ford's widow runs the place. You remember Ford, Hootie..."

Hootie must've been stumped for a minute. He was quiet. Thinking? Maybe it was a slow process for his one-track mind. "Somebody to cut," was his feature this night. "Huh?"

Arlin's voice butted in, "You know. You wuz with us 'at night Ford got shot. Down south a here. I don't know 'xactly where but Buck 'n Ford both got shot 'at nite. Ford's one 'at died."

Hootie was still as lost as the new postman on the rural route. "I weren't with ya on that 'un."

"Yeah, ya wuz," insisted Arlin. "Roscoe got up a meetin' and somebody waylaid us."

Hootie nodded. "Yeah, yeah. I know whatcha talkin' 'bout but I didn't know 'at Ford boy."

" 'At's 'cause he lived out here in Cotton Row. That was his first time with us—and his last."

"Oh, oh, he wuz leg shot and bled ta death 'cause he wouldn't go to the doc."

"That's him, lava breath. You 'bout stupid."

"I didn't know that fool, ok? It ain't like we wuz introduced or nothin'."

Arlin laughed. “Ya musta been drunk ’at nite.”

Hootie laughed. “I git drunk ever’ nite ’fore we go out huntin’.”

I knew what they were hunting. Mostly colored people. But sometimes white people, too. They mighta been with our recent committee that tried to burn a cross in front of our house to intimidate us. I was in a fix. More than a fix.

I was in deep, deep trouble.

“What’s ’at got to do with anything?” Hootie asked.

“Let’s go on down ’at gas station,” Arlin said. “We gotta meet somebody there anyway.”“

“What about ‘light-in-the-loafers’ here funny boy?

“He ain’t nothin’ to us. Take his bike if you want to and let’s get on outta here. I’m with fat woman back here and I need some grub.”

“Fat woman!” she screamed. “Who you calling fat, you beanpole? You have to run back and forth in the shower to get wet.”

Hootie laughed and Arlin tried to backtrack. “Be easy now, sweetheart. We’ll get you fed tonight and Hootie’ll give ya some sparkin’. Ain’t that right, Hootie?”

Hootie laughed diabolically. “Yeah. Shore...”

“Let’s get outta middle of the road,” Arlin suggested. “First car comes along’ll hit us and ruin this beautiful limo.”

“Don’t start in on my car, Cherokee!”

“Don’t start in on my name, Hootie!”

“Half-breed... half-breed...”

“Shut up, Hootie... Convict... convict...”

The “fat woman” intervened, “Both you dimwits shut up and let’s get outta here.”

Hootie must’ve agreed. “I reckon we need ta get on down to ar’ meetin’ with that kid.”

I felt a relief beyond thankfulness as the wicked ones seemed on the edge of departure. But before the car could ease away from Harry S. and me, it suddenly lurched and the driver's door flew open. It was such a worn out piece of transportation that the interior lights didn't come on and I still couldn't make out any faces.

A dark hulk of a man appeared before me, and I thought I saw a glint of metal in his hands.

"I got my shotgun on that there dog, boy. You tell 'im to get on outta here."

"Why should I?" I asked without thinking.

"Cause you goin' fer a little ride with us and I ain't likin' to git dog bit 'fore the nite gits started good."

Man, I thought, this isn't good. "Go home, Harry," I said sternly to the protective dog beside me.

Harry didn't move.

"What kinda name's 'at?" Hootie asked.

I ignored his comment but I had trouble looking past the shotgun pointed toward my dog. I picked up a rock and tossed it at Harry S. He saw it immediately and quick-stepped to avoid my throw. But he did not leave.

"Git home, Harry!" I raised my voice, but my dog continued to eye the big guy and to growl menacingly.

"Come on, Hootie," Arlin called. "That dog's got more sense than you got. He knows it ain't right to snatch somebody off the road."

Hootie was angry.

"Shut up, Arlin. I'm handlin' this. Look here, boy, you gonna git in the car with us. I know ya can help us find that other cat. I'll kill that there dog if he jumps at me."

I was tired of their mess. "Why don't you folks just go on and leave us alone. I'm not looking for a ride and my dog's not leaving me."

"Sure he is," Hootie said, walking around the bike so he could get a sight on Harry.

Harry S. realized his position was poor, so just as the blast of the shotgun momentarily deafened me, the dog disappeared off the road and into the woods. I didn't think he was hit, but I was steaming mad at the convict. I wanted to find a stick and smash his face.

He must have figured I'd rebel against him because while I was still searching the darkness for Harry, Hootie moved quickly to seize my arm.

"You gonna git in the car, kid, or you want some a this shotgun, too?"

Without another word, I stepped toward the stinking car, pulled the front seat forward so I could get in the back, and sat down in the darkest hell of my young life.

What else could happen to me?

We hadn't gone far before I could make out the occupants of the car. They were all smoking and I was desperate for air. The thing just stunk.

I didn't pay much attention to the girl beside me, and the one called Arlin seemed to have some sense. He kept trying to convince Hootie that it was wrong to pull an innocent kid in off the road. Hootie didn't pay him any attention, however, and pushed the accelerator to the floor. The car rattled, vibrated, and gave new meaning to the term "death trap".

While I was busy sizing up the boys and how I was gonna get outta this mess, I felt the warmth of the body next to me and a hand touched my hair. "Hey, sweetie," she said softly near my ear. "You're kinda cute. Where've I seen you before?"

My eyes were about adjusted to the dim light of the dash so I looked-into the pudgy face of the anointed fat woman. She had pudgy cheeks with evidence of acne growing on them and she had the throaty voice of a heavy smoker. It was Margie of the Sandwich Shop—Jack Daniel Margie. Motorhuming Margie. Great. Now her motor was humming next to me. I felt doubled-locked to my circumstances.

For once, Hootie did something for me. He looked up at the rear view mirror and saw his woman stroking my head. His anger flashed.

"Get your fat rump off the kid," he yelled.

Margie laughed and touched my hair again.

"You know what'd be fun, Hootie. We need to carry this here cute boy up to the hangout with us. I dig his pretty hair and white teeth. I bet he's never had a real Friday night woman date."

"I bet he don't want none a your honey," Arlin laughed, looking over the front seat at us.

Margie went belligerent, screaming vile words and swinging her fists at both Hootie and Arlin. They just ducked out of range of her rage and Hootie let the car drift over the middle of the road, narrowly missing an oncoming car. Margie ended her tirade with an admonition that she wanted both men dead before morning and by the most painful means possible.

I retreated as far as I could on the armrest and kept quiet.

With Margie locked down angry and Arlin studying the terrain, Hootie wanted to know how much farther we had to go.

"You shore forget things easy," Arlin said. "We wuz up this way not long ago. That filling station's up ahead here on the left. You oughta see the lights soon. Better slow this tater-hauler down."

Hootie tried the brakes, and the wheel jerked hard right and started vibrating even more than it had been.

Arlin whooped and laughed. "This car ain't fit for the junkyard, Hoot. I seen wrecked war jeeps better'n this cow."

"Shut your face, Cherokee. I need to sell some beer and rite quick. Where's that boy? What's his name?"

"Moorefield. His name's Moorefield. I sold him a six-pack for two bucks last week. We need to go to a dollar a beer. His old man's rich—big shot up town..."

Did he say Moorefield? I was having more bad connections than the phone company. Then a miracle happened. The jerky motion subsided and we crept, humble like, into the dusty lot of Evil-Eye Ford's Split-Nickel filling station and Country Store. If Dirk the Jerk and Moorefield spied my young carcass in the roller derby of inmate city, what else could befall me? Third time's the charm, Moorefield had indicated. Third time! Rand had given me excellent advice, most recently as the narrow light of day left the tomb of our enclosing valley. Not heeding him a bit, here I was in the middle of my poor judgment and convicted felons—and Moorefield was just a judge's gavel away from equal justice himself.

Sure enough, Golden Boy's Red Stallion was standing in the back shadows of Ford's store, the omnipresent glow of cigarettes dotting the interior of the showroom-fresh automobile. How could creature punks enact such blasphemy upon the fancy interior? If it were mine...

Hootie got out first and ambled over to the car, his swagger one he'd developed inside the big walls, I guess. Arlin the diplomat got out as quick as he could and followed Hootie's wake like a hound trailing his master to the hunt. I couldn't hear enough of the exchange to gauge the reaction Moorefield had to the price proliferation of bootleg beer. After a while the lights inside the red car came on and two silhouettes cleared the car and came toward where big Margie and I were camped.

Margie had lost interest in me as soon as Moorefield's name came up, and now she was straining to see through the glass that got washed the last time it rained. Me, I was praying for it to be darker as I slid toward the swirling pit of regurgitated beer that waxed the floorboard beneath me.

"Honey love," Margie whispered as Moorefield's profile broke out of the shadows and came into our partial light in the settling dust.

She changed positions to see better, but when Hootie opened the trunk to expose the beer, I suppose she got angry, because she said the "s" word. I wanted to say it, myself, but I was busy being the chameleon of the night, hiding in the vile repugnance of the stinking car while awaiting the departure of the rich and defiled one. I did notice that Margie's dress rode up her thighs as she squirmed to look around the opened trunk lid, but the sight of her bloomers lit on me with the same effect of a gnat whipping around me as I played right field in a summer game in the pasture. She was one big love machine.

Then the air got tense.

First Moorefield’s voice lifted up, then Hootie’s, then the trunk slammed with an authority that made the car jump, Margie and me with it. I covered my head thinking I’d hear a shotgun blast at any minute but there was only muted conversation, and after a while the trunk got opened again and normal conversation ensued. Then a bit of laughter creeped in and I figured the big time bootleggers were through extorting their price from Moorefield or negotiations had settled down to an acceptable level.

Then luck had to have somewhere to go so it ran out on me.

Not that it had been near my questing soul for the past half hour, but now it just flat abandoned me. Dirk was coming around the corner of the car and showing some interest in what was inside.

Arlin stopped him with a word and the two wandered back toward the red car likc old pals, but the flashlight hit my face from the opposite side and I recognized the voice before I could see a face. “My school chum,” he said and held the light so it blinded me.

“Get that friggin’ light outta his eyes,” Margie protested beside me, leaning forward to block his intrusion into my dungeon.

“She sweet on the choir boy?” I heard Moorefield ask.

Hootie’s gruff voice responded. “Get outta there, boy. I done traded you off to a caravan crossin’ the desert. You off to Egypt.”

His laugh was cold. I wondered if somebody had read him the Joseph story from the Bible—the Old Testament lesson where a boy’s jealous brothers sold their youngest sibling into slavery. Who would have read it to that felon? I was sure he couldn’t do it himself.

And what was I to do? Margie was trying to protect me like she wanted me to hang around. Why? And Hootie was losing me after he gained me for no profit. Why was I a medium of exchange?

“What’s going on?” I finally had to ask.

You’ve got a new ride,” I heard Moorefield say. “We got another little game for you to play.”

"Why don't we play that one where I go home and you boys drink beer and jerk each other around and everybody stays happy," I ventured.

"See," Moorefield pitched in. "That smart mouth's starting to kick in. He would insult the Pope face to face."

"I'll fix his smart mouth," Hootie threatened, but Margie bucked up again in front of me and her bulk blocked his reach for me.

"This here's a good kid," she said in their faces. "He ain't a pot of crap out looking for trouble like you two. I ain't allowin' neither one of you to lay hands on him. First one touches him gets a stick in the eye. Biggest stick I can find."

"Get your fat self outta the way," Hootie said, getting impatient.

"I'm 'bout tired a you callin' me names, convict. I'm good enough to be with in the dark but I ain't good enough to be seen in the daylight? Well, you don't need to go tarnishing this sweet boy just to prove you tough. I'll slap your eyes out before you take him."

The two backed off from the car and whispered a while, then Arlin got in from the driver's side and began trying to crank the car. The battery did its best to move the motor to life, but it just wasn't strong enough. Like me, it didn't have the power to overcome a heavy resistance.

The door slammed and Arlin kicked the body of the car and cussed considerably. Then he rejoined the group behind the car that must've been discussing Margie and my future because it was a deep session marked with cussing and laughter. After a while, they all moved over to Golden Boy's ride and talked some more, their cigarettes glowing in the shadows.

"Thanks for helping me," I said weakly to Margie, who was watching the group but not straining to see them like she had been. In the halflight she smiled and some of the harshness left her face.

Strategy session complete, the dynamic duo headed back toward the car. Hootie was almost conciliatory as he opened the door and pulled the seat forward for me to exit.

"Them other boys are leavin'," he said. "Get out and help us push this thing so we can start it. Margie can stay in but we need more backs to push this jalopy... Get out."

I saw Golden Boy leave the lot and Margie's eyes found mine with a questioning look.

"Come on, fuzzy cheeks," Hootie said, impatient again. "I'll take you home soon as we get this thing runnin'."

I got out of the car and he motioned me to the back bumper. Arlin had his door open and he was pushing on the A-pillar just as Hootie was on his side. I turned my butt to the car and lifted with my arms cupped backwards under the bumper. I strained at the thought of freedom coming to me as Hootie extorted us to give it one big shot.

Slowly, the nearly-moribund beast inched forward until we got lucky and caught a little dip and it gained some speed. Hootie hopped in, found second gear, popped the clutch, and surprised us all. The split muffler roared to life, and the black death trap was highway bound again. Only it was heading out of the high dust without me. I heard Hootie's insane laugh and what sounded like a hearty "Hi-yo, Silver" as the lightless wonder faded into the darkness that took Highway 9 southward.

Stranded.

Great. What was a body to do? If you couldn't trust a convicted felon, who could you trust? What was the world coming to?

The other side of the coin was that I was free of that bunch. Margie had tried to help me, and I owed her something for that—maybe a kind thought and a kind word the next time. All she got now was verbal abuse and physical abuse. I felt a bit of remorse for her situation but it was one she had developed herself.

I had a long walk in front of me back to my bike, but at least I had my freedom—and that was something. I wouldn't even tell Billy Rand when he got in from his heavy date with the Blue Branch twins.

Of course, soon as I took my first step, hell came back to visit. The red Impala had turned itself around from its north heading, and there it was, cutting across my path in the dust of the lot, sliding its tires, looking for braking traction. A door flew open, and a blade came at me as Dirk grinned and motioned me toward the yawning sanctuary of the back seat.

Out of the pigpen into the penthouse, I would've thought on a clear day. But this was butt-deep dark, and the forces of evil were ganging up on me. "I ain't going," I heard myself say.

"Sure you are," Dirk grinned. "Third time's the charm, sweet boy. That fat gal can't save you. You're my date now."

"You just talk that way because you got the big boys listening," I tried to smart mouth back, figuring I didn't have anything to lose.

He lost the grin. "Get in the car or I'll stick you right here."

I shrugged. "I meant to say that I can't wait to ride in Golden Boy's high-powered vehicle that his daddy bought him." I took a step toward the car. "Who's that in the back seat?"

A rabbit of a fellow was on the back seat behind the beer-drinking driver. I had seen him around school, but he hung on the fringe of the fast crowd so I didn't know him well. He was a bootlicker if I recalled correctly—eager to please—eager to be accepted. His presence gave me some strength. "What they got you for?" I asked him as I slid into the plushness of the new Chevrolet, after the junkyard decor of the convict's ride. "To help pay for the gas?"

"Shut your gap, Holmes," Dirk said as the car accelerated smoothly out of the lot and back north on 9. The exhaust cutouts were capped this night so the exhaust pushed through the factory mufflers. Instead of a roar I was used to in Weldon's beater on most Friday nights, I was privileged to hear the high whine of the red Chevy as it gathered speed.

And gather it could.

Moorefield didn't say a thing as he was watching the road ahead and mashing the power pedal. I could see the speedometer at an angle as it climbed over the top of the circular gauge and started toward the big numbers. I would've enjoyed the break with inertia and the thrill of quick acceleration except I didn't know what my future held. That uncertainty overrode the thrill of being in the fastest car in the valley.

I decided I might as well piss Dirk off 'best I could. He was busy chugging a longneck and belching like he had massive gas buildup.

"They say that stuff won't hurt you," I said to the front seat. " 'Course I have reservations, myself, about drinking stuff that looks like a by-product of farm animals."

Silence. Then Dirk's hand snaked over the seat like he was going to slap me. He laughed and retracted when I flinched.

"Margie the Largie," Dirk said. "You been sugar-lipping big Marge there in the back seat, Hot Rod?"

"They say that stuff won't hurt you either," I replied, not really caring what the Jerk said.

"Smart mouth. Marge's got the cool mood for you, trash boy. She likes 'em young and innocent. I reckon you're innocent, but you know what they say about preacher's kids. I seen you lockin' eyes with that White Oaks girl. She's too hot for you. She needs a seasoned vet like me to show her the dark spots on Friday night."

"Her IQ runs a little bit beyond moron, Jerkie. She wouldn't be seen with you if you were related to the pompous one here. Or, are you related?"

Dirk looked at me but didn't quite know what to say.

Moorefield laughed at Dirk but kept his attention straight ahead like he was after the sound barrier right there on the valley floor.

I figured I might as well load up on Dirk. He was too stupid to respond and I might score a few points off his slow wit. Jeremiah Nobert, the other back seat prisoner, was as far out of grace as the planet Pluto. He was looking off into the stars like he wished he was on any other planet besides this bondage that seemed to hold him quiet and trembling.

"Margie is the kind of girl," I started up, "who likes to conquer and crow about it."

Dirk looked funny in profile but didn't question my meaning. So I explained. "While we were alone back there, Jerkie, she told me all about your secret love—well, secret lust—for her. Just you, her, Jackie D. and the quiet of the sewing factory parking lot. She gave you strong marks, Dirk, very strong."

I got the right reaction—'cept to the extreme.

He turned like a snake on a mongoose and wrapped strong hands around my throat.

"I woulda choked your lying mouth back at Ford's store the other night, big talker, but that sick-head uncle of yours got in the way. Now you ain't got no backup. I wanta see your eyes pop out afore I turn you loose."

I did my best to get free of his sudden attack but he was much stronger than I was and he was angry to boot. Just as I thought my air would never come again, Moorefield slapped Dirk with his backhand and ordered my release, "Don't let that little liar fire you up, Dirk. Can't you see he's just playing with you? He can't back up any of that school-boy talk. He's just a weak little sissy boy that holds hands with a preacher's daughter and recites Bible verses. He won't be so smart when we get him up to the high perch and he has to be indoctrinated. Then we'll see how big britches he is. In the meantime, have a beer and leave that mouse alone."

Indoctrinated? What'd that mean?

Indoctrinated into what?

Wouldn't hurt to ask about the "what." One more human violation on my form would not cause the earth to tilt off its axis. "What are you indoctrinating me into, Jerkie?" I asked.

He laughed without looking back at me. I knew he didn't intend to answer when the laughter stopped.

I glanced at the pale creature next to me. He looked like Tom Dooley with a noose around his neck waiting for the preacher to finish up on the 23rd Psalm.

"What is it," I said, looking at his pale face. "What you in here for?"

He didn't speak. Instead, a look of defiance flitted across his face and he looked back off into the night.

The night was busy getting out of our way. We were courting a hundred miles an hour on a short straightaway, and while I wasn't sure what stretch of valley we were covering, I knew we'd soon run out of straight-ahead roads and the curves around the hills would be impossible for even the new car to hold on to. We were about to be launched into a cow pasture like a renegade satellite. Moorefield was pushing the limits on General Motors engineering.

"Hey, Hot Shot," I yelled toward Moorefield, wanting my voice heard in my impending disaster. "I'll stop spreading stories about your momma if you'll slow this thing down."

Not spoken soon enough.

The red missile hit the first curve toward Rabbittown and the right side of the road gave way to a terrible rupturing of physics. The tires were screaming, and the big engine was straining in its traces as it tried to swing the rear end around and keep the nose pointed northward.

I don't know where all we traveled.

The road was ahead and then behind, and trees were in the windshield proper, then gone, and the tires, in agony, lost touch with reality. We were in the air in a ride not meant to fly.

And this was no ride in the park.

We knocked down a fence with the stout chrome bumper and ate up the farmer's field as we skidded like a greased-down bumper car at the county fair. The front seat thought it was as funny as a ribald comedy, hanging out their arms to brace themselves while the ride spun like a compass needle looking for ninety degrees north. The shouting subsided after a while and there were two pale figures in the back seat when the final action was played out. We came to rest somewhere between a rock and a hard place.

Moorefield let out a rebel whoop and looked around for a beer to drink. Dirk got up off the floorboard and searched his face like he was checking to see if any parts had left him during the crash landing. Finally satisfied that he was all together, he pulled another longneck out of the floorboard, miraculously found the church key still magnetized to the metal glove box, popped off the top of the glass container, and started life with another Pabst Blue Ribbon beer.

"Y'all may call that fun," I said nastily as I rubbed my sore head and shoulder that had come in contact with something hard during the glory ride, "but I think you're both crazier'n a flock of gooney birds flying north."

Moorefield reached for my shirt while I was still mumbling and reconnoitering my physical being. His hand was strong and he drew me forcibly toward his face as he spoke, "I'm about tired of you and your mouth, Holmes. I'm tired of seeing your white-trash family creeping around school. And that simple-brained, half-soldier Uncle of yours belongs in the loony pen—behind chicken wire. But I've been promising you some of my attention and I think your number just came up on the wall."

"You should have a number on your chest, outlaw," I responded, angry over his disrespect for me and my family—not to mention his despicable attitude that said the world was his to control and manipulate to fit his momentary interest.

"Never shut up, do you?" he said coldly, turning loose of my shirt while he swung a fist at my face.

I couldn't remain the pacifist any longer. My anger grew within me until it was a force that lost its control and direction. I swung back in heated anger, hoping my blows would find some mark. But I realized I was simply breaking wind off a deserted mountain top. I felt a heavy weight on me. The three of them were pinning me to the seat, and someone was ratcheting my head around like it was a ping pong ball in a hotly-contested game.

I closed my eyes, and in great anguish I tried to scream out my fury, but a fist in my stomach cut short my breath and I felt sick. I was about to pass out. The night air swirled around me as I was dragged from the back seat and thrown into the muddy field.

"Let's leave his butt here," I heard someone say as I groaned in agony, but another voice overruled that idea. They talked among themselves, and I felt someone kick repeatedly at my ribs with the strength of open hatred.

"Get up, you little weasel. Time to be a man and play our train hang game."

I tried. After awhile I could almost stand upright by myself, but my breath came to me with pains as real as damnation. And I couldn't force my legs to move me forward.

"Where's the clever banter, welfare child?" Moorefield said in jest. "Is it difficult to catch that big breath of air with that broken face and those tender ribs?"

"Hootie doesn't look like much," I said between gasps of air, "but he knows how to stay out of the ditches."

The kick caught me in the crotch, and besides the jolting pain, I thought of the first time a bicycle seat did that same thing. I could only grab, the classic way, and bend forward, searching for relief.

"You're lucky, little Holmes," Moorefield said. "Although I detest you with every fiber and with every sense that my body and brain possess, I decided to park close to the night's entertainment area. You don't need to raise your head to thank me. Simply struggle forward."

"I'll still manage better than you," I said, spitting out the blood that had appeared in my mouth sometime during the beating.

"He never shuts up," Dirk said. "Let me cut his tongue out."

"No, no. We need him for climbing and hanging. We need to initiate him into our secret fraternity with the Southern Railway. You, too, Jeremiah. What are you being so quiet about? You haven't said a syllable since we picked you up at the store."

Jeremiah looked like he had a "rendezvous with death." And not on some "forgotten hillside" as the poet lamented. It was as if his rendezvous was creeping through the dark toward him. He remained quiet and pensively weak, as if the night wind that came down off the forested hills also whispered his name. I glanced sideways at him, and he was even paler than he'd been in the car as it hurtled through the night and slammed to its last rest in the unlit field.

A train's sharp whistle rode through the far trees and called to us—apparently the signal we were waiting for. Dirk found my abused ribs with the point of his switchblade and without further talk, we started across the field toward the trees and the tracks beyond.

I was literally in the dark as to why we made the sudden break for the tracks, though I didn't say anything further. All I could think of was that if I survived this night, I'd spend my free time getting even with these punks. I didn't know exactly how, but all Christian spirit toward them deserted me and I was as wrapped in evil as they were. For a moment, in the scuffling, struggling movement toward the bluff, I knew hate that could severely lance my soul.

The searching beams of the big diesel train thundered into my brain.

After a walk that hurt with each step forward, we suddenly came to a bluff overlooking the tracks. The air vibrated with the energy of the huge engines as they rushed toward our vulnerable position. The ground shook under my feet and I thought, for a wild moment, that they were about to throw my body down onto the passing train. Instead Moorefield gripped my arm tightly and pointed toward Jeremiah who was standing at the edge of the bluff as if he was looking for a passage, a trail down to the thundering freight train.

After Jeremiah teetered crazily on the edge of the bluff, like a diver checking his balance on a diving board, Dirk approached him with his switchblade and the pale boy shouted into the night. Though the words tore out of his mouth, in the noise of the rushing metal cars I couldn't hear a sound he tried to utter.

Suddenly, Dirk grabbed the reluctant inductee, and together they slid on the seat of their britches down toward the black hole the train was speeding through. It was like a giant panther that streaked past with the thoughts of the hunt in its brain, foregoing our little prey as worthless as it raced toward another part of the world.

I saw Jeremiah's light shirt reflecting some of his being as Dirk stood near him, goading him onward. I couldn't see what they were doing at first, but I soon realized that Jeremiah was climbing a metal railroad signal tower, an apparatus that was rooted to our side of the tracks but extended like an arm over the thundering freight. Halfway over the tracks it stopped and hung its great signal lights to the trains that sped past it.

What was he doing?

Slowly, slowly, Jeremiah ascended the tower, looking back countless times toward the safety of the ground behind Dirk. His clothes were nearly torn away by the momentous wind the train generated, running its path of appointed time, never wavering from its constant speed, simply rocking in its traces like a baby's crib that travels its short path in the security of a mother's watchful eye.

When Jeremiah had reached the top of the tower, he bent forward as if the flying wind would rip him from his grip. I thought I heard a long scream of fear from his lips, but my mind was doing strange things to me. I watched in terror as the death on wheels licked its jaws at him, cruising incessantly under him with the constant threat of the beast that was never still or satisfied with its victims, always straining to pull fresh bodies to its great bosom.

I had forgotten that Moorefield was beside me, but he began shouting over the bluff toward the pit where the devil ran his course. Apparently, they wanted Jeremiah to release his grip and either stand up or hang off the tower, his head in close jeopardy to the speeding boxcars below.

No wonder the reticent Jeremiah had been pale-faced all night. His was a rendezvous with death if his grip faltered at all and he was caught under the stampede of the runaway freight.

Moorefield left my line of vision for a moment as I watched Jeremiah, hoping he would simply hang on until the freight had run past and he could lower himself to the safety of the good earth.

Moorefield, however, had other plans.

I saw his arm come forward as he threw something toward Jeremiah. I looked at him in disbelief as he tossed a second rock toward the speeding freight and the figure that was pressed against the black steel of the tower.

I stepped toward him to prevent his throwing anything further but as I turned away from the tracks, his head rolled back in great levity and the night was filled with his heinous laugh, piercing even the dancing steel of the rails as the freight fought its way through the night.

When I looked back toward the tracks, Jeremiah was missing from his perch on the tower. Stepping closer to the edge of the bluff, I looked down, hoping to see him safely next to Dirk. But Dirk was scampering back up the hill toward us like his life was being threatened by the constant roar of the unforgiving rails.

He was suddenly on the bluff next to us. Then he was in Moorefield's face, screaming and waving his arms, his voice muted by the noise but his eyes wet and his face covered by tears that he didn't bother to wipe away. He pushed Moorefield backward and started toward him with the switchblade but they both stopped and stared at each other in the blackness of the bluff. Dirk suddenly threw his blade away into the night. Moorefield said something to him, but Dirk was walking across the field in the blackness of the far ridge. I was left looking at the person who knew no soul—who had no connection to morality.

What had become of Jeremiah?

I looked back toward the tracks again and felt a killing hold on my neck and throat. Strong hands penned me motionless from behind, and a voice came to me so close to my ear that I could hear its message like the words were implanted in my brain through some surrealistic means. It was Moorefield's voice that gripped my soul like the devil had risen up out of the pit of night and stopped my heart as he spoke, "You say anything about this night to anyone, anytime, any place, and I'll kill your entire family, starting with your mother and working my way down one at a time. You hear me, Holmes? You nod your head real easy-like. Then I'm leaving you right here. Remember, I can get to you no matter where you run or where you hide. Nod your head that you heard me and then keep your eyes off me as I leave."

I did as he instructed, cemented to the spot like a statue left to rest in a forbidden garden. I was too scared to move, too stricken to think, too tired and too sick in my soul to envision what had become of Jeremiah. Moorefield's words stuck on my immediate thinking and went 'round a short course, circling past me again and again.

Finally, I heard the car come to life across the field and the spinning tires as they tried to grip the slick surface of the farmland. When the noise had subsided, the freight train itself played out its time and the sounds of the night rails diminished as the heavy freight cars went off into their place in a night beyond the horizon.

I stood trembling for a few minutes, the coldness of the evening surrounding me as I peered off the bluff into the abyss—now quiet as a grave—as solemn and as black as a tomb.

I knew what I had to do.

I was afraid of what I would find. I was afraid I couldn't stand the sight of Jeremiah in his altered state, in his ruination there somewhere on the tracks or near the tall grass of the field that led up to the bluff. What could I do for him? Run for help? How long would that take? What could I say?

Nothing.

I could say nothing, but I had to tell, had to get help.

How could I do that? What could I say?

The important thing was Jeremiah.

I forced myself down the same path where he had walked only a short time before. I thought of him before, when he was a pale, breathing mortal like me, when he was a frightened mortal like me, amidst the throwbacks of trash, the wicked wastefulness of youth.

I felt sick again.

My stomach hurt and I was at the bottom of the bluff next to the quiet tracks. I threw up without shame, both from my fear and from my earlier beating. My stomach wanted to be free of its contents much as my mind wanted to free of the sights, and thoughts, and words that had made up the horror of this night.

I started up the tracks in the pitch black.

Someone once wrote, "The paths of glory lead but to the grave."

Thomas Grey? Did he pen that?

Jeremiah? Did he live that?

Did he take his shot at glory there in the darkness of a winter evening when the enormous, inexorable energy of a blasting freight train bolted under his life, pulling at his grip with the suction of a whirlwind cavern, of a whirlpool that wound downward into the blackest hole? Jeremiah had been locked into an immutable position, a few scant feet over a living river that raced beneath him.

And where had he hurtled to?

Had he lost his grip on the cold metal that pried his icy fingers off the sooted frame, a frame that crooked its alloy finger over the abyss like an oak tree, cragged and broken in a winter wind, giving itself to a greater strength, to a way that was demanding, to a thing that borrowed itself from mankind in the form of deadly hurtling steel and made nature a partner in its making of a fearful being?

Fear? It was real to me, whispering to me, making me understand that life and death ran side by side. One had the advantage over the other because there were forces willing to help destroy the other. And that had to be death at work because life was chasing the light that gave it a worthwhile name, and death was simply destruction, out to remand mankind in the narrow tunnels of the broken earth.

I shuttered and pulled my jacket tighter to me as I ascended the gentle rise of the railbed. I would consider the whispered threat later. Now, I was consumed with the thoughts of finding Jeremiah, the pale one, the one who had his life taken on a roll of the dice in a deadly game.

How could he have disappeared?

One minute he was hanging there like fruit on a pear tree. In the next instant I turned my head and he was no more. He was history, his life an unreal effort to obtain.

Why did it happen? Had he joined their insane circle? If my Sunday school teacher was correct, God had a plan for everyone. Was this the plan for Jeremiah, or did Moorefield cut Jeremiah's plan short? Where, then, was the guilt?

I don't know exactly what I mean, but Jeremiah did not need the agony of marching in Moorefield's army. At the end, was Dirk having second thoughts? How was he going live with this? Would he speak, or had Moorefield threatened to kill his folks, too?

One thing was certain, when evil came to bear, Moorefield was Satan's match. Hootie was mean, too, mean enough to cut a man's guts out and drastically abuse my new friend Margie. That was mean. But Moorefield? Deliberately trying to knock Jeremiah off that perch. Why? They could have just bounced him out of the herd. He never said a word in that back seat. Like he knew. He just knew.

And he didn't do anything to stop it. But what could he have done?

Maybe pride was more important than life.

He was caught in the tree limbs like a fly in a spider's web.

There wasn't any light and if I hadn't been scanning the side of the tracks I would've missed him. I didn't want to go up to him. I just couldn't. I was sure he was dead. There was no wind and no movement. And his arms and legs didn't normally bend in those grotesque directions. Nobody argues with a freight train and wins.

Jeremiah had failed the initiation. Now he had failed life, too.

Standing watch with Momma against the hatred and threats of the cowardly Klan was nothing to standing vigil over Jeremiah's fatal perch in the unloving arms of a spindly oak tree.

10

"Cruelty has a Human Heart...

—William Blake

I'm not sure how they got Jeremiah out of that tree.

I didn't want to see. My mind had an image of him hanging there that would outlive any sights that might try to replace his final, singular appearance surrounded by nature.

The sheriff tried to be compassionate while straining to understand my nebulous story. I didn't blame him for being confused. I was confused. And that horrible feeling of watching death at work consumed my mind and froze my spirit.

Finally, the sheriff sighed, resurrected his last fragment of patience, and decided to take me home.

I was still so involved in my shocked frame of mind that I did not consider the deeper trouble that would await me. Momma's children did not ride in sheriff cars, or spend time in jail, or denigrate the family in public. Even hard-working Dad often paused long enough between jobs to tell us about the Biblical admonition to choose a good name over great riches.

What riches awaited me now?

What punishment awaited me?

If I survived Momma's fury, there was always Moorefield lurking back there like that panther that stood with the night, invisible, but real and lethal.

"I don't fully understand what happened," the sheriff said as Momma looked across the room at me. "We ain't putting no responsibility on your boy, Miss Tallulah. Not just yet. We'll have to do more investigation. There was some car marks back up the ridge where somebody spun off, but Oliver claims he don't know them boys, so we'll just have to see what we can find out. I'll let you know what we come up on. Meanwhile, Oliver might want to stay close to home. Sometimes these boys get into things that ain't easy to get out of. Oliver's a good boy so I'm sure he ain't in no trouble that'd require the law or nothing, but right now I just don't know."

That was enough. He might as well have said that they'd just skip the trial and hang me the next clear morning with just enough time given to draw a crowd. And they'd use that oak tree that shaded the courthouse. And they'd bring picnic lunches and stand on the grass and watch me plunge into infamy with that killing rope on my neck—the only one of Momma's children to die in public, drawing the biggest crowd to witness it as any old person could recall.

Momma looked at me across the table.

Billy Rand looked at both of us.

I imagined, off in the distance I heard a train's whistle. I wished I was on that train. I'd ride with the wind in my face and never look back. I'd ride until I was the oldest rail hobo in existence, and they named stations after me, and made statues of me, and asked me if I'd kindly attend their hobo celebrations. And they'd show how my beard was white and longer than Moses's and had to be cast back over my shoulder to keep it from brushing up against the clicking, rumbling wheels beneath me. And off I'd ride, that long, harsh, uncaring ride of the steel in the chill of the night and the heat of the sun, over the blue of waters, and deep muddy rivers, and hills that toted each other off in the distance, and valleys as vast as God's greenest earth could stand. And back again, too, until I lay me down to rest.

Except I couldn't rest. Couldn't get Jeremiah off my mind, out of my mind's eye. He might as well have been cast in bronze, heavy on my eyelids. He was in the blackness that hid everything. Except I could hear that silent scream when the wind tore the words from his mouth. It was the unheard scream that ran loudest through me. Jeremiah, why didn't you just stay home?

"What is the true story?" Momma was saying as I avoided her eyes. She could see to the turned-under parts of my soul, so seeing through a lie in daylight was no trick at all for her.

"I told the authorities what happened, Momma," I repeated.

"You're not telling the truth, Oliver. Everybody knows that's the thinnest lie since Satan invented the thing. You're not fooling anybody with that tale. I want the truth or I'll have to punish you. You won't like it either. You know I'll do what I say."

I looked away from the table and out the screen, through the winter window. Another grey day outside. Grey as my mind. As confused as my mind. How long could I hold out?

"We'll sit here until the truth comes out of your mouth," Momma said, leaning back and up straight in the chair. "I've got your time, Oliver. Tell me when I can turn you loose."

I looked briefly at Billy Rand, but he simply scrunched his bushy eyebrows together and looked back at me. No help there. He should know. He should realize I couldn't say anything. But I hadn't told him anything. 'Hadn't told him that Hootie, Arlin, and Margie had picked me up, or that the Moorefield gang forced me into the Impala—the red-flamed devil of the night.

Moorefield's dad was rich. They could get to me, to my family, to anybody. They had the power. We had none. I had nothing except a screaming, falling image of a dying youth meshed with the hurtling freight and the cold of a deep winter night.

That's all I had.

"He's still in shock," Billy Rand finally defended me. "He's not mentally ready to talk yet, Momma. Let's give him some time. It's a tragic thing when somebody goes as a youth. I remember you read us a poem about dying young 'before the crown of youth is tarnished'."

"Words of a cynical poet," she responded. "But perhaps you're right, Billy. This boy gets into more predicaments than anybody I've ever heard of. And mostly, I think he's minding his own business. He's a tragic figure and he just happens to belong to me."

She rose from the table and while her words offered some comfort to me, her touch was not forthcoming. Momma was not a big one on the touch of love. It was her eyes, when kind, that were her gentlest loving feature.

I looked into her eyes for that reassurance, that kindness, that love. She was too upset. All I saw was her perplexity and wondering. She would give me some room to recover, but her spot was reserved for future questioning. I knew this, but I welcomed the temporary reprieve.

I mumbled my thanks to Rand as he got up and followed Momma out of the room. I felt sick. My stomach hurt. My head buzzed. When I closed my eyes, deep in self-pity, tears reached my eyes and escaped, rushing down my feverish face.

They let school out for Jeremiah's funeral.

I wish they hadn't. I didn't want to go.

But I did, sitting with Billy Rand and Weldon, with people staring at me and whispering. All the girls were crying, and when the preacher talked interminably about wasted life and fruits of evil, I could've stood up and echoed his words except I, myself, was buried emotionally, and I didn't need Jeremiah's funeral to remind me of it. The hardest part was when Mrs. Nobert passed out on the front pew after they dragged her off the coffin and closed it.

That little country church was bursting at the seams with school kids and relatives filled the pews, and flowers overflowed at the altar. And black cars, even the sheriff's car, parked out in the grass and listened to "How Great Thou Art." And that just about broke it for me. I tried to think of other things but all I could see was Jeremiah hanging on that trestle arm and hear his silent scream of terror as the black hole of hell pulled him from below.

I don't know if Moorefield and Dirk were there or not. I kept my head bowed like I was apologizing to Mrs. Nobert for being alive when her son wasn't.

When everybody finished singing songs that are intended to console the ailing spirit but end up tearing your heart apart, the congregation went forward as one to touch Mrs. Nobert, and the whispers of remorse cut me deeper as accusing eyes turned to me. I was glad it was a cool day outside and I could breathe the churchyard air and fill my lungs again because if I had counted the breaths I took inside the church, it wouldn't have been many.

After a while they brought Jeremiah's wooden casket out and several men helped carry Mrs. Nobert the hundred yards or so to the place under the pines. I hung back at the edge of the throng. I wanted to run off into the woods that surrounded us, but Billy Rand caught my eye and threatened me with a stare so I had to be respectful and follow the mourners out to the yawning earth and endure the looks of pure hatred that washed over me— knowing the heavier grief that washed over the Nobert family.

I stood silently with the others, smelling the freshness of the turned, red clay, put aside for the acceptance of Jeremiah's body. I looked briefly to heaven as the preacher made one last appeal to God, thinking perhaps my prayer went heavenward more rapidly if God gauged those things on sincerity.

11

“A guilty conscience needs no accuser.”

—English Proverb

I was sitting in the library trying to read *The Caine Mutiny* when Evie came in.

She was with some other cool girls that dressed neatly and flirted innocently with the football players. Evie didn’t flirt much.

When she saw me, she started toward my table. I couldn’t help but notice that her friends touched her arm, cautioning her to hold up. I was sitting by myself in the far corner of the leprotic colony. For a reason. No one wanted to get near a chronically-diseased person.

Evie smiled at the girls but continued walking. She approached my table with a cheerful spirit. She placed her books quietly across from me and whispered a genuine greeting while everyone in the library was busy experiencing drop jaw.

“How’s life at Jamback?” she asked as if I was simply idling away till the next class.

I tried to smile.

“Things are great down White Oak way,” she persisted. “ ‘God’s in His heaven; all’s right with the world.’ ”

I looked at her pretty face, at the freckles that ran over her petite nose like wildflowers growing on a distant mountainside. I felt better just looking at her. I had known all along that I would. “Copy cat,” I said. “I read that somewhere the other day.”

“I’ve been showing you too much English lit lately,” she almost apologized. “You love the language as much as I do. Isn’t that ironic? We’re both lit nuts, yet we both speak the King’s English with a Southern accent. Can you imagine Milton or Shakespeare showing up in this tiny country school and sitting in on Mrs. Murray’s class? They wouldn’t understand a word we said.”

“You’re in a jolly mood.”

“And you’re sitting over here like you’re waiting for a ride to the guillotine.”

“I was thinking of the gallows—noose and cut loose, you know.”

“That’s not going to happen. The Lord looks out for fools—and boys that do foolish things.”

“What do you think I did foolishly?”

“I don’t know exactly, but hanging out with the wrong crowd? Shame on you.”

“Isn’t it wrong to judge people—to judge if they’re good or bad? We’re preached at daily about those we’re to associate with. Isn’t that judging?”

She frowned. “You don’t judge people. You ‘simply discern’ my momma says.”

“What if you don’t get much choice on who you hang with?”

“We all have choices, Oliver.”

“Not if someone puts a knife to your throat.”

She studied my eyes a minute. “Oh,” she said softly.

When I looked around the library to ascertain who was looking and straining to hear us, she gave a quick look as well, grasping my arm. "Is that what happened?"

"Watch your voice," I said. "Sugarlocks is prowling around."

Sugarlocks was our librarian, a weird little man who was nearly bald yet covered his gleaming skull with a conspicuous comb over. He looked like a toad wearing a greasy wig.

Her eyes got big. "Tell me about it."

I shrugged. "Which time?"

"You mean there was more than one coerced ride?"

I nodded. "Yes."

"Good Lord! Oh, excuse me. Tell me, Ollie. Who?"

I was torn. Should I? Should I not? I couldn't think fast enough to see all the way through my dilemma. "You heard of a guy named Hackett?"

"Of course not."

"Try convicted felon."

"What'd he do?"

"Enough to put him in jail."

"My Lord!"

"Sssshhhhh..." Sugarlock was eyeing us from across the room.

"He had a shotgun, tried to kill my dog, and forced me into his beat-up car."

"What happened then?"

"I was groped by... by this girl."

"You mean...?"

"She... ah... got funny with me."

"Oh. Did you get funny back?"

"Lord, no. She was his girl. And she wasn't someone I wanted to encourage."

"Oh. I didn't catch that. Go on with your story."

"Where's Sugarlocks?"

"Who cares? Tell me more."

I looked around again. "We drove down to Evil-Eye's store."

"You, the girl, and the guy with the knife?"

"And another man... To The Split Nickel. Hackett sells another guy in a hot car some beer."

"What guy?"

"Can't tell you."

"You drink any?"

"No... No!"

"Go on."

"Then the girl says a good word for me and they let me out and Hackett, with his bunch, drives off into the night. I thought I was safe, until..."

"Did he come back for you?"

"No. The guy in the hot car comes back and his buddy gets out of the car and puts a knife to my back and tells me to get in. He gets in, too, and there's another guy in back. Jeremiah.

"On down the road, this guy drives his car off into a field and we all get out and go to the bluff overlooking the railroad tracks."

"I understand. Go on."

"I'm not clear, but somehow I end up on the ground, where they all take a swipe at me. Ah..."

"Go on."

"Well, the guy takes his switchblade..."

"What's that?"

"A special knife."

"Oh."

"Anyway, the driver shouts directions, and the one with the switchblade forces Jeremiah down over the bluff, up this signal tower, and onto this arm-looking thing that stretches out over the tracks. I'm standing on the bluff watching this mess while the train runs along below us. That's when the driver starts throwing rocks at Jeremiah."

"Why'd he do that?"

"Who knew? Anyway, I tried to stop him but it was too late. And when I looked back, oh Lord, Jeremiah was gone."

"Oh!"

"Then the driver grabs me by the throat and threatens to kill me if I tell anybody. Me and all my family."

"Oh no!" She looked at me with tears in her eyes. "All you've been through... You've got to tell the authorities."

"I can't."

"Why not?"

"I told you. They'll kill me and all my family."

"They can't do that. Who are they?"

"You know them so I can't say."

She looked around. "Are they in this room?"

"No."

"You didn't look."

"I knew before I came in, okay?"

"Older boys with cars," she mused.

"Don't start pushing me. I tell you all this in confidence."

"I listened in confidence and in knowing I've got to help you."

"Oh, no. You're just my listening friend. I'll figure it out."

"No, Ollie. I'll help you."

She was way past listening. I could hear the gears humming in her head. "Promise me you'll be quiet about this," I pleaded.

"Sure," she mouthed, but it seemed disingenuous.

I felt like I'd screwed up by telling her.

"I know what to do," she said, quickly. "You need to just rise up and strike back at those that accuse you of wrongdoing. Sitting in a corner by yourself sulking won't impress anyone."

I considered her admonition a while. "What happened to 'turn the other cheek'?" I asked.

"What happened to Jeremiah? Look, Ollie. I wanted to talk to you

Sunday at your house, but you know how parents are. They think all kids are out answering the call of the wild. Regardless of their opinion, I wanted to tell you that I know you didn't do anything wrong. I still don't know all that happened but somehow you got caught in the web."

She straightened up and looked right through my soul. "Whoever you're covering for is not worth your sacrifice. Get up off your knees and spit in somebody's face."

Was this my Christian friend speaking? Was she really a wind-in-the-face night rider? I thought long suffering and sealed lips was the only way I could respond to Mooreland and his cronies.

"Look. I'm sympathetic to your trouble, Ollie, but somebody's pulling a net around you and holding you down. If you don't tell the truth... Well, remember, 'The truth will set you free.' "

"You don't understand," I said.

"What's to understand? You're not one to knock people off railroad towers. You're not even one to climb up on one of those things. The worse thing you've ever done is get in a race car with that greaser boy and break the law drag racing. That's pretty mild compared to covering for a bad person."

I was surprised. "You know about the Silver Run races?" I asked.

"I was there that night you rode with Voit. 'You think, just because I'm a preacher's daughter, I just sit home on weekends and study my Bible?"

"Who were you with?"

"None of your business. He was a nice kid."

"I don't remember seeing you there."

"I saw you hanging out over by the store like you were scared to death. When you got in with Voit, I thought you were either scared not to or Voit coerced you. Which one was it?"

I nearly smiled. Evie wasn't all ponytails and Proverbs; she knew the night calls.

"Here I was all this time thinking you were innocent little Orphan

Annie on a mission to bring love to the pagan world. You're out there feeling the night wind in your face, too."

"I have fun, smart mouth, but I don't go too far. That crew you were riding with Saturday night is *way* out there. They go all the way and then back again. You were like a choir boy at a Satanic ritual."

I winced, but I felt better about my situation. If she saw me this way perhaps others did, too.

"Seriously, though," she said. "You gotta tell me who these kids are."

"I can't. I've already told you too much."

"Then I'll fill in the blanks," she said. "I'll do some snooping around. 'Can't be too hard to figure out in this regressive valley."

"You fill in too much, you'll be writing my death certificate."

"Don't worry about a thing."

Sugarlocks interrupted. "Oliver Holmes!" came the loud voice, "Mr. Gorman wants you in his office."

I made it to the library door before I noticed my escort. Sara Kate. Every senior boy's mental pinup. Full, luscious lips, eyes that'd shine in a cave. If she even spoke to a rag-tag Jambacker like me, her reputation would take an irreversible hit. So I ignored the picture-perfect figure and started down the dark hallway.

"What in the world's wrong with you?" her hurt voice stopped me as soon as we were away from Sugarlocks's lair.

I paused and looked back at her. "What do you mean?"

"You were the only one there, and yet you won't talk to anybody. Don't you have any feelings?"

She was crying. Real gosh-darn, down the perfect cheeks and over the silky jaw bones, tears. And in front of a Jamback Road boy. Did she have the right person? I wondered. Did Gorman want me or did she?

She leaned against the wall near the door of the chemistry lab and produced a well-wadded Kleenex from her pocket. "You did not even apologize to his mother. I saw you at the funeral, looking like you wanted to be a hundred miles away. And Jeremiah just laying there in that coffin. He didn't do anything, and he was dead. And you were alive. And now you walk around school not talking to anybody, not caring about anybody. How do you do that?" Her voice trembled.

I looked away from her.

"Me and Jeremiah were talking about getting married in the spring. He was gonna get a job at the filling station and I was going to junior college. We were gonna run off to Georgia—just the two of us. We been steady since the ninth grade..."

There was a long silence as she sobbed.

I still didn't know what to say.

"I guess an ignorant country boy like you couldn't understand how it is to love somebody. All you got is a house full of brothers and sisters. No indoor toilet to bathe in. No future in this world. And there you were watching an innocent person die right in front of you. You know what happened. You saw it all. Why is it you can't give me his last words or the thing he did before that train..."

The tissued Kleenex was finished. She threw it away in the dim light and searched for another one. I watched her over my shoulder, as confounded confused as a dude could be. I wasn't being cool or heartless. I was simply overmatched emotionally. I was speechless.

She started slowly toward me, her voice escalating as she approached my seat on the stairs. "Say something, you stupid boy! You killed my boy friend! I hate you! I hate you! I'll always hate you! Say something, you coward!"

I steadied myself to ward off what I thought was a coming physical attack, but as I held my hands out in a defensive position, the door to the Chemistry lab burst open and the young lab teacher rushed toward us.

I backed away carefully as the bespectacled teacher glared angrily at me. "What have you done to this girl?" he shouted at me, reaching for my arm.

I didn't resist or say anything. Sara Kate was leaning against the stair-rail crying her heart out.

"Why'd you hurt Sara Kate? I don't know you. What's your name, boy?"

When I failed to respond, the man gripped my arm in a proverbial vice and started down the stairs, literally towing me with him.

"You'll come to the office with me, mr. smarty pants. We don't allow boys to hurt young ladies in this school!"

I allowed myself to be manhandled all the way to the office at the bottom of the stairs. When we reached the outer door, the man threw it open and continued across the outer office until we reached Mr. Gorman's private door. Without hesitating, the angry teacher threw the door open and propelled me into the presence of the principal with a final hefty shove.

I stopped as quickly as I could and looked toward the desk. Mr. Gorman was up to his sleeve garters in paperwork. He didn't smile or move as we burst into his presence. He simply looked slightly dismayed and drew his abundant eyebrows together. He seemed more interested in the red-faced teacher than he was me.

"What do we have here, Mr. Avair? An abysmal threat to the safety of our school?" Gorman asked.

"This person injured Sara Kate in some way. She is upstairs crying her eyes out!" Mr. Avair's face was hot red as he explained his problem.

Mr. Gorman sighed as if he had better things to do than dry Sara Kate's tears. He never looked at me.

"Did you see this boy strike Sara Kate?"

"Well, no, sir, but he did something because she was bawling. I heard her shouting through my lab door."

Gorman pushed his torn vinyl chair, with the well-worn cushion, back from his desk and stood up. His lean frame towered over that of the animated lab teacher.

"I'll take it from here, Mr. Avair."

"He needs corporal punishment plus a suspension. He's not fit to be in our good students' presence!"

Gorman seemed frustrated.

"I'll handle him, Mr. Avair. You go see about that chemistry lab. Might be an explosion up there. Somebody could get hurt."

"What about Sara Kate?"

"Mrs. Moore will see about her. She's seen crying seniors before."

"Well, I want this young person to pay for his unnecessary..."

Mr. Gorman guided Avair back through the door that he had rudely pushed through. When he was gone from our sight, Mr. Gorman returned to his shredded vinyl-backed swivel chair with the torn cushion and resumed his work on the stack of papers before him.

I stood motionless a few feet from his desk.

Several minutes passed before he looked up from his work. He got up, gave me a quick look, then went out the door that led to the outer office—the one most people used when summoned into Caesar's chambers.

I continued standing for several more minutes, taking in the dour surroundings. The office was small, smelled of peppermint at odds with the polarizing scent of dried chewing tobacco. There were black and white photos of past dignities on the wall behind the desk. The single window to my right had the heavy shades drawn so that the most focused area of light was the dusty, spindly lamp that luminated the papers Gorman had recently deserted.

The door soon opened to readmit its principle occupant and a thin, attractive lady. She wore expensive-looking clothes, and her hair was put in place by someone who meant for it to stay there. I had seen this person in the halls, but she mainly talked to seniors so I didn't figure she knew me. Now she smiled at me. My first impression was that she was genuinely devoting time to me. Her face was warm. Her demeanor the same.

"Please sit down, Oliver," she said, motioning toward a chair directly before me.

I went to the chair and waited for her to sit. She hesitated, confused for a moment, then realizing my manners, she smiled and sat across from me as far removed as the small office allowed.

"I'm Mrs. Moore," she said. "I'm the counselor here at school. I help students that have problems."

I looked from her, then quickly to Gorman. He was back on those infernal papers, scratching his head and dialing out of our conversation.

"Would you like to talk about anything?" she continued pleasantly when I returned to her attention.

I did not. I looked down at my hands in my lap.

"If you're bashful, or if Mr. Gorman intimidates you, I can take you to *my* office. It's close by."

I didn't care to move. "I have nothing to say."

For a moment, there was silence in the dour surroundings.

"I know about your trouble with the Jeremiah Nobert incident," she said softly.

Jeremiah. All anybody wanted to talk about. And me in the middle of it. Over and over. Like my nights weren't bad enough. They couldn't just leave me alone and let the great Grendel of time encompass me and spin my soul out of me? Did they have to keep prodding me in the side with their questions, with their sinuous smiles that meant nothing to me? Their condescending attitude left me vulnerable to my own weakness. I leaned back on Genevieve's remark to me one day in the library. "Ollie, people can't make you feel inferior unless you let them."

Yeah, I had thought. Poor white boy from Jamback, living in a house nearly falling down. A rutted, eroded front yard, and an uninhabited barn that reminded us daily of our predicament. But she was right. I needed to get over the self-pity. Even Sherman T. thought self-pity was a sin.

I brought my attention back to Mrs. Moore and thought I'd be the devil's advocate.

"I met a man the other day. He called me a boy without honor."

She looked surprised. "Oh?"

"He said I could do a lot of good just by giving up the truth. What did he mean, Mrs. Moore? What is truth?"

"Truth is... what we all seek..." she offered.

"Momma says God is truth."

"Well, Oliver, I suppose you could say truth is of that, but in counseling, we try to get to the truth through..."

"Questions?"

"Well, yes, I suppose, we..."

"You want to ask me questions about Jeremiah, correct?"

"Well..."

"Will those questions help you or me?"

"I don't see how they could hurt..."

"You think I haven't been asked every question about that night that can be asked?"

She straightened up in her chair and tried to regain control of the student-counselor relationship.

"You can be feisty, can't you?" she asked, anger flaring in her eyes.

"I don't mean to disrespect you, ma'am, but I'm going to sit over here and be real quiet about any questions coming out about Jeremiah. Just so you won't waste time on me that you need to use on the seniors."

She turned her now-sparkling eyes toward Gorman who looked up from the confusing papers.

"Watch that tongue, boy," he warned, his glasses riding low on his hammered nose. "Lady's trying to help you. Be respectful."

I didn't say anything in response. Gorman held an ace on me. He could still elect to punish me for the Sara Kate thing.

I glanced at the window with its impeding, dusty slates. I was finished with Miss Good News from the counselor's office. Mrs. Moore sensed my withdrawal and requested that Gorman meet her outside his office. I figured they needed to talk about my smart mouth and come up with an adequate solution. Apparently, she had come around to the lab teacher's school of thought: guilty until proven innocent.

In my troubled mind I didn't really give a good fox hound about what they thought. They hadn't been out there that night. They didn't have to be concerned about Moorefield hiring somebody to wipe out my entire family. And Golden Boy could do it. If Harold-the-felon could cut up people and scare people to death in a Klansman uniform, it wouldn't take much effort to prey upon a desolate family sequestered in the obstinate poverty of Jamback. Evie had said that God had a plan for me. What that plan was I couldn't figure out. I was in a bigger maze than the dumbest rat in the science lab. Some enlightenment had to show up soon or I was leaving the track.

The private door to the office opened behind me but I didn't bother to turn around to see who it was. I figured Gorman had been out fashioning a hangman's noose and he would throw it over my ears at any minute and watch me roll around on the floor like a snake with its head caught under a fat Buick's tire.

When the noose failed to appear and no further sounds of movement reached me, I twisted in the chair to see a person of unknown identity stood looking the place over.

"You Oliver Holmes?" he asked, smiling and walking toward me.

I grimaced.

"I heard they had you locked up in here. What kind of office is this? Place smells like body odor and old mattresses."

He was tall, had an intelligent face, wore expensive clothes, but they looked like he'd simply selected them off a pile in his bedroom floor and put them on. He was not in Moorefield's school of charm, but he had an air of knowing certain things, and his smile and darting eyes seemed as disingenuous as the counselor's. He held a battered notebook in his right hand and a stubby pencil that needed attention in his left. I'd never met a person quite like him. He sounded Southern, but he had the quick eyes of the cynic.

"I'm Mitchell Rimple," he said, swapping out the notebook so he could shake my hand. "I'm a writer for the newspaper."

Rimple. Where had I seen that name?

He sat down across from me and opened his notebook. The left hand stood ready, as if expecting dictation. He made some sweeping marks over the page in an awkward southpaw motion and grinned heartily at me.

"I used to get sent to the principal's office, myself, when I was in school. Preacher's boy. You know how that is. We meant well but the other kids dragged us down."

He chuckled at his remark.

"What kind of school is this? You got real teachers here, or just Mommas that come in and teach how to can figs and starch shirts? Or does the preacher's wife come in to teach English but gets confused and ends up teaching about Jesus and the wickedness of evolution? And then she gives homework that can only be found in the Bible."

I looked at him in amazement. He must have enjoyed hearing his own words.

"I'll bet the principal has a cattle farm down the road so he goes home every now and then to check on a saltlick, or a fence that needs mending, or sees about the colored boys he's got out picking cotton in the field down by the creek. Every good piece of farmland's got a creek near it. Cut down the forest, throw out the seed, and make enough money to order up a year's supply of life for the kids and Momma."

He took a quick breath and continued, "My daddy was a preacher. You go to church, Oliver?"

Swap a demon for Satan, I thought. How'd he get past the people outside? No refuge in the principal's lair?

"I heard you were great friends with Beatrice North. Lucky boy. I tried to date her one time but she was way out of my league. What'd she see in a kid like you? No offense intended. I meant that strictly as a compliment. I hear good things about you and your family. I know you live back in the woods, have old-timey values, good grades, good manners. I know your old man works two jobs to pay the rent. Older brother is already through college. What's the secret?

"I met your dad. Nice guy but he doesn't strike me as a huge intellect. 'Must have a great Momma. Speaking of which, what does Momma think about this latest incident you got yourself mixed up in? You get in more ruts than a busted wagon wheel. How'd you ever get up to Chink's Gap to fight with that freight train? I heard you were a smart kid, so why'd you and Jeremiah climb up on that overhang and get yourselves exposed to death running right along under you? Boy, I did some stupid stuff in my day, but rail-hanging wasn't one. Whose idea was it? Jeremiah's?"

He paused as if he wanted my response. I simply looked at him.

"What kind of person was he? The kids around this school are mighty shook up. But you know, it's not uncommon for farm sch... I mean rural schools, like this, to have tragic things happen to their students. Poor roads with ninety degree curves, unmarked bridges, no road shoulders, excessive speed, inexperienced drivers. I can see where it's easy for the young adventurous spirits to get out of sorts and end their lives tragically in accidents. I nearly did the same thing myself, showing off for the girls, drinking beer and throwing the cans at the cows we passed down those country roads. You ever throw a full can of beer at a cow? You can knock it to its knees if you hit it just right."

He paused briefly, waiting for my answer.

"But you didn't answer me about Beatrice. I met her in college. Her name there was Emily—Emily Brubaker. Came from a well-to-do family. Her father was some kind of banker. Must of kept a lot of funds for himself. His wife was a looker, too. I could see where little Emily got her physical attributes. Excellent reporter and award-winning writer. Of course all writers have those same aspirations. Doesn't always happen but we head out with that intention. What are your intentions, little Holmes?"

My intentions were to ignore this pompous person.

He hesitated for a moment.

"No remarks. No impromptu sagacity from the alleged smart mouth of the class? Are we retreating to the humble pie, taciturn, self-pitying role that a stern country momma has drilled into us? Are we not to speak to the newspaper reporter? The liberal reporter who is an avowed agnostic? A danger to the children? Children unable to think for themselves?"

"Think about this," I said. "No comment."

"Ohh," he laughed back. "Family policy invoked. No comment. How original. You all practice that line every night before you go off to bed? Say your prayers and go off to sleep? What do you dream about, Oliver? Butt-naked torsos or an innocent boy falling off that hang-rail?"

I didn't hesitate to answer, "I dream about the days when I can go far away from newspaper reporters and live my life with some privacy."

"Ohh, he speaks. And where is that place you seek, young Holmes? Where, say, is Utopia?"

"Anywhere away from inquiring, obnoxious miscreants."

He chuckled and leaned toward me, but before he could try to assault me with more dialogue, the office entrance door came open and the principal was standing in silhouette against the outer light.

"Who the dickens let you in my office?" Gorman said in a highly-agitated voice.

"The office girl," the reporter said, standing up to defend his territory.

"You're a liar. Nobody told you to come in here. You're just harassing my student. He's got enough of a load on him without a slickster like you piling on more emotional garbage. Get out of my office and stay out!"

"Apparently, sir, you are unaware of the power of the press."

"You'll be aware of the power of my boot up your rear if you don't leave campus immediately. Leave this here boy alone."

"I'll be talking to Southern Association about your lack of professionalism," Rimple threatened as he edged toward the door he'd come in.

"Never heard of them," Gorman replied. "And don't invite them over here. I got enough paperwork to fill out now."

Rimple left the battlefield without further firepower covering his withdrawal. When the door slammed shut, Gorman approached his desk without looking at me.

"Didn't know that rascal was in here bothering you, Holmes. It's about time for English. Get on back up to your class."

I got up quietly and started for the office door.

"Oliver," Gorman said, stopping me as I reached for the door knob. "Anybody else give you any grief today, tell 'em I said to kiss your..."

He thought better of his phraseology. "...foot."

Evie was waiting in the main office.

"I know who it was, Ollie," she whispered, proud of herself. "Preston Ward and Clifford Mize. Right?"

I just stared at her. What had I done? We had been great poetry writers and tea-drinking literary lovers together. And now I had unearthed her real talent: criminal investigator. Somehow I knew she wouldn't leave it alone. "Look, Evie, I know I told you a bunch of top secret stuff, but you can't go sticking your pretty nose in my business. I was just letting off emotional steam. I thought I could trust you."

She put her hand over her nose. "You don't like my freckles, do you?"

"Of course I do. They're cuter'n a new puppy."

"New puppies are all wrinkled and blind."

What was a boy to do? "Are you going to promise to leave this inquisition alone?" I asked.

She studied the ceiling as we started away from the office area. The hall filled up with other noisy students. We could talk as securely as if we were inside a giant cement mixer.

"Oh. Preston Ward doesn't drink beer," she said, thinking out loud.

"How do you know?"

"I've ridden a few country roads with Preston."

"At Silver Run?"

She politely pushed me aside. "Ollie. You're ruining our relationship."

"How's that?"

"Questioning me about Preston. He's a nice boy."

"He kiss you?"

"No. Well, maybe. Just a peck."

"Okay."

"You upset?"

"Why should I be?"

"We're just literary friends, right? You and me."

"Sure. We write bad poetry and lie to each other about it."

"See! You're ruining our relationship. I wanted us to be friends. I'm older than you."

I shrugged and we started up the stairs. "How about Clifford?" I asked.

"What about him?"

"He drink beer?"

She looked at me strange-like.

"What kind of question is that?"

"An inquiring one. You kiss him, too?"

"No! Well... Maybe."

I shrugged big time and felt hurt.

"Ollie, I'm nearly seventeen."

"So. I'm nearly sixteen."

"You're ruining it for us."

"Revoke my membership in the Choccolocco Poetry Society."

"Why are you being sensitive and pouty about those boys? We've got a major problem to deal with. As soon as I figure out those two boys' names, I'll start to work on a solution... strictly through the power of prayer."

"I didn't know you were such a nosey busy-body."

"How am I that?"

"I wish I hadn't told you anything. Sooner or later you'll tell Suzanne, and she'll tell Audrey, and she'll tell May and..."

"What a perfectly horrible picture you paint of me, Oliver Holmes. I thought we were poetry pals in the deepest sense and here you go calling me names."

"I'm not calling you names."

"What about 'busybody'? Is that Spenserian?"

"I don't know what that means."

"I don't think I do either but it sounded good."

"I gotta go to English."

"See. You're doing better already. As soon as I made you jealous over those other boys, you forgot your troubles for a few minutes."

"I'm not jealous."

"You were."

"Was not."

"How come you kept asking about the kissing thing?"

"I wanted to know if you were that kind of girl."

"What kind?"

"Kind that kissed boys at a Saturday night drag race."

"Where and whom I kiss is my business."

"Well, my mission was accomplished, too. For a few seconds I got your mind off the train thing."

"How's that? Oh, I don't care about... Say, how about Margie the Largie groping on you? You kiss her?"

"Emphatically no! For two reasons: one, she's an acne queen..."

"She can't help that."

"Two, her boyfriend would've cut my lungs out if I'd touched that girl."

"I've changed my mind."

"About what?"

"About helping you."

"Why?"

"I think you made the whole thing up."

"What!"

"You just wanted to be big boy on a backwoods campus. No sports. No who's who..."

"I work in the afternoons. I can't play sports."

"Consider me crying, but save me the effort."

"I don't want to be in Who's Who."

"Good. You won't be disappointed."

Evie's friends came by and reminded her to hurry on to math class. She smiled and waved, then said her last words to me before she darted for the classroom, "See you about this investigation right after school."

She stopped at the door and grinned. "The one I really kissed was Delno."

She disappeared into Blue Nose's inner sanctum.

But I couldn't see Freckles that afternoon.

I had a physical problem.

My ribs hurt bad where Moorefield, the Jerk, and Alvin had kicked me while I was on the ground at the train scene. I could pedal my bike over my afternoon paper route, but whenever I slowed the activity, I had trouble breathing. Getting out of bed required a testament of torture. Who knew those muscles were necessary to perform such a simple task?

"Oliver," Old Doc Francis said, grinning and dropping down beside me in his living room that served as his patients' waiting room. Old Doc was a real doctor but he was retired now and, to the detriment of his sweet wife who tried to watch his diet, increasing in size. But the doctor had an incurable disease—hunger. He was friendly and gentle to work on your wounds and such, and he didn't charge much because the valley folks couldn't afford much. He just doctored and didn't worry about money. He was a good man to me. "What's done happened to you, boy?"

"I'd like to get you to check out my rib cage, doctor, but I'd have to pay you back by doing afternoon work after my paper route."

He examined my face carefully. He knew about Jeremiah. Everybody in the valley did. He also knew that I had no money.

"Your momma and daddy know you're hurting?" he asked, looking away.

I didn't say anything.

We sat in silence a few minutes.

"Well, come on in here to my operating room and let's take a look at your skinny rack of bones."

He had trouble getting up and walking back to the next room, and he insisted on talking as he went. He and Mrs. Francis loved to keep up the chat. "Had me a news service once," he said, lightly, "standing on the corner of a big city hawking *The Daily Tribune*. Made twenty cents a day. Cold and hot the same. Stand there and pass out the latest news. Communication at its finest, or rubbish at its greatest, 'cording to how high you stacked that paper before you threw it out. How much ol' Moon pay you, boy, for helping him?"

"He gives me three dollars a week, sir."

"Right respectable sum. Which days you like best—winter—summer?"

"Uh, I like the transition seasons better, sir."

He laughed. "Nobody calls them transitional around here, Ollie. Sit down on that ironing board over there and take off your shirt."

It was a frail table with a sheet on it. I took off my shirt and sat down.

"How's your sweet momma doin'?" he asked, starting his look-see over my body with his low-riding spectacles on. "Heard y'all had some night callers other night."

"Yes, sir. She's fine." I figured that covered that.

But Doc didn't think so. He wanted more information. I'd forgotten that the doctor considered himself the news center of the valley. Older farmers having a slow day in the winter fields would stop by the waiting room for the latest chat and hottest coffee. Old Doc would keep a patient waiting while he got the latest news on Harvey's fresh calf or Brewster's restive mare. After a while he'd wander off to the other room and pretend to be interested in Ethelene Pound's aching back or her painful hip or her headaches. He'd laugh that great laugh of his and tell her to resume normal marital relations, knowing full well that Mrs. Pound had been a widow over ten years and the placebos that he gave her would do as much for her "condition" as any miracle drug would.

Along with his medical practice, Doc had great practical wisdom. For all he'd done for my family, I figured I owed him a better picture of what had transpired that night the West End Klan came calling. The news alert per Ollie's personal viewpoint, I guess you could say. Doc lost interest in my exoskeletal system and stopped to study my face.

"They came up through the creek and stopped out at the barn trail."

"Many of 'em?"

"No, sir. Maybe six or eight. Most of 'em hung back out at the trail but a short little guy and a bigger fellow came up to talk."

"What'd they say?"

"Well, Momma kinda intercepted their little 'raid'. She told them to get off our property before the Good Lord's angels came down and chased 'em off back across the creek."

"I can hear Miss Tallulah saying that. Then what happened?"

"I'm not real clear on their mission. The taller man said they thought we was livin' with a bunch of hollow fellows or something like that. I wasn't sure what that meant."

"Those rascals don't need much prompting to light up a torch and try to scare people. Buncha skellums. Melon-lovin' chickens."

"Anyway, the big man must've figured Momma was home alone with a house full of kids 'cause he decided to take his boys and leave us alone. It was the little man that started cussin' and sayin' bad things and pointing at me and talkin' about Seth and that other killer, but the big man called him 'Fly' and said to get on back away from this innocent family."

"Fly? Who's this Fly?"

"I'm not positive, but I think this character was the one that tried to run me and Sherman down on the roadside that day of the big snow."

"When that Snow Girl got put down in the woods near the dam?"

"Yes, sir. The following evening we were walkin' 9 and this jalopy tried to run Sherm and me over. We had to hit the ditch to keep from gettin' killed. And then I saw this same car later on out in West End and this guy's uncle called him 'Fly.' He looked like a punk to me."

The doctor looked away from me and thought a few minutes. "He's gonna be a dead punk when the Troop gets through with 'im."

"I hope I haven't told too much," I said suddenly, trying to backpedal. "I don't want any more trouble for me or my family."

"Don't worry about that, Ollie. There's an old standing law between the West End bunch and the Valley Troop. We don't mess in each other's business. If they's to come over this side of the mountain, then we got fellows that'd take exception to their violating that law. This punk must've told some mighty big lies to get up a crew for Choccolocco."

I thought maybe he was thinking of Sherman's dad. If a no-good tramp came along and lived in a dark hollow somewhere and started stealing chickens or tractor fuel, or camped and hunted on private property where he wasn't supposed to go, well, unless that person showed up in church on Sunday morning and confessed his sins and sought atonement, then it wasn't too long before a neighborhood party showed up at his shack and showed him the road out of our valley.

I wasn't sure exactly what commandments these folks had to violate to get the road out, but somebody kept score and levied severe penalties. I didn't want to say much else and the doctor caught my reluctance so he eased up on the details except he wanted to know one last thing. "One more question, Ollie," he said. "Who was it broke up the party?"

I thought a minute. He was asking about Ole Cooper. “Well, sir, just as the big man was calling off the hunt and the other Klan members were going toward the creek, here comes a white figure down Jamback Road. From the porch it looked like a ghost was gliding down toward us. The boys really got spooked then and they hit the trail running. But it was just that... pardon... crazy man from the war. I think he’s a Cooper.”

Doc nodded his head and smiled. “Know him well.”

He laughed a pretty good laugh and decided he’d heard enough. He got down to my business like he was satisfied with what I’d told him. Then he looked at the bruises and abrasions on my body and got serious with his examination.

“I’m not the one to inform you, but there’s some people in this world don’t deserve to draw air every day... Mighty sorry you’ve had to learn that first hand.”

He lifted my arm and felt my ribs.

“You’re allowed a grunt or two on this side, Ollie. Somebody did a right competent job of trying to break your bones right in here.”

I held my breath and tried not to make a sound. The examination hurt like crazy, but I didn’t want tears to register in my eyes.

“I’ll give you some medicine to put on those scrapes and such. I don’t think those bones are fractured, although something or somebody tried hard enough to make you scratch around for your breath... Who or what done this to you, son?”

I didn’t say anything so Old Doc continued to check my upper body all over and hummed a Christian hymn as he worked.

“Some pulp wooder didn’t drop a load of pine on you, did he?”

“No, sir.”

“A car fall on you? Weldon puttin’ in his own transmissions now?”

“No, sir.”

“Well, that don’t leave much to question. I guess some freckle-faced girl took exception to your advancements upon unclaimed territory.”

He laughed at his metaphor and finished his examination, turning back to a cabinet where he gathered up a bottle of medicine and a small tube of something.

"One of these deals goes inside—the other out. You're a smart boy. I reckon you'll figure out which one goes where."

I took the medicine and buttoned up my shirt.

"When can I start to work for you, Doctor?" I asked.

"Well, Ollie, considering the condition your condition is in, why don't we just wait until one of them transitional seasons comes around. Reckon I'll have plenty yard work to do then... In the meanwhile, you go lay that battered bunch of bones down a while and take it easy. Can't say much for your mental part, but if I was you, I'd be talking to Captain Bishop. He likes to interrogate folks that go 'round beatin' up fifteen-year-old boys. Some say he's right good at it."

"Thank you, sir."

"You know, Ollie, the Good Book talks about the meek inheriting the earth. By being meek I don't think the Lord meant to substitute the word 'weak.' I think he meant that a strong person could still be subordinate to those over him, but he could still be strong."

He waited a minute as I bowed my head in silence, unsure of what he was driving toward.

"Seems you got a nestful of problems eating at you, boy. But best I heard you ain't letting nobody push you into a bad step. I find that mighty admirable.

"You'll be all right. You know why? 'Cause the Good Lord Himself is gonna look after you. He ain't sending no Gabriel or anyone of them fellows He trusts to patch things up. No, sirree, Ollie. I believe the Good Lord's got a personal interest in you and you couldn't get any better help in the universe. You stay strong, boy. You ain't alone."

I listened to Old Doc on all of his advice. I respected him. I just didn't feel as confident about my future as he obviously did. I knew the Good

Lord looked after the infirm and ones that did foolish things without intending to hurt anybody, but sometimes I also thought that I must've used up God's good grace to me.

There I went sinning again. Self-pity. I had a lot to be thankful for.

Doc tried to cheer me up further as I pulled on my clothes. Then, too, he was looking out for himself as well. "Say, Ollie," he laughed as he washed his hands in the big sink. "You know what'd be mighty handy to me sometime whenever you and Billy Rand are out prowling on this end of the valley?"

"What's that, sir?"

"If you was to get me up a sackful of your momma's hot breakfast biscuits loaded up pretty good with butter and wrapped up in wax paper so they won't get cold before you get here. Now, that'd make this old country sawbones as happy as a new-born colt."

I smiled as the tone of the conversation shifted. "Yes, sir," I replied. "I can handle that real soon."

"Don't go pushing them aching bones now. Just when you get a good run at some spare time. Yes, siree, your momma makes the best brown biscuits this side of Tarpin Creek. I can almost taste 'em right now."

I was halfway home, walking the treacherous 9, when a jalopy roared up behind me and eased over beside me as I got off the road outta the way. I recognized the driver of the old beat-up car immediately. Raike.

"Hey, Ollie," he said brightly. "Get in and I'll give you a ride home."

"Thanks," I said as I got into the wreck.

The door wouldn't close properly although I went through physical anguish slamming it two or three times. The car coughed and sputtered several times before the clutch caught and we were up and heading down the road. When I looked down I could see the pavement passing under my feet.

"Watch your feet," Raike said, grinning.

He was proud of the jalopy, having worked the past summer to have wheels his senior year in high school. He drove Evie and himself to school most days.

'Made our bus ride seem tame compared to this death trap.

"How you feel, Sport?" he asked with a laugh.

"Right on top, Raike. Right on top."

"Well, I know you had a hard row to hoe lately. Evie tells me you ain't talking much about the other night. I'm sorry but if I can help in any way..."

"Thanks, Raike. Everything's fine."

He looked at me fully as the death trap vibrated and the steering wheel shook, severely limiting our speed.

"Hold her, Maude, she's a rearing!" Raike hollered out as the car bucked and rebelled against working for us.

"Man, Raike," I said seriously. "If you can stop this rolling wreck, I'll take to walking again. It ain't safe here."

"Aw, it ain't nothing bad. It hits a spell every now and then, but we'll get there."

I wasn't convinced.

Several cars came up fast behind us, honked lightly, and passed us on a straightaway. We were actually creeping along, trying to soothe the wheel problem that had shaken the steering.

"Where you been, Ollie?"

I pointed vaguely backwards. "Back there."

"Back where?"

I hesitated. The car got up a slight momentum and I hoped I might not have to walk dangerous 9. "Back at Doc's place."

"Whatcha doin' way up there?"

"Trying to schedule some yard work for him," I said, honestly.

Raike laughed. "That yard of his needs a bushhog. I hear he loses one or two patients a year out front in his wild shrubs. He's got wild hydrangeas that come down off Cheaha and squat by the handrails so they can snatch people up on the way to his office."

I grinned. "That's a big story, Raike. And not even funny."

He agreed by nodding slightly as he fought the renegade steering wheel.

"Hey, Raike," I asked suddenly, another thought hitting me. "Who's that boy at school named Delno?"

Raike looked blank for a minute. "There's no boy named Delno at our school."

I waited a minute as he seemed to be searching for the correct answer. "You sure?" I asked.

"Wait a minute."

"What?" My heart held up its job for a minute.

"There was a boy up at Bible camp last summer named Delno something. How would you know him, Ollie?"

I shook my head, disappointed that someone had popped up in Raike's head.

"I heard Evie knew him."

"Genevieve? My sister?"

I nodded.

We rode a few minutes in silence.

"He was a college boy, I think. His dad was a preacher of a big church in Birmingham. He and Evie were prayer partners at chapel."

More than prayer partners, I thought.

"Maybe I know him," I lied, searching. "Describe him."

He thought a minute "Oh, he was a lady's man. The girls fell all over him."

I was disappointed. My face must have turned down.

"You look sad, Ollie. What's wrong? This dude wouldn't know you, would he? He lives way over in Mountain Brook."

I shook my head and watched 9 skate along under my feet.

"He had a crush on my half-brain sister. I caught him kissing her out back the chapel one night and beat the tar outta him..." He looked at me sharply. "You won't tell dad, will you?"

"No."

He laughed. "You know what she said after I put that Romeo on the road?"

I didn't really care. He'd kissed Evie. She'd admitted it and Raike had seen them. I was probably as important to her as a...

"She said he kissed like a movie star. Now, what's that mean?"

I was crushed. Might as well scratch that one.

"Where'd you hear about Delno? He hasn't been lurking around school, has he?"

I shook my head but didn't comment. Another few minutes and we'd be near Jamback. But just as I thought, the motor conked and Raike had to plow through the roadside bushes until the beast died. Little as I knew about being a mechanic, I tried to help Raike work on the moribund vehicle. But I think everything about it was shot. It needed a decent burial at Hewberry's Junk Yard just off Mint Gap Road. I expressed as much and Raike reluctantly agreed. We left the hood up and started hitchhiking toward our respective homes. Thankfully, we got lucky when a lady in a Mercury came along and we got aboard quickly. I hopped out at Jamback and Raike stayed aboard for White Oak.

As I started down the road toward the house, I wondered what next great challenge God had lined up for me. A load of pine off that pulpwood truck, Old Doc had said. Yeah. That was pretty much the feeling.

After the aborted ride home with Raike, I spent the evening moping around so low that even Rand noticed. Most of the time he was quiet at home. I was usually the one keeping the other kids stirred up.

"What's wrong with you?" he asked as I sat on our bed and tore up notebook paper, wadded it up and fired it across the room toward a trash can. I was lethargic and didn't really care if I hit the target or not.

On top of everything else, I had the Delno blues.

"You ever really like somebody at school and they didn't like you back?" I asked, ripping another sheet out of a used notebook.

He studied my face a minute as he diverted attention from his textbook. "You still stuck on that senior?"

I didn't indicate anything, just adjusted my aerial attack to include his drink on the table. My first shot bounced off the rim and hit the floor.

"Hit my RC, fuzzy, and I'll fix you so all the kids at school will be looking at you."

I took deliberate aim and looped another wad off the lip of the glass.

"I've got problems," I said, studying the floor.

"Don't compound them."

"You know Genevieve?"

"Raike's sister. Sure."

"You think she's cute? Pretty? Luscious? Cool?"

"Which one am I suppose to answer?"

"She anything to you?"

"No. She's nothing to me. My radar only works for Lexie from Blue Branch. You know that. But I used to think she was prettier than Sherman T.'s sister, and that girl'd stop a Greyhound bus on a Kansas highway."

"But is Evie really...?"

"You're the one knows her. You're the one writing her poetry and making moon eyes in the library. I got my own problems. That Duncan Moorefield's trying to hook up with the Blue Branch girls. Guess which one?"

"Lexie the Sexie."

"Don't use that term around here."

"I don't. I only use that tag around Weldon. Answer my question."

"Answer *my* question. What do you know about Moorefield?"

I was startled upright. I looked at him. What did he mean?

"You think Lexie will go for the rich boy over me?" Rand asked.

"Of course not. Moorefield's too wild and reckless for Lexie. Her daddy'd take a shotgun after Golden Boy if he showed up at her door."

I didn't convince Rand. He shook his worried head.

"She asked me a lot of questions about him at study hall," he said, sounding mournful now.

I was sorry I'd started the conversation.

"What about Moorefield?"

"I asked you first," I said. "Give me a rating on Evie."

"Evie's top drawer," he said, but not with conviction. He had Lexie the Sexie on his brain.

"Why do I even talk to you?" I asked.

"Go ask Ryder then. She knows everybody in the phone book."

"Ryder'd tell me anything just to trip me up."

"Trip her back."

"I can't. Did you know the boys in her class are scared of her. She couldn't get a turn at a spin-the-bottle party."

"Talk to Raike then."

"I talked to him today."

"And?"

"You ever ridden in his piece of crap convertible? Don't. It's death on four wheels."

"Anybody know you rode with him?"

"Are you kidding? I came home on the back seat of a nice lady's station wagon."

"Where'd you been?"

"To see Doc."

"Why?" He seemed concerned.

I hesitated.

"How'd you pay him?"

"That's my business."

"Why are you going to the doctor? Momma doesn't know?"

"Don't tell her."

"Pay me."

"What do you mean?"

"Find out about Lexie and Goldilocks for me and I'll keep quiet on the Doc thing."

"Find out what?"

"You know. What she thinks of both of us. Who has the inside track to her hot little motorjammer... Stuff like that."

I knew I couldn't begin to engage Golden Boy. However, Lexie was cute. I'd like to talk to her.

"Tell me now about Evie and I'll do it for you," I offered.

He thought a minute. "Truth is," he finally said. "Evie has a lot of great qualities. But the senior boys think she's a few stars short of a constellation."

I frowned. "I don't want to hear that," I said. "My whole life's upside down."

"You're the one tilted it, big boy."

"Okay," I agreed. "I'll check on Lexie tomorrow."

He went back to his book. "Why'd you see the Doc?" he asked without looking up.

I wasn't sure what to say, so I said nothing.

The old ghosts came back and sat down beside me.

12

"Foolishness lays a deep trap for the spirit of misadventure."

—Ron Miller

I was feeling blue again. School was as much fun as an Asian death march.

Guess I was sulking around like I was about gone myself. Sherman T. said I was feeling sorry for myself and to come by his house. He had something to show me. So I convinced Miss Ordie to let me off at Sherman's stop, but I had to swear that it was all right with the iron woman.

I put a finger over my lips toward Ryder so she wouldn't rat me out soon as she got home. But I knew she would. When you're already the underside of shelf paper you might as well get yourself lined up with some foolishness.

I didn't feel any better as I stepped off the bus, but Sherm grinned like he'd just found out the powers at school were moving his locker space next to Miss Bonnie's. "Wait till you see her," he grinned and punched my arm in a show of good-buddyism.

"Her?" I questioned. "Your parents adopt?"

"Naw, dung breath," he replied. "I got me a friggin' hot rod. I been trying to tell you all day at school."

"Great," I said, flat talking. "Another bicycle."

"Bi means two, don't it? Well, this deal has four wheels."

"With you..." I started. "You mean a real hot rod?"

"Bet your sweet buns," he said. "If you had sweet buns, which you don't, but since we're old buddies..."

"It ain't April Fool's Day," I said. "That's weeks off."

"Can we say 'coupe'?"

"Coupe DeVille? That ain't a hot rod."

"Coupe as in Ford. Engine as in Chevy."

"You're going to hell for lying."

"I got the kind of rod you drive fast and wreck frequently." He grinned wickedly.

I dropped the blues on the spot. Life was good again for a moment. "Where'd you get it?" I had to know. "You've been holding out on me."

"Man owed Pop some money for winter feed. Been owing 'im two, three years so when he couldn't pay and he got ready to move off to town, he told old Monte to come over and get the car for payment."

"Cool, cat," I breathed excitement now. "It run good?"

"Well, wait till you see."

"That means it doesn't run," I said. "But we can make it run."

"Well," Sherman T. hedged a mite. "This is gonna be a challenge, Gooberman."

"Engine blowed up?"

"Naw."

"All there? Carburetor? Distributor?"

"Sure. All there."

"So? What's missing?"

"Transmission."

"Where is it?"

A shrug. "Man claims it's over at another boy's house. I'm not sure."

"You kinda need that," I understated.

"Well, something else, too."

"How's that?"

"Right door won't exactly close."

"Exactly? It either will or it won't. Which is it?"

"It's a won't."

I almost cussed. "Great," I said. "What else?"

"Well, the rear end is kinda strange."

"How strange?"

"It may be a Chrysler."

"May be?"

"He wasn't sure what it was."

"Does it have axles? Does it roll?"

"Oh, sure. Now the brakes..."

"You don't have any."

"Well I do, but..."

"I'm going back home," I said, feigning disgust. But I couldn't wait to see the coupe. We were a quarter-mile away through the woods or closer if we chanced the road that took off by Brewsters' house. The Brewsters had a dog that ate steel and spit razor blades. And me, I hated mean dogs, especially those that were in my slipstream and closing fast.

"Where's the hound from Hell?" I asked as we neared Brewsters' place.

"Let's hit the woods," Sherman directed. "I'm gonna sneak over there one night and pitch him a poison wienie."

I don't know what Henry was thinking but Sherman T.'s Ford made "ugly" a compelling term. The back slope could launch skiers. The front grille was a no show. But the kicker was the thick cotton rope that was bound around the passenger door to hold it against a body so rusty that the body mount and the door striker were things of no ones recent memory.

"God, Sherm," I said. "It's beautiful."

"Told you so." He was beaming.

"How'd you get it home?"

"Pop supplied the pickup and I steered the '38 Special."

That must have been a trip of small wonders, I thought, referencing Mr. Monte's driving skills. His license had come through the rural route postman, courtesy of Sears Roebuck Company.

" '38 Special," I copied his praise. "I like that. It ain't a '40 classic but it's a rod."

"Dig that engine," he said, pointing to the orange-painted valve covers that spelled out "Chevrolet" in script. The carburetor was mounted where it belonged, but the air filter was missing and pinestraw and birdnest stuffings seemed to be sprouting out the carb throat. Needed some housekeeping for sure.

"Engine locked up?" I queried as I dug out part of the mixings in the intake area.

"Hellfire no," he blurted out proudly. "Jest been sittin' around. It'll run like a scalded dog."

"You hear it fire up?"

"Naw. Old butt breath said it'd haul donkey."

I didn't want to lance his bubble. "Reckon it'll run with that little Powerpack in it and 265 exhaust manifolds."

"Yeah, buddy."

"Well, I'm impressed, hotrod. Can't wait to go for a ride."

"That's why you was invited," Sherman said. "You gonna help me tow this thing up Butternut Hill and we gonna coast back to the yard."

I looked at him like he was crazy. Then knowing for sure he was, I shook my head and backed out of the shed where the hopeless wreck was parked.

"Come on, chicken dung," he prodded. "You ain't got a hair on your butt."

"I'm not in this one," I said. "I've been shot at, chased by tanks, eluded various sized dogs, been beaten to a noodle by scoundrels, and implicated in Jeremiah's sudden demise, but I'm telling you here and now I'm not riding in a car with no brakes, faulty steering, and a nut behind the wheel, being kind in my personal reference, of course. You're actually clinically insane if you think I'm riding that death trap off Butternut Hill. Change the name to Butts'n'Nuts Splattered Hill after we ride down it."

Sherm wasn't deterred. "Help me hook this chain to the tractor," he said. "Pop's off chasing Olivia the mad bull. We'll have his tractor home before he misses it."

Mumbling and cussing, I grabbed the chain. "Gotta have papers on me," I said as we hooked the two vehicles together and prepared for its long run down the hill through the woods.

Butternut Hill was a slight challenge for the farm tractor. Maybe it was my driving or the unlikely Ford coupe it was dragging, but with more confidence than I cared to admit to, we started out of the yard, across the wooden bridge and up the hill that touched the property on the north side.

Nobody lived up the rutted dirt road, so I guess it was just a loggers road or the way to the family dump down the hidden hollow beyond. We'd hunted up that way the past fall and killed a few squirrels and shot at some wild turkeys, but Sherm and I both were such bad shots neither one wanted to get out of the other's sight. So after we ran out of ammunition, we walked home through the woods and gave the squirrels to the dogs to eat because I read once that squirrels were in the rodent family and I was fresh out of intent on snacking on rat meat.

The tractor struggled and belched smoke, but I held it in the middle of the ruts and Sherman hung out the good door, grinning and pounding on the metal of the old car as it put its butt against the tractor's butt and we hauled off up the incline. After we spun rocks and debris until I thought the antiquated tractor was gonna give up the life, we made it to the top of the hill. Sherm locked the brakes hard as he could. I let out the chain slack and undid the rusty Ford.

After I parked the tractor under a pine tree, I walked back to Sherm who was imagining he was Fireball Roberts ready to fly down Daytona's back stretch.

"How am I getting in?" I asked. "That door's tied shut."

"Crawl in the window. I'm letting the brakes go. This pedal's starting to go down, faster'n..."

"I can't crawl in there."

"You can't ride then. Get back outta the way. I'm leaving the chute."

"Hold up," I corrected myself. "I dragged that piece of sewage up here, reckon I can ride it back down."

My next mistake of the afternoon came fairly soon. I was halfway in the window on the roped-down door when the brakes left town permanently and Sherm let out a whoop. We started down Butternut Hill like a runaway trolley in Frisco town.

"Stop this thing," I tried to say, but we were hitting ruts like they were speed launchers and Sherm was screaming like an eagle with the steering wheel spinning like the paddle in a washing machine and having no effect at all on the front tires.

We reached halfway point as I righted myself on the seat next to him just in time to feel us get airborne as we contacted the lip of the road. It threw us into the air like we were the Wright Brothers hoping for eternal flight. But the old car settled on a short flight path, cleared out some pine saplings near the muddy ditch, and then got its best speed as it bit a clear stretch of incline, sending us barreling at a speed that made my heart get up my throat and take a lookout for where we were headed.

'Course we had no idea or control as to where we were going. The wheel was useless and Sherm was pumping the brake pedal until it pounded through the rotten floorboard, but we continued to reach speeds unimagineable by a real car handling the same long stretch of grade.

When I saw the woods rushing toward the windshield and the water of the creek near the bridge splash over the hood like a giant bucket had let out its contents on us, I covered my face and tried to brace myself for the landing. No use. It was like the time I was learning to ride a bike and went full speed into the barn. When I woke up that time, Billy Rand was standing over me with concern on his face.

I guess the lights went out a second time, because I saw the water and the trees approaching us fast. And when I woke up, old Sherm was leaning over the seat toward me, a grin on his face made peculiar looking because a line of blood was crossing his forehead and nose and falling onto me.

"You all right, Ollie?" he was saying. "Talk to me."

"I was knocked out, Dip," I said, laying in the floorboard and trying to take stock of the situation. "How do you think I am?"

"You look fine."

"You look like crap. Quit bleeding all over me. You're ruining my shirt."

"Bleeding," he questioned, reaching for his nose. "Thought that was snot. You know—knocked the snot out of me."

"You knocked something else out of me," I replied, angry at myself for letting him talk me into riding a mad bronco down a ferris wheel of a hill.

Sherm reached for his nose and up into his hair and when he saw the mangle of tissue and blood of his scalp in the tainted rearview mirror, he did the noble thing. He passed out on the seat.

"Well, Oliver," Doc Francis said as he looked me over in his patient waiting room. "Your buddy's gonna have a headache for a while. I want you to sit here and don't fall asleep. Keep yourself alert. I wanta be sure you don't have a concussion. Looks like just a bump on your head but we'll wait and check it out after I run a sewing machine over Sherman's head."

He laughed and slapped my leg. "Heard y'all got you a real hot rod to drive. Better get a safety check before your next race."

He was still laughing as he went out the door to his operating room. I didn't think it was so dern funny. If that water hadn't slowed us up, we'd hit those trees full force and really been buggered up.

Mr. Monte had been kind to us, helping us out of the wreck and being gentle with us, not cussing us and carrying on like some dads would've done. And I wouldn't have blamed him if he had been upset. Burning up his tractor, tearing up his bridge, rerouting the creek. Let's see, what else stupid did we do? Probably be Sherm's last Saturday cruise ride with us boys, though. The '38 Special would go to the field where old farm machinery retired—never to be touched again.

I didn't notice the lady as she came in the door. I heard it open and heard the screen door slap closed, but that was just a sound I heard a hundred times at home so I was doing what Doc said not to, had my eyes closed and was leaning my head back, hoping the pain would ease up and the knot on my head would go down before I made it home. Lord, the beating I was going to face. Maybe I could join the Chinese Navy under an alias.

"Excuse me," the feminine voice entered my painful state. "Is this the Doctor's office?"

I opened my eyes and saw a pretty lady wearing large glasses and a curious half frown, half smile. "Yes, it is," I answered, watching her closely, sensing an attractiveness. She could be a knockout without those telescope lenses she wore. Petite body—but shapely. "He's in sewing up my friend," I said. "What's your ailment?"

"Oh, I'm fine physically."

As Sherman would've said to that line, and I thought it, "Bet your sweet buns you are, honey." But I was a gentleman.

"I understand that the Doctor's the valley guru," she said, sitting a few chairs over from me.

An appropriate distance, I thought.

"I'm searching for some local ornamentation."

"Advice to the lovelorn?" I questioned. "Lady that reads the tea leaves moved to California."

She wasn't sure if I was teasing or not.

"No. Local things," she said. "What happened to you?"

"Bull kicked me in the head," I lied.

"Mercy," she said. "You all right?"

"I'm fine but they had to shoot the bull."

She was confused. "I don't understand," she said.

I started to continue when she snapped her finger.

"I know who you are," she said. "You're that famous farm boy. Don't tell me. Yes, Sherman Monte."

"What?" I said, incredulous.

"Yes, I met your mother today. A sweet lady. 'Thinks the world of her baby boy. Tell me, out of curiosity, what happened to your older brother?"

I was mortified. Mistaken for Sherman T? An insult. "You're way off base, lady," I said, almost indignant.

"Don't be bashful. Your reputation runs way out in front of you. Your fan club's hard at work as we speak."

"Stop it," I said.

"You're the one that found the body in the snow. I remember reading about you."

"You're further off than a Mars landing strip," I corrected.

"The bodies in the cave then. Local hero. Newspapers. Radio. I'm so proud to be sitting near you."

"Who are you, lady? You sound like a Yankee."

"I'm an intern working for your local paper. The *Times*. What's the last thing you've witnessed that I can put in the pages of history?" she asked, appearing serious.

When I declined an answer, she changed gears and hit on another topic. "What can you tell me about the Valley Troop?"

I had tipped over the milk bottle and couldn't put the spill back in. I studied a spot on the wall. Maybe she'd go away with the silence.

"Would you say they're gaining in numbers and popularity? Or have they begun to decline as the world shrinks in the glare of new technology?"

I was still mum.

"Have you personally dealt with these scalawags? Have they harmed you or your family?"

I looked at her and made a face like my head hurt, which it did. More so now.

"Whatever you say," she assured me, "will be kept in the strictest confidence. You can trust the media. But you know that. You've had experience there. Trusting reporters. Miss North, I believe, was your recent ally. What do you hear from her?"

I shrugged and my eyes found the ceiling again.

"Shame about that Jeremiah." She'd changed directions again. "I hear the Holmes boy is taking it hard. I guess he's the only one who knows about what really happened and he's not talking. But he'll have to talk when the Grand Jury convenes in a few days and an inquiry starts up. Very bad business."

I looked at her. She knew who I was. She was working me like a jazz master works a bass and my heart was playing her rhythm.

A Grand Jury? That sounded serious. Was it true? I'd ask Billy Rand. He'd know for sure if she was playing me.

"Do you know this Holmes boy?" she asked. "Does he attend your school? I'd like to speak to him."

"What would you ask him?" I ventured.

She shrugged. "About Saturday night, Jeremiah,Valley Troop, West End Klan. A few things like that. Give him a chance to get people off his back and onto that low-life Klan, that hate-mongering outfit that needs final exposing and eradication. Like vermin!"

"How would you do that?" I asked.

" 'Pen is mightier than the sword," she replied, taking off her glasses and leaning toward me. She was beyond lukewarm. She was approaching cool.

"I never trust the media," I countered. "Not that I've had an occasion to test them, but my dad doesn't like you folks."

"Just doing a difficult job. Everybody tries to hide the truth from us. You think it's easy trying to discover the truth? It's almost impossible."

"Makes you try all the harder, I'm sure," I replied.

"Take you for example," she said, looking into my eyes.

I wished she wouldn't do that. Cool women made me nervous.

"I'd say you weren't kicked by a bull. Maybe an automobile accident? Two adventurous boys in a dangerous vehicle. One gets stitches, the other gets a concussion. Am I warm?"

I almost smiled. "No, cool," I wanted to say. Instead, I ratted out. "How quickly you found me out," I said. "Holmes made me do it."

"It was your old coupe?"

I nodded.

"You were lucky not to be killed. People say you had no brakes and no steering."

"Exaggeration," I said. "We had brakes for awhile. Steering when we started out. Things went bad fast."

"Is your father upset with you?"

"He will be when he starts repairing that old bridge and burns up his tractor trying to drag that hot rod outta the creek."

"As he should be. You boys were wrong to do this."

"Life is dull in the valley," I defended. "We needed a ride in a wild car. We got it. More fun than the circus."

"Do you ever have fun riding with the Valley Troop? That would be an adventure."

"The Troop's about died out," I said. "It's the West End crew that needs death by the sword."

"Why is that?"

"They were over at the Holmes house the other night," I said. "Tried to scare Mrs. Holmes and her kids. They got run off by old Lyle Cooper, though. They were about half-crazy drinking or they wouldn't come up in the valley territory."

"What do you mean?"

" 'Talk is the Troop's gonna get even with the Klan..."

"Interesting. How and when does that happen?"

"Ain't out yet. Maybe pretty soon. Troop don't like scaring innocent people—especially women and children."

"I heard that somewhere else, too. Must be a Southern thing."

" 'Bet your sweet buns," I said, then caught my expression. "Sorry. 'Got carried away."

"That's okay. I've been called worse, and in this area, too."

"You promise you won't write this stuff?" I asked.

"I promise, dear. You just get that head seen about. And stay out of dangerous cars."

"They're the most fun," I said.

"You boys." She smiled, apparently happy that I'd given her some press fodder. "Anything else you don't want printed?"

I grinned through my headache. Who was fooling who here?

"Spell my name correctly," I said. "Sherman T. It's what my friends call me."

She winked at me and got her things to go. "Glad to finally meet you."

"Likewise, I'm sure."

She was headed for the car when my betraying mouth went against my good sense. “Ma’am,” I said loud enough to stop her.

She paused and looked back at me, her face saying she was puzzled at my attempt to halt her leaving. I walked to the door, within ear shot, and looked down as if deciding what to say next. I knew I had to apologize for lying, and for pretending to be someone else. That was wrong, just hoe-down wrong. Where did I start to right the wrong conversation, the wrong assumptions?

“I’m not Sherman T.,” I said, looking at those big eyes.

She waited quietly with one of those slight smiles that could take a conversation in either direction. A crossroads smile, I guess you could say.

“I’m Oliver Holmes,” I confessed.

She nodded her head and her eyes and smile together left the crossroads and ganged up on me with the compassion of feminine softness well placed.

“I know.”

“I couldn’t leave you with the lie. It wasn’t right. I’m the one agreed to pull the car up the hill and I’m the one was there when Jeremiah...”

“I realize that, too.”

Her face went quickly to concern and I thought I might begin to like this lady if she continued to use those enslaving features of hers to unravel my soul. Her obvious compassion was shaking loose that stone wall I’d built around my own emotions after Jeremiah had disappeared off that hanging arm over the tracks.

“It’s complicated,” I said, pausing enough to let her know the levee was not completely broached.

“You want to go inside and talk?” she asked, politely.

I shook my head. I loved Mrs. Francis, but her mouth ran full gear when the brakes should’ve hit in. She was not a valley gossip, just a loquacious person, trying to help others spiritually and emotionally—where her husband was busy always stopping the physical bleeding. If we went inside, she would hear everything I said to the reporter.

"Don't push this Klan business too hard," I said. "You don't know how mean these people are."

"Have you experienced them at work?"

I nodded my head and looked down again.

"They don't care if you're a man, woman, or child. If they figure you're out to harm them in any way, they'll take steps to make sure you lose interest quickly. That was true what I said about the hooded men that came by our house the other night, but I've also been trapped in a car with their kind and I can assure you their cruelty goes through the flesh and all the way to the middle of the bone. Their hatred is that severe. And try if you can with your newspaper, you're not going to change things by writing about them."

"How do you change such a society of evil?" she questioned, probably already knowing I had no answer for that question.

I shrugged slender shoulders and looked in those now sympathetic eyes.

"I know you're under tremendous pressure, Ollie. I won't press you to explain anything that's happened. I won't mention this meeting, either. You're right, adults can be very cruel. I hope things work out so that you don't get caught in the legal mess that will follow all of this business."

She stepped toward me and offered a cool touch to my shoulder.

"Why don't you take care of yourself and stay close to home a while. Too much foolishness going on around here."

We both smiled, and she stepped back to the door and prepared to drive the company car off into the late afternoon shadows. She must've been a farm girl. She worked the gears and clutch perfectly and the car responded just as the engineers had intended.

I thought of Beatrice North and the way she had used and abused the same car. But Beatrice could smile and change the world.

This lady was getting cool, but her smile was still in the developmental stage. She'd get to the point where her big eyes and pretty lips could paralyze a full-grown man. Not quite there, but she'd already done it to me.

13

"Wisdom denotes the pursuing of the best ends by the best means."

—Frances Hutcheson

A couple of days went by and my head got to feeling better, but Sherman T. looked like the mummy walking around.

'Course he played it for a joke, spooking grade-school kids whenever he saw them in the hallways and asking girls if they wanted to feel his wound. He didn't have many takers on the feeling part, so he milked his injury through the teachers by complaining of a headache and such so he could leave class early. I figured he got about what he deserved—trying to kill us in that old rod.

I heard Mr. Monte got hacked off when he found out his tractor was about used up engine-wise. It took several mules from a neighboring farm to drag that water-logged hot rod out of the creek. They just left it to dry out under some pines and forgot about it for a while. Sherman T. wasn't ready to give up on his hot licks, however, visiting the old Ford every afternoon after school and piddling with it best he could. Of course, that rusty ragpot on wheels needed major work done to it. We both knew it, so Sherm was cool and laid low about it.

I was just leaving school one afternoon, heading for the bus home when I noticed the state highway patrol car in the parking lot. A mighty uncommon sight.

I was hoping they were there to pick up Moorefield and put him back in the jailhouse. But my stomach did a turnover when the next thought hit me. Maybe they were out here looking for me to question me about Jeremiah and all.

Of course, my favorite cuss word came to mind. I was walking fast toward the wayward bus when a grade-school kid called my name and said the state lawman wanted to talk to me. I felt like I was under arrest for something evil and didn't have any choice. I walked timidly to the car where the giant state trooper was leaning back on the fender and grinning.

"Hey, Ollie," he said, and offered a handshake.

I tried not to shake. He had to be there to arrest me. I just knew it.

"Don't look so guilty," he said. "You're in no trouble. I need your help on something."

"I thought you were here to pick me up on the Jeremiah thing," I said, relieved to find that he was not.

"We can talk about that when you're ready," he said. "I don't want to put too much pressure on you. But I need help with some other business. You know a kid at school named 'Boother'?"

I thought a moment, my gears changing, trying to catch up to his. "Boother," I repeated. Boother Ledbetter. Dumbest kid in school. Failed every class every year. Borderline white trash.

"Yes," I said, not figuring to cause myself undue harm. "Yes, sir, I mean. I know Boother Ledbetter. That's the one you mean?"

"Does he live out on Slow Mile Road?"

"I don't know, sir. I get off the bus before it winds out into the big woods."

"So he's not a friend of yours?"

"No, sir. We've got gym together, I think. He doesn't talk much."

"Could you get yourself invited over to his house one afternoon?"

I was startled. Word was he lived in a shack with his widowed mother and his retarded brother. They didn't bathe much or ever change clothes. I usually avoided both the boys if I could. "You seen where he lives?" I asked.

The big man laughed and nodded his head. "Look," he said, leaning forward so he could lower his voice. "You handle it the best you can, but I need for you to look inside his house and find out what contents were in a purse that he and his brother found near Owl's Creek down by his house. It has something to do with the Snow Girl case. I'd be mighty obliged if you could help us out."

"You know I'd help you, Captain," I said, but hesitated.

"You help me," he replied. "I'll help you with your problem."

What problem? I thought. I looked questioningly at him.

"I know you, Ollie," he said. "You didn't have anything to do with Jeremiah's death. Somebody's putting pressure on you to carry a burden, but I know you well enough to see you're free of blame. You help me wind up this Snow Girl business and I'll take that other monkey off your back. Wouldn't take more than one or two guesses to figure him out, anyway."

I always thought the captain was mean but smart. He had some wisdom, too. He had me figured out in two minutes flat. I trusted him. I felt relief just thinking his way.

"I'll pedal over to Slow Mile this afternoon," I said. "What is it I'm looking for?"

He told me two or three things to pry loose from ole Boother. I put them in my head and started for the bus before I got left.

"One other thing, Ollie," he grinned as I departed. "Stay outta those death-defying hot rods."

I didn't say anything to Sherm. I just got off the bus at my stop and left him to go home and tinker. Actually, the captain's words had parlayed some other hot rod thoughts that had dropped in on me during gym class. I had been outside sitting against the wall to keep the wind from howling down my back. Some of the senior boys were talking about a nasty, mad-dog Chevrolet that was being built in a junkyard shop up in Blue Mountain. I wasn't sure where that was, but I thought it was just north of Bentonville in a mill village area.

Of course I tried to muscle in closer to hear the bulletin, but the seniors gave me an ostracizing look so I shrugged and walked away. But I didn't go far. When the smoke of profanity cleared somewhat and the circle broke up at the coach's calling, I went over to Weldon and asked about the car.

"Leave me alone, Ollie," he said. "I'm trying to catch the eye of Lydia over yonder. Man, she looks tough in that gym outfit."

"I'll go talk to her for you," I offered, "if you'll give me a touch of news on this mad-dog Chevy in Blue Mountain."

"All I know, it's a straight axle '55 Chevy with a Chrysler hemimotor."

"What's a straight axle?"

"You'll find out Saturday night. It's gonna be at Silver Run."

I sincerely hoped I was at Silver Run on Saturday, but my life was strictly day to day. If somebody ugly, mean, and nasty wasn't after my butt, somebody cool looking, Satanic, and wicked was. And now Captain Bishop had laid an "assignment on my heart" as the preacher says.

What was a cool cat to do? My cool was running short.

Slow Mile Road was well-named.

You had to go up the county road that crossed the same creek three times, push the low branches out of your face as you crossed the dilapidated old wooden bridges, and clear yourself past a yard full of dogs that were chained to a fence post. They snarled and yanked on those chains, but by and by I got past the protected shack—wondering what it was that needed protecting—and started by the cotton field clearing. 'Course there wasn't any cotton this time of year, just an old black-soil field with the bitter stalks of the fall crop poking up out of the ground like tobacco weed near the Indian burial ground. The ghosts of the Indians didn't bother with a lost soul white boy like me, having better prey to haunt, I reckoned, because I didn't see a branch snake toward me or any weeds folded over where the Indians were stalking their prey through the tall grass. Even old man wind got down off his high horse and left me alone to pedal in the silence of the isolated country road.

I wasn't sure about this Boother fellow. Talk around school was he and his brother didn't come to school but once a month and that was just to keep their names on the roll. Then they just sat in the back of the class like social outcasts. They never said anything. The girls kinda giggled at them and the boys ignored them. Why bother with them? They'd be out of class again tomorrow and maybe not come back till spring.

I think that I had played on the same team with Boother once, but he didn't do much. After a while he just sat down and looked off up the field like he belonged out there in the deep woods and not there in the social confines of the school. I guess most folks agreed with that because they left him alone.

Now, I was supposed to buddy up to him and try to figure out some stuff for the big captain. The things I did to avoid jail.

Theirs was the last and only house toward the end of Slow Mile.

I nearly gagged when I smelled the pigpens out in the backyard and saw the chickens strutting around the yard and into the house like they were Sunday company. I didn't see any dogs. I was glad of that because I was still practicing being invisible to those "Hounds of the Baskerville" that had tested their chains pulling after me as I had passed the other shack.

I stopped in the road and hollered for Boother as loud as I could. Nothing. A few chickens looked up to see if I'd feed them, then they went on about their business. The single pig in the thick, black mud didn't bother to look up to check the new voice. I made an impression on nobody.

I tried again and waited a while. Finally a woman came halfway out on the porch, all stooped over and shuffling along like the world's oldest person, until she was full on the porch looking at me. She didn't say anything but stood there all humped over with her hand over her face. All I could see was her eyes and an old scarf pulled tightly over her hair. Her clothes appeared worn and dirty and she was "as the peasant that lived in misery and saw no light to guide her."

"I'm looking for Boother," I hollered again, 'loud as I could and still sound respectful.

She used her free hand to point toward the deep woods up the hill behind the shack. But she did not make a sound.

"He out yonder hunting?" I asked but she made no further motion.

When I was fixing to ride back down my lonely road toward the wild dogs in chains, another woman came out on the porch and looked questioningly at me.

"I go to school with Boother," I explained myself to her. "I wanted to talk to him."

"He's gone off with Brother. They out huntin' for supper."

"Which way they go, ma'am?"

"Back there in the woods—where they always go. What you want with Boother? He ain't got no friends."

"We play on the same team together at school," I half-lied. "My name's Cleveland, Grover Cleveland. We got class together." I full-lied. Desperate times were these, I rationalized.

"Follow 'at thar trail," she waved toward a pig trail that wound off into the snake grass.

"Sure," I thought. "Enough snakes in there in the wintertime to chew my shoes off me."

"They got guns," she cautioned me. "Don't go sneakin' up on 'em quiet like. They liable to shoot ya."

"They liable not to see me," I mumbled. "Can't shoot a blue streak."

I wanted to give it up and go back home, but Captain Bishop had sounded urgent, and way back in the rear of my brain, I seemed to remember boasting to the fellows that I was gonna solve the Snow Girl case. The reality of helping do that was handling danger in squalid working conditions.

I pedaled slowly down the path and called out ever so often for Boother until I was up under the thickness of the woods where the limbs blocked out the failing part of day and the bike had done all it could do. Trail ruts, tree stumps, and hanging vines were an overmatch for the Western Flyer.

I called my pseudo-friend a few more times and propped my foot up against a fallen tree trunk and was sitting quietly there when I heard the movement behind me. My heart froze up on me and my brain died. I was locked in a vacuum somewhere in the darkest Alabama hills. Was that old taciturn Boother behind me with his rifle, or was a haunt from over near the burial ground sneaking up on me with just enough sound to cause my blood to lock up on me?

I heard the rifle bolt and the sound of the metal casing going into a chamber. Somebody was fixing to shoot my butt. I raised my arms slowly and tried to sound jovial.

"Ease up, Lone Ranger," I said in a quivering voice. "A good guy here."

The bolt locked down and I felt a barrel training itself on my back. Crap, I thought. I've got to move. Slowly I eased my upper body around until I was picking up the person in the shadows.

Darkness seemed to have run in deep under the trees and got itself a place for nightfall. I could see no sunshine in the trail behind the figure. He was tall and lanky, his clothes worn and dirty, his right eye making its sight down the rifle barrel straight toward my head.

"I'm looking for Boother," I said in a faltering voice, my mouth dry. "You ain't his brother, are you?"

He started toward me with the rifle carefully sighted and his step was cautious and skillful—a seasoned woodsman. He was a teenager, too, but older than Boother and bigger in size. He had that idiot look about him like in-breeding was the accepted thing in his family.

When I thought he was gonna put the gun barrel right up in my face and pull the trigger, I heard another sound and a hand crossed before my eyes and pulled the gun off to the side.

"Stop it, Brother," Boother said, the most words he'd ever uttered in my presence—and also the sweetest. "This here boy goes to school with me."

"I was just funnin', Boother. I weren't gonna shoot 'im."

"Well, *he* didn't know 'at. Ain't no sense scarin' him like 'at."

I was mighty relieved that Boother could talk. Defending me even in front of the rifleman.

Boother looked at me in a questioning way. He was smarter looking than his brother, but neither one'd win the smart citizenship award. I was sure he thought I was crazy for coming out looking for him.

"Why you out calling me up?" he asked, holding his brother's barrel toward the ground.

"I was just ridin' by. 'Thought I'd drop in."

"Nobody don't come 'round here."

"Yeah, well, I was free this afternoon. Thought I'd get in some visiting, and you were on the top of my list."

He backed off a step and spit tobacco juice onto the stump near me. "You lyin'," he said as if it was a fact everybody present knew.

"Well, yeah, I guess I was," I admitted. "Actually I was out here to see if you boys had found any more lady's purses out by the creek. There's a reward for what was in that last purse y'all found."

"What 'at?" Boother asked, frowning.

"Oh, that little leather number y'all pulled off a tree limb down Owl Creek," I said truthfully.

"How'd ya know 'bout 'at?" Boother asked again.

"Heck, boys, it's all over school how y'all found a purse full of money and jewelry and got to keep it all and sold the purse and made money off it, too. I'm surprised there ain't a line of cars pulled in at y'all's house, people trying to get a look at two rich fellows that found a pot of gold."

"Weren't no gold in it," Braska disputed my tale. "Lessen ya count the earrings."

"Shut up, Braska," Boother said. "He's tryin' to trick us into tellin' 'im how much stuff we got so he can go tell the sheriff and he'll come git it all back."

"That just flat ain't so, Boother," I said quickly. "I just figured you was lucky enough to find some good stuff and I just wanted to look at it so I could tell everybody at school tomorrow that I seen the loot."

"What's it ta 'em?" Braska asked. "You full of somethin' smells bad."

"God's truth," I said. "I figured you boys hadn't heard about the reward."

"What's 'at?" Boother asked.

"They're payin' five hundred dollars for anything found that came outta that purse."

"You're lying," Boother said. "What's it to anybody? Just a little ole pocketbook."

"If you'd noticed, that ain't your everyday ordinary pocketbook. Made of Italian leather and imported over here. Sold through a big store on Fifth Avenue in New York City. Just a few bought. That particular one belonged to a rich girl that lost it and she wants it back."

"Why'd she loose it so easy then?" Boother asked. "Looked like somebody throwed it in the creek and it got caught on the tree limb. I had to wade water to git to it."

"Well, this girl's from a powerful rich family and she wants it back because it's got pictures and private stuff and she's paying five hundred big ones to get it back."

"What if we ain't got it no more?" Braska asked.

"Then you just missed five hundred dollars," I said, shaking my head.

"Bull crap!" Braska yelled in anguish.

"Naw," I said with a straight face. "They won't pay for that. Just the purse."

"But we ain't got it no more," Braska lamented.

"Too bad," I said. "Money just took off up a wild hog's butt."

"Hold up," Boother said. " 'S'pose we still have 'at stuff was in it."

"I ain't sure," I said. "I don't know if I can trust you boys. Y'all could drag anything outta the house and tell me it was the contents and how'd I know? Naw, we need the purse itself."

" 'S'pose we done used up some a th' stuff," Braska asked.

"Like what? You ain't puttin' on lipstick, are you? Be mighty funny. Like puttin' underwear on that pig y'all got in the backyard."

"We ain't funnin'," Boother said. "We still got lots of stuff."

"I can't evaluate what I ain't seen," I put back to them. "Y'all could bring out your momma's makeup and say it was the rich girl's and how'd I know the difference?"

"This here's real all right," Braska said. "We still got some money and other stuff."

"I don't know," I said. "Money's money. How you tell one person's from another?"

"This'n here's hern," Braska swore with his hand lifted up like the other one was laying on a Bible.

"Now, maybe," I said. "If I could see some pictures. That could prove it was hers because pictures don't lie."

"That's true e'nuff," Braska said. "Where them pitchers, Boother?"

"I told ya I burned 'em."

"Ya lyin' lizard. I seen ya put 'em under yore sheets like ya was gonna take 'em out nights and look that pretty face and get fired up."

"Shut up, Braska. You the one wanted ta sell them boots and the purse. Six dollars for all of it. Big dealer you are. You the one give 'way five hunderd dollars. You flat stupid."

"Well, this here boy can git it back fer us."

"This here boy can't do squat fer us. He'll take our stuff and keep the money for himself."

"Well, just a minute, boys," I said. "If I was out to cheat you, would I go to all the trouble to come out here in snake country about dark, look y'all up knowin' ya totin' guns, and not be ready to make you a deal?"

They both stared at me, unclear about what I was saying.

"Maybe I can work around this missing purse thing," I said, rubbing my chin like I was thinking.

They were quiet, watching me think.

"Tell you what," I said. "I think I got it evened out for all of us."

"How's 'at?" Braska asked.

"Let me think now. It's comin' to me. I gotta find a way to protect you boys and myself, too, so y'all won't think I'm running off with the reward."

"How ya aim ta do 'at?" Boother asked.

"Well," I said. "Let's see what I got on my side. I'm the one heard about the reward. Without me coming out here, y'all would just be out hunting turkeys for supper and not know a small fortune was just waiting to make you rich. We together so far? Good. Now, if I was to go back and tell them I ain't got the purse, but, I got the things that was found inside it, and you boys keep any money you already found. That's it. Y'all keep that ten dollars or so..."

They looked at each other and grinned.

"I won't mention no money. I'll just say, 'Here's the contents' and I want five hundred dollars. Then I bring y'all back four hundred dollars to split and I keep just a hundred dollars for myself."

"How we gonna know ya'll bring that four hundred back?" Boother asked.

"How I know y'all don't give me the wrong stuff to turn in?"

"It's there all right," Boother guaranteed. " 'Cept 'at money you said we'd keep."

"Praise the Lord," I said. "Y'all keep that whole ten dollars."

They grinned again.

"An' I'll just have to trust that you're givin' me the right stuff."

They looked at each other, still not sure.

"Look at it this way," I said. "Suppose I hadn't never come along here today. Y'all would spend that ten dollars next trip to the store. Right now we're standing nearer a gold mine than the gold rush boys. I take stuff y'all ain't got no use for and bring back four hundred American dollars. That'd buy you both new guns and enough beer and whiskey to keep you cocked and ready for action for several months. Whatcha say? You ain't got nothin' to lose. If I don't show back up here this time tomorrow afternoon, you both know where to find me. Just bring your big guns to school and shoot my butt if I'm fooling with you."

"You know we'd do it, too," Braska said.

"I know you would," I agreed. "I'd sooner kick a bear in the nuts than cross you boys."

They bought it.

We went back out the pig trail like greased lightning and the two of them disappeared into the darkness of the shack. After a few minutes of voices cussing at each other, they returned with a nasty bag of stuff and handed it to me.

I took it and made my last play. "You see now," I said. "I'm trusting you boys. I ain't even looking in the bag. I'm just gonna take it to the sheriff like you handed it to me. You see how much I trust you. Y'all both can trust me, too."

I started to pedal off.

"Hold up," Boother said.

He reached into his back pocket and drew out what looked like a folded picture. "I forgot one," he said timidly.

I opened the bag and he dropped it in.

I got out of there like I was on the edge of hell and Satan's cavalry was gearing up to chase me down.

14

"Truth is often eclipsed but never extinguished."

—Livy

When it was pure darkness in the valley, the night was laid in deep.

Deep enough to hold its ground for a while, so I slipped out the front door and strolled up the rut of a road that led up to Highway 9. I wore a light jacket, but it needed backup support in order to assure my skinny bones weren't chilled. I walked hunched over and quick as I could. My one dominating thought was that the word had gone through the chain of command and somebody actually showed up at our turnoff to pick up the goods.

Feeling like Algier Hiss must have felt, I walked with the diligence of faith in what I was doing. If Captain Bishop was right, what I had tucked under my arm in the dirty, wrinkled paper sack was an answer to that overriding question of the moment: who had placed the Snow Girl in her wintry grave?

Of course my curiosity had summed up its best intentions, though I tried to push it off my mind. That sack was sitting there on the dresser, keeping up a steady conversation with me, whispering for me to unravel its folds and peep into its innards—to ascertain that the Ledbetter boys had not pulled a fast one on me.

I resisted per the Captain's instructions and didn't listen to the calling of curiosity, hoping that when this business was cleaned off the slate, maybe the big man could help me out of the fix with Moorefield. Sure sounded like he was willing to put that horse in the traces and see if it would run.

I wasn't past Jamback but a few minutes before a car cranked up a ways down the road and started up toward me. Boy, these guys were serious about wanting to get hold of this information, I thought.

It was a county car. Deputy Jack Short pulled up next to me on the gravel and reached over to unlock the door. I opened the door carefully and looked inside. "Hey, little Holmes," he said. "Captain Bishop said you'd have a package for me."

"I guess you folks are working together," I said as I laid the sack on the middle of the seat.

"Them the goods?"

"Yes, sir. I haven't looked inside to see what's there. I did what the captain said so the evidence wouldn't get fudged up."

"You done good," Deputy Short said. "How'd you weasel these things outta them boys? They swore to me they didn't have nothin' left."

"They weren't too smart, sir," I said. "I kinda promised them a reward by this time tomorrow. 'Didn't think ahead how I was gonna pay it when the time came. They may be looking for me with their high-woods guns come sundown tomorrow."

"Wait," Short replied, taking the sack in hand but not opening it. "I think there may actually be some reward out there for this case. I ain't sure. But you can tell them it takes time to run the paperwork and then the governor's gotta sign the papers, too."

"That's good for me to say, sir, but I kinda promised payment tomorrow.

I don't imagine patience is one of their virtues."

He thought a minute then took out a business-size card from his shirt pocket and wrote something on it. "Here," he said. "Show 'em this. This says I've acknowledged receiving the evidence and that a reward is pending. Explain to 'em what pending means. I've signed it and dated it to make it legal."

I took the card but couldn't read it under the car's dim dome light. "Yes, sir," I replied. "I reckon that'll buy me some time."

"If they give you a hard time, call me and I'll come out or send a car to warn them off. Maybe they'll understand that."

"Thank you, sir. Good night."

I started to close the door.

"Little Holmes," he said to stop me. "I'm not knowin' what's in here either but I wanta say you done a good job getting it for us. Much obliged."

"Where you been?" Rand asked as I sat down at the table.

"Out to watch the coming of night to my native land."

I wondered for a minute how I could distract him so I wouldn't have to reveal the truth. A few lines from the William Cullen Bryant poem "Thanatopsis" came to mind. I knew he hated poetry. "The golden sun, the planets, all the infinite host of heaven, are shining on the sad abodes of night."

Rand looked at me like he wished he'd not asked. I decided to play the line further, adding my own thoughts to Bryant's. "They wait at twilight for my eyes to see; they flaunt their beauty before the night's cool breeze."

He gave me a nasty look. "I heard Momma and Dad talking about you the other day," he said.

"How brilliant I am?"

"No. Dad said come spring they're gonna tie you to the barn door and let the rats eat you."

I ignored him as he went back to his algebra.

Algebra.

I could do that stuff if I wanted to. I didn't want to. Mrs. Jones was a cool enough teacher, but algebra meant taking time to concentrate. All I wanted to do was read books and discuss them with Evie. She was a smart girl. Even if she was older than me, she saw fit to include me in her tight group of two—the two of us. I felt a shot of pride. Spring would follow this terrible winter and I half-thought, when the junior-senior social came along, Evie might—just maybe—ask me to escort her to the dance.

I smiled in my smug daydream, thinking of how awkward that would look in reality—me escorting a dressed-up Evie through the door of the decorated gym. Me smiling like I was somebody as I reached to sample a pastry or one of those mangled sandwiches, so small it got lost on the tongue. Or the senior football players, with all the knock-out girls, pointing at me dancing with the freckle-faced Evie. Not envying me as we whirled around the gym floor, but eager to pull me aside and question why we were there—Evie being the embodiment of Christian purity and me, despite my notoriety, about as likely a candidate to be social as God was to be kind to Satan's wicked angels. Me—fighting the battle of social anxiety and pretending to know how to dance and how to dress and...

I stopped the daydreaming as abruptly as I got it underway. Boys at the hoedown had to have smart dress trousers, shiny shoes, a starched white shirt, and a light wool jacket over a dressy tie. One thousand percent, I had none of that stuff. 'Couldn't afford it, either. I might as well dream of bebopping with a movie star in Hollywood.

Evie would be gracious with me. We were good enough friends for that. But all dressed up and social? Well, I couldn't afford the tie, let alone the entire wrappings. Might as well cost a million dollars. Why was I even imagining such? Why waste time with something that wouldn't happen?

And what if Moorefield was there. Who'd be his date? One of the hot chicks that went around school like their air was rarified? 'Couldn't stand near them—socially unacceptable. But Moorefield could. He was as cool as a California subculture. Neat, fine woven things all over his athletic body. If I had a sports jacket, it'd look like it was still on the rack in the closet when it lay on my skinny shoulders. But not Golden Boy. That thick blonde hair, those perfect white teeth—the girls all looking for him like he was cubic money. Gliding over the gym floor, massaging the marble with those shiny shoes. And his date's feet gracefully in the air as they danced into the pages of the prodigious year book. Year book. There I was—humble-jawed acne, cow-licked hair, and a confused social demeanor.

"Who'd you go meet?" Rand asked, interrupting my dream and inquiring into my recent departure.

"There was a little man in a uniform that stopped by to see me," I said.

"Why?"

"He was just being friendly."

"Yeah. Sure. Why?"

"You wouldn't turn me in, would you? What have I done to you lately?"

"Everything you do at school embarrasses me. Heard about the trouble with Mrs. Finkle."

I shrugged it off. "Last week's garbage."

"She sent you and Sherman to the office."

I shrugged again. "She talked a good game," I replied, "but I got out of it. My innate charm."

"Inane charm, you mean."

"What's that word mean?"

"Look it up." He shrugged and looked back at the algebra. "I heard

Sherman T. got licks off Gorman," he said without looking up from his papers. "Why?"

"Inquisitive little spelunker, aren't you?" I said with a grin.

"What'd he do, butt breath?"

" 'Told Mrs. Finkle off in front of the class," I said truthfully.

"Was he defending you, you little waffer?"

"Naw, he just wanted out of class a while so he spit out his usual venom and got hauled into court. Gorman accommodated him with the air lift and Sherm moseyed on back to class—smile on his face—blush to his cheeks."

"You lie. How can I believe you?"

" 'You don't like answers, don't ask questions, Rand."

He looked up a minute and concern was in his eyes.

"Ryder got into some mess today. I haven't figured it all out yet, but she'll hear about it at supper." He paused and looked down at his work. "Stay tuned."

I was elated.

"Give me a hint, spacelander. I owe that girl over a hundred tattle-tells. Be good to see her smugness sweat."

"I ain't saying," he said. "Just wait and see. But don't bring it up. Momma's had a hard day."

"You think I just got back from the Caribbean?" I said, sarcastically.

"Just leave it alone. Leave it alone."

Sure I would.

There was a solemnity to the air that I detected immediately.

I ran my eyes around the table and tried to figure out the source in my immethodical way.

Billy Rand was out—he never felt the edge of the sword on the back of his neck. Mary Ellen was a perfect match to my friend Evie at school; her constant smile was worth some weight on the scales of justice. Little dark-skinned Peterson was as innocent as third grade could fathom.

And there sat Ryder—as quiet as a nun with a prurience encounter that must have scorched her vows.

Momma was busy pouring tea and checking the kitchen for the last of the pan-fried potatoes. I almost smiled as I took in Ryder's grief.

"Heard there was trouble in sixth grade today," I whispered.

Ryder's head came up and her thin lips set themselves for denial. "You can't wait to tell Momma, can you?" she said bitterly.

I grinned and shrugged. "All things are not clear to me," I said, pretending to be interested. "Maybe you could explain before Momma comes back."

"Hush your face," she said, her voice strained with emotion.

Billy Rand looked puzzled. He did not want a full scale encounter for anyone at the table. "Y'all be quiet. Momma doesn't feel good tonight."

I pointed my fork at Ryder. "Is there a mystery to unravel?"

Ryder glared and bit her tongue in anger. All that was left was for her to throw her food at me.

Momma came back into the room and sensed the level of intensity, but her grey eyes were tired. "I met a teacher from school today," she said calmly. One by one, we all stopped eating.

Ryder looked at Momma like her world was had just been covered by the blackest clouds in the sky.

"She was a sweet lady," Momma said as she served herself some of her freshly-fried potatoes. "She didn't say a stray word about the condition of this old house or the sofa with the stuffings sticking out. She just wanted to meet the mother of Ryder Holmes."

Ryder's face went from crimson to ashen. Her fingers trembled slightly as she placed her fork on her plate. For a millisecond I almost felt sorry for her.

"Tell us about the incident in the hallway, Ryder," Momma said.

Ryder stared at her plate. "Mrs. Anderson had to go across the hall to the office for a minute," Ryder mumbled. "She told everybody to be quiet while she was gone, but there was a lot of laughing, and talking, and pencils being thrown around. I sat in my desk and didn't say a word, but when she came back into the room, she raised her voice and told everybody to line up inside the coatroom, that she was going to paddle every single person in the class. And...ah.... Everybody except me lined up and took their paddling. When Mrs. Anderson and everyone else came out of the coatroom, she asked if she'd missed anyone. They all called out my name.

"Mrs. Anderson came to me and asked why I didn't line up like the others. I told her that I had done nothing wrong."

Those were the seminal words. We all looked away from our unrepentant sister, but Momma didn't say a word. She just kept looking, with no emotion on her face, at Ryder.

"The teacher said she was going to punish everybody, including me. I said I couldn't get a paddling at school. She looked at me for a minute then she told me to go with her out into the hall. She asked why I disobeyed her. I told her I didn't disobey, that I'd been quiet at my desk. 'How about the paddling?' she asked. I told her that my mother said I couldn't get a paddling at school or I'd get another at home. She drew back a minute then asked me to repeat myself. I did, then she stared at me for a long time.Then she smiled and said, 'I'd like to meet your mother.' " Ryder's voice trailed off. "That's all she said."

When she stopped talking we all started breathing again. All eyes went back to Momma. She smiled. "She was a sweet lady, Ryder," she said.

It was dark and we kids were sitting at the dining room table doing homework. I was trying to do algebra but I might as well have been trying to figure out how to fix China's economic problems. Both were beyond me.

The knock on the door caused us all to look up. Rand was the only one allowed to answer the door when Dad was off at work and Momma was busy. I followed along behind him to the door hoping the algebra book would self-destruct in my absence.

I looked out as Rand opened the door and there in the light of his own flashlight was the world's meanest man and the only state trooper who'd take time to look up a dip like me to help solve his murder cases.

"William," he addressed Rand in that deep voice that could make women faint and men run for cover. "I must talk to your mother," he said. "Sorry to be calling so late."

"Come in out of the wind," Rand offered as Momma came into the room from the girls' bedroom.

The big trooper apologized again, this time to Momma. She smiled like he was welcome to come in. I guess we'd all come a long way since that rainy night months back when he kinda coerced me into showing him the way to that death hollow up Nance Creek.

"I need to talk to these two boys, ma'am," he said, gesturing toward Rand and me. "I'm sorry if it upsets your little folks."

"They're fine," she said. "Ryder, girls, y'all go to your room. Just leave your work on the table."

They disappeared and we four sat down across from each other at the dining table.

"Guess we can start with Oliver, here," the captain said, smiling toward me. "First off, Ollie, I know you didn't have anything to do with Jeremiah Nobert's death. But I got a feeling it's time you told us who did. It seems somebody knocked him off that railroad trestle. Who was it?"

That was a quick blow and it hit me hard. My face went red and I tried to breathe in deep but my lungs quit on me.

"Tell us the whole story, Ollie," Momma said. "The captain's right. It's time to know it."

I looked at the ceiling for a few minutes then decided my world was too crowded with screwed-up people to keep on holding them hostage in my mind. I turned to the big man. Then I told them the story of that night

—from the time Harold forced me into the car until I found Jeremiah attached to that old oak tree.

They all listened with keen interest until I finished.

"I figured something along that line," the captain said. "That Moorefield boy has been in trouble with the courts before. This incident should give me plenty of latitude to get up several warrants on him."

Captain Bishop was enjoying his treasure trove of criminal information, and I was enjoying the relief that comes when a secret must no longer be held. I felt a release that would give my spirit a new awakening. Now that the tall trooper was taking over, I felt like I was safe to look beyond the shadows.

"Let's see. First off, our friend Harold forced you into the car."

I nodded affirmatively. "The other guy, Arlin, tried to stop him," I said, "but Harold was not to be denied. He was on a blood hunt."

"We'll blood hunt him. That misdeed alone will be enough to get him back in the penitentiary. That will eliminate his presence in the community.

"Now, this Moorefield kid. He forced you into his car after the first abduction."

"No, actually, Dirk had a knife—a switchblade—and he threatened me if I didn't get into the car."

"But Moorefield was driving. It was his car."

"No mistaking that," I said. "Spankin' new Chevy with the big motor."

"Just rehashing details here," Captain Bishop said, casting an eye toward Momma and Rand. They were listening intently, solemn and silent. And I was eager to clear myself now that the captain had opened the first lock of the dam.

"You were forced to witness Jeremiah at the train scene?" he questioned.

"Dirk forced Jeremiah down the bluff and up the train tower with that same switchblade," I said.

"Did it look similar to this one?" the captain asked, producing a knife from his pocket.

I didn't touch the switchblade, only looked at it in the palm of the captain's big hand, but I could not say positively if it was the same knife.

"It looked... similar to that one," I said slowly. "It was dark and all I saw and felt was the point of the blade. He held it closely to my ribs. But come to think of it, Dirk was so upset when Jeremiah fell that he ran back up to where Duncan Moorefield was and I thought he was going to stick him, but he changed his mind and threw the knife away into the pasture or field where we were. I'd forgotten about that."

"I examined that field and the bluff," the captain said. "On my second trip out there in the daylight, I found this knife about fifty feet from the hillside that Jeremiah went down."

"Dirk may answer some questions for you," I said. "He was very upset when Jeremiah disappeared. He must have blamed Moorefield for going too far."

"We'll make it a sure thing to talk to him. I have his parents' address. I suppose he's living with them?"

"I'm not sure," I said, "but as far as I know..."

"If Dirk refuses to talk about the incident," Captain Bishop said, "I may need you to testify about the whole deal. How is that with you and your family?" He looked from me to Momma.

Momma looked away to consider the situation while the captain waited patiently.

"I know you're proud folks, ma'am," he said, "and I appreciate the fact that all of this negative, devil's business puts you right in there with that element you want your kids to avoid. Believe me, people in this community know your family is God-fearing and law-abiding. This boy was simply riding his bike on a country road when this entire business started. He has nothing to be ashamed of. As a matter of fact, you should be proud of him."

Momma looked at me, studying my face for a long time. There were tears in her eyes. I didn't know if they were tears for all the confusion I'd endured and the evil I'd witnessed, or if the family creed had been violated so badly that irreparable damage had been done to her pride. She looked straight at me and nodded her head.

"About Harold, 'Hootie' again," the captain said when the tense moment of permission-giving passed. "Would this girl Margie be willing to talk straight on the incident? The first abduction?"

I thought a minute. "I think so. He was not treating her well. She may like the idea of Hootie leaving town again. She really did try to protect me. She was very adamant about helping me stay alive."

The captain nodded. "I'll speak to her from your perspective. She may help us tremendously on quite a few items." He smiled and turned the questioning to Momma. "The Klan been around lately?" he asked.

Momma shook her head. "Not since that night."

"Let's just say they won't be coming back over here," he said. "I imagine they've learned what valley not to operate in. And I'll say no more on that issue."

We all looked at each other and felt relieved again that peace was settling in on our community. I wouldn't question the captain but I knew who to chat with later about the Klan. That would be an easy determination.

Just as I felt a ton of weight lifted from my shoulders, and my life felt almost normal for a moment, the captain withdrew a large envelope from a folder and started a new phase of the domestic inquisition. "I hope this is the final item on our agenda, ma'am. Boys, I've got to ask y'all about these Snow Girl pictures. The sheriff and I have studied these items under a microscope and we can not discern the identity of the person standing with her. With your permission, Mrs. Holmes, I'd like to show all of you the photographs. Don't touch them, but please take your time and study them."

Momma seemed reluctant to start up another criminal investigation, but her civil mindedness must have overridden her reluctance. “This the last item, Captain?” she asked, her voice sounding weary.

“Yes, ma’am,” he said. “Absolutely the last.”

He placed the photos on the folder and stepped back so the three of us could see the black and white pictures.

I was anxious to see what the Snow Girl looked like but I hung back until Momma and Rand had examined them as closely as possible under the light of the low-hanging bulb. When they had gotten their fill of the two photographs, they pulled back without saying anything and let me have room—as if I would know any more than they would. They seemed to be unaffected by the pictures. At least their eyes did not reveal any revelation to me.

“Where did you get these photographs?” Momma asked. “Were they with the body? I thought I heard she’d lost her purse. Or it was never found.”

I paused and looked at the captain’s face.

“These photos come courtesy of a very smart young person that fanaggled them away from two poor souls of the backwoods.”

Momma thought about the answer and smiled. “ ’Guess that statement would cover a lot of folks,” she said.

I breathed an old fashioned sight of relief and stepped to the table.

She was a beautiful girl.

That full, brilliant smile said I come from a secure family and therefore I’m secure and my personality is one of openness, confidence, and optimism. Her eyes were dark, but if I’d ever seen them in this world, I’m sure they would’ve been as lively and active as her smile. The hair was light, easily tossed around her shoulders, and her clothes appeared precisely joined to the overall picture of perfection.

The man at her side must have been her father. He had that confident look, too. Plus he wore a sport jacket and open shirt that said he was on his way to the country club, but he’d been glad to stop and have his picture taken with his beautiful daughter. Perhaps it was a lazy summer day. They stood in front of a measured and groomed estate that spoke quietly of wealth and position.

I didn't see any expensive jewelry on the girl's wrists, but perhaps they were being given the afternoon off while she went for a ride in the British sports car that belonged to the fellow next to her. Except... something was amiss about the obvious young fellow. His face was prominently obscured. I didn't know if someone had taken a sharp metal point and deliberately defaced the image or if they simply folded the picture and tore his face away. The paper backing was folded a couple of times, and I thought back to Boother's reluctance to give the photo up at all. Had Boother fallen for the beautiful blonde in the picture, knowing full well that a person of her stature and beauty would never be on his arm? Or had the young lady herself gone into a rage against the young man and sought to alleviate his face from her memories of afternoons of soft drinks on the veranda and kisses under the magnolias? Naw. Boother probably did it. He had discovered the girl and he may have wanted her all to himself. She was beautiful and I was sorry I'd never know her. I was sorry she'd never live to see her own beautiful children run under the summer shadows or grasp the hand of the friendly grandfather. Whoever had placed her in the snow needed seeing about.

I wished that I could have helped the captain in his pursuit of justice but it was mainly just a shame that the beauty of the girl had been overcome by the beauty of the winter night—a beauty that had waited patiently for someone to wake her from her slumber by the quiet water.

"Examine the young man next to her," the captain's voice directed. "If he was her boyfriend, maybe he had something to do with placing her in the snow. Maybe he's the tie to her appearance here in a county where no one knows her. That's our only hope, anyway.

"The older gentleman is probably a father or uncle, obviously well-off. He could be anywhere. The estate could be anywhere. The background doesn't seem to help us at all."

"Such a shame," Momma said. "No one should have a child turn up this way. This girl was very beautiful. A full life ahead of her. I hope you can find the person that left her by the dam, Captain. He deserves the wrath of the Good Lord."

Captain Bishop tucked the photo back into the folder. "I agree, Mrs. Holmes. It takes a cold-hearted person to do this sort of thing. God is not letting him rest easy—now or forever."

15

"Whoever fights, whoever falls, Justice conquers evermore"

—Ralph Waldo Emerson

They came to get Moorefield and Dirk at school.

They probably acted as quickly as they could so Moorefield's dad couldn't pick up the whole family and run out of town—never to be seen again. At any rate, it was a glorious sight for me. I was sitting in algebra class when Evie tapped on Blue Nose's door and, with her winning smile, informed the scourge of the math department that Ollie Holmes was required in the office.

Of course I wasn't.

"What are you doing?" I asked, once I was clear of the bombing range. "Who wants me now?"

"Quiet, you handsome boy," she said, her sense of urgency so great that her two-toned Oxford shoes squealed on the slick tile floor. "We must hurry down this way. A sight awaits you that will restore your faith in Jesus."

"Who said I'd lost it?"

"No time for Sunday school. Come on. I was being my usual helpful self as an office aide when that giant captain and that pudgy sheriff came in to see Mr. Gorman."

Now she had my attention. While we walked quickly down the dark, deserted hallway, I listened closely to each word.

"They went into Mr. Gorman's office, so I hurried over to another little office where you can put your ear against the glass and hear what's being said. Glory-be! They were there to arrest Duncan and Dirk!"

"What?"

"Sure 'nuff! The sheriff had papers in his hand and the captain stood beside him like a giant enforcer. Mr. Gorman sent Sara Kate's little sister Peggy May to get both boys out of shop class. Mr. Luthin wasn't sure where they were at first, but Peggy May said that some of the younger boys said they were out back smoking. So they finally got hold of both boys and brought them to the office.

"I was standing around innocently in the office when the boys walked in. You shoulda seen their faces. Dirk started crying when they told him why they wanted him. Duncan Moorefield just had a smirk on his face as if he wasn't worried. But they handcuffed both boys and started for the car.

"Hurry!"

Our timing was perfect. Just as we came out of the dark hall near the office, we almost ran into the arresting posse. We put on the brakes and went undetected as the two boys, heads bowed, were pushed toward the door. Dirk was crying like a child and blabbering something about his innocence. Moorefield had a defiant look like he had experienced incarceration before and it was no big deal.

As Evie and I stood back out of sight, Moorefield glanced at the shadows. As he turned his head, his dark eyes found me, freezing me to my spot. That one look said everything to me. He was not defeated. He would admit nothing. His father was a lawyer. They'd do that tricky lawyer stuff and get him back out. But for just a moment in the pale light of the grey winter day, Duncan Moorefield had lost.

I knew I had not won. The prize was not mine to win. But for just a momentary flash, I witnessed my nemesis in handcuffs and under someone else's control. That was enough.

Evie squeezed my hand in that dark hallway and moved excitedly against me. "My prayers worked, Ollie," she said.

I waited until the boys were closed up in the back seat of the sheriff's car before I squeezed her hand back and echoed her exact thought.

"Mine, too," I said.

I couldn't wait to see the next day's news.

When Mr. Moon came by to give me my route papers, I took out the top edition and sat down by the store to read it. Mr. Moon didn't object. I reckon he figured I deserved to know what happened after the law picked up Duncan and Dirk at school.

There it was on the front page—in big headlines.

Apparently, Captain Bishop had helped the sheriff get up enough evidence to tie all of the business together. He'd found the switchblade at the scene, had observed Moorefield's wrecked car, noting its damage exactly matched my description of our landing in the field after plowing through the barbwire fence. There were beer bottles at the scene and tire tracks matching the Impala's. And old Evil-Eye at the store had seen the beer bootlegging on her property, had seen me leave one car, and saw me being forced into another—corroborating my exact story.

Margie had been a tremendous help as well. Although she was not at the death scene, she told the captain that I had not gone voluntarily with Hootie. That he had threatened me, and my dog, with bodily harm. She was pleased to be contacted about Harold. He'd been abusive to her, and she felt no loyalty to him.

So Harold was arrested, taken off parole, and was being shipped back to Kilby State Prison.

I also read that an eye witness would appear in court to reconstruct that fateful night by the tracks. I shuddered in fear, but I knew what my future held and I knew what Jesus would've done. He would never bow out when courage was required. Besides, He said He'd be with me all the way.

I could be quiet from the fear of evil.

Good news travels in bunches.

A few days after the big arrest scene, I had finished my route and was turning my bike onto Jamback when I saw Mr. Monte's farm truck headed my way. I got off the road a piece and watched him plow through the lower ditch, enter our rutted road, and coast toward our house. Staying back a safe distance, I felt a little apprehensive. Mr. Monte didn't stop by to see us unless something big was going on.

When I got there a few minutes after Monte got out of his truck, Dad signaled me to go on into the house. He was standing on the porch waiting to greet Monte, and he didn't want me listening to their conversation. Naturally I went through the house and doubled back outside.

Mr. Monte never came inside when he visited, and we didn't own any porch chairs, so the two men were standing near the porch steps. He was talking. "I'm right glad your boy got cleared up on that Nobert thing," he was saying.

"Me, too," Dad said. "Ollie was bad shook up around here for a while."

The two stood silent for a few minutes, Monte chewing his tobacco and Dad just looking toward Jamback.

"We got a whole lot of freedoms in this country," Mr. Monte started up after a while.

"Yep," Dad agreed.

"We got a lot of freedom here in this valley."

Dad nodded his head and looked away from the late afternoon sun. If he saw my quick glance around the corner, he didn't say anything.

Mr. Monte took a little breath and spoke again, "Right now I'd say we got more right to feel safe in our homes."

Dad looked at Monte, unsure where he was headed.

"I read this book one time after Vester died in the war," Mr. Monte continued. "Seems to me that book was saying that sacrifice is a big part of the soul."

Mr. Monte's oldest son Vester had been killed while fighting with Patton's Third Army in France. One of those hell-raising German machine guns had taken him out. The Montes had never fully recovered from the loss.

Dad looked puzzled at the words. I was myself.

"Ahh, Isaac, you know how me and Martha 'bout got buried ourselves when that Uniform come by in the winter of '44 and told us 'bout Vester. It don't matter none if they said he was a hero or not. Just dyin' for your sins for a Christian nation is reason enough to show honor and courage. It worked hard on my Martha, though. She took to bed for months, neglectin' us other folks and cryin' most the time. 'Weren't no good to it. Vester weren't coming back on that town bus. He weren't gonna see no more plowing or watch a twilight bird on its way home. That good part of our days was over."

If I had been closer, I probably would've seen tears in Monte's eyes.

He waited a sufficient time before he spoke again. "After readin' that there book 'best I could and 'best I could understand it—I'd already been through the Bible kinda handily—well, I figure if Vester could see his way into heaven by dying over yonder, I reckoned the least I could do was give my time to seein' that thar freedom he fought and paid for weren't tainted by no sorry folks here in this valley.

"I couldn't go overseas and fight them Huns, but I could stakeout my territory right here in God's green valley, an' if anybody thought they could act like Cain and raise up against the good-hearted and defenseless, then I'd see to it that they didn't do their evil and go out brag about it, and come back to hurt the weak again.

"I believe God gives strength to those that rise up against evil. Ain't nothing to a man that can't defend his folks—even if it means giving up one part of life for another. Life just runs on out there. 'Pull the curtain back and see the other part just waiting.' That's what I told Martha. She talked how she hated that boy that pulled the trigger on her son—hated the person that made that bullet that killed Vester—hated the government that took his life—and hated the government that caused him to be put in front of that bullet. That's how bad it was for Martha. Took a long while but love overtook the hate. That's my feeling of it. Love. Peace. Don't go messing with things that upset that. That's when you sacrifice."

His voice had moved from emotional to strong as he spoke. He looked solemnly at the ground—but he was serious.

"I don't follow you, Monte," Dad finally said. "I know about Vester and I don't want to lose none of my boys to the ungodly, but what is it you're trying to say?"

Monte kept his head bowed and did not reply for a long while. "Used to be a family in the church. They'd hold up their tithe every Sunday and show it off before they put it in the plate. 'Wanted folks to know they done their part returning right to the Lord."

Dad nodded slightly.

"Well, I never took it as right to be boastful before God. I jest done what the Book said and went on."

Dad still was not clear. But after awhile, he must have found the thread Monte was revealing to him. He spoke back more strongly than I anticipated. "Somewhere in there," Dad mentioned, "the Lord says 'Vengeance is mine.' It ain't necessary to hunt down every dog that barks. If we did, that's all we'd do. Life's too short."

Monte looked up and saw the two paths that were laid out. He smiled and spit tobacco near the truck. "You work your side of the road, Isaac, and I'll work mine. I ain't sayin' either side is the only way to follow. I'm just sayin' that when the women and children get hurt by the cowardly wicked, there's a plan to handle the work."

Dad nodded but seemed uncomfortable. "I believe God will take care of my family," he said.

This time Monte agreed, but he looked straight at Dad's eyes and said his last words. "My Vester didn't die so some lowlife could come harm my family or my neighbors. He died so we all could have peace in our souls. That's the way I understood the whole thang. Anyhow, I got cows to see 'bout. Sun leaves early on these winter days. But ain't life peaceful here in these blue hills? I told Martha today, I wish Vester coulda lived to take over the farm. When it's quiet in the mornin' and the sun's comin' outta the mist, I git a little piece of heaven ever now and then. And that's enough for me. Tell Miss Tallulah we said hello."

Mr. Monte made it back to his truck and left.

Dad went into the house, his head bowed in thought. I wanted to go after him and ask him about the conversation, but he was my father and I'd never question his words.

As I walked back down the unpainted side of the house, however, past the dormant fig trees and the early evening shadows that followed me, I thought I understood what Mr. Monte was saying.

Fly would never come into our valley again.

16
Silver Run

I didn't know it would be my last race at Silver Run.

Weldon talked us up about a night out of the valley, and the first thing we did was skip the Bentonville hangouts and head for the Run.

Big news. Eness Voit was set to run the Blue Mountain Boys in their big "hemi." I didn't even know what a hemi was until I looked it up in the school library. But I was in the back seat by myself, the night wind was blowing cold on my face, and the loud echoes of the night monsters were waiting somewhere up ahead. I was nearly ready for Saturday night.

I say nearly because just under my feelings of anticipation for Eness' showing out at the drag race, I had an uneasiness in my stomach. Evie. Would Evie be there with Preston?

"I traveled the country roads with Preston," she'd said. "Well maybe he did kiss me..."

I was fifteen going on the age of freedom. Could I ever be the one to drive Evie around in the pure shadows of night, see those freckles under the neon lights while cruising the hangouts? Experience that sweet smell of femininity that made the senses buzz?

No. Of course not. Evie was older than I was. She'd be gone off to college somewhere while I was still a footnote in the country schoolhouse of nonachievers. Immaturity and dreams against the reality of a flowering woman. Why even think about that? But Preston? He was such a sweet, sweet boy.

"How's your woman, Ollie?" Weldon suddenly asked from the front seat, his sly grin enhanced in the yellow lights of the dash.

He was trying to get my goat. I knew it. Rand knew it. And after I refused a reply, Rand defended my dreams. "Leave him alone, Weldon."

Weldon laughed. "You seen them kids sporting around school like a couple? Your little brother's the cat's meow out there strolling and talking to a senior. Wonder them other seniors ain't looking to tweak his frame."

"Him and Evie write poetry."

"Ohhh, ain't that nice. And here I thought Preston was the fair boy of the school."

"Evie's just a nice girl," Rand said. "She ain't like that Margie that dates ex-cons and pulls her dress up for every hube that wants a look."

Weldon flared up at his reference. "I ain't dating no ex-con's girl," he fired back.

"You would if you had the moxie to ask her."

"That was way back a while. I ain't interested in her."

"You were until you found out Hootie was her nighttime friend."

"I ain't scared of no Hootie neither."

Rand laughed. "Yeah. He ain't much of a threat to you in Kilby, is he?"

"Say, little boy," Weldon chided. "How was it riding 'round with them criminal types? They have more fun than us pretty boys from the valley?"

I still refused to answer.

"He won't talk about it," Rand said.

"Just gimme a short picture of what it's like to have big Marge licking your ear while gooney Hootie's pointing a pistol in your face."

"Hootie didn't point no pistol," Rand said, defiantly. "Why you all excited about what Ollie's been through? You ain't got the nerve to join the jailbird society? Why don't you dial up ol' Margie and see that lifestyle first hand?"

"I've moved on from Margie. I'm fired up 'bout them Blue Branch girls. Lexie or Lydia. Ain't no difference to me. All the cookies in the cookie jar taste the same."

Rand didn't say anything. I knew he was sweet on Lex. "You really think they been switchin' out on us, Weldon?"

"Who cares. Either one of 'em knock the eyes out of a Holy Roller preacher."

"Yeah, but that don't seem right. I mean, how can they take it so lightly? Reckon they do that with other boys?"

"Other boys? We only ones crazy enough to go that far out in the woods for some late night sugar."

"Ain't like we're Cary Grant or such. They could get real boys if they wanted."

"Why you worried thata way? We see 'em on church nights, other nights we troll the hangouts or go to the races. Might go off down to Georgia next weekend to see Blue run."

"You don't know where Dallas Drag Strip is."

"I can ask, can't I? Besides, who cares? Might meet some a them hot drag strip girls. I hear ones hang out at the strip don't think nothing 'bout riding in a hot car or sparkin' in a big back seat."

"We got one problem, sport," Rand said. "This ride ain't exactly hot."

"Well, you can just smooth around with that sad look of yourn and them navel-showers'll be on you like cedar smells on Christmas."

"You want me to hook 'em and you reel 'em in?"

"Worked so far, ain't it?"

Rand was still thinking about the twins. "We gotta earmark them Blue Branch girls. Surely one of 'em's got a birthmark or a scratch here or there that's different. Maybe a mole on the shoulder or something."

Weldon coughed fake-like. "I ain't never seen nothin' but what's uncovered at church. I don't know about the back seat but neither one of 'em in the front seat'd make a good drag strip girl."

Rand laughed.

"You must've seen glory!" Weldon protested. "You didn't tell me."

"I ain't seen nothing," Rand replied.

"Come on now. Kiss the sister, kiss the twin, what kinda love am I really in?"

"What kinda mess is that, Weldon? You been right there with me. All I did was kiss on the girl."

"I'm curious now. Let's go pick them twins up and set junior lover out here on the road. We can come back for him later. Less'n he hooks up with Marilyn Monroe or such while we're gone. Can't trust that boy. He gets around more than the tracks on a roller coaster."

"We're goin' to the drags." Rand corrected course. "We'll worry about those Branch girls tomorrow night. Tonight I want to see Eness get aholt of those Blue Mountain boys."

Weldon was ready to agree to that proclamation. Seeing the Branch girls was never a nailed-down thing. In spite of the argument over their log cabin in the woods, those girls were so popular at school that the front seat honey bees had to stand in line. Getting lip time was fully optional—in spite of their purported fantasies.

"What do you hear about those Blue Mountain boys?" Rand asked—back to the immediate concern.

Weldon twisted his face up and didn't say much at first. "They're all right fellas. Don't mess with 'em, though. Couple of 'em like to fight. I don't know which ones will show up tonight, but word is the big one'll bloody your nose in a heartbeat."

"What's all the rap over the hemi?"

Weldon gave a low whistle. "I don't know how they done it, but them boys put a hemi in a '55 Chevy."

"Never heard of that."

"They ain't neither but they done it."

"How?"

"Ask the good Lord. It's a secret between Him and them."

They were quiet for a minute and I went back to thinking of Evie. What should I say or do if she was there with Preston.

"Say, Goober," Weldon called on me again. "What's your girlfriend's real name? What's that 'Evie' stand for?"

I didn't say anything. My face felt kinda red because he was talking about her. I was glad it was dark.

"Genevieve," Rand said for me. "Her name's Genevieve."

"What in King Hill kinda name is that?"

"They moved in here last year from outta state," Rand offered. "They're a real fine family. Her daddy's preacher at White Oaks Baptist plus he works at the foundry in Bentonville."

"What's he do at the foundry?" Weldon asked.

"How should I know?" Rand snapped back. "I told you all I know about the family. You already know Raike."

"Don't get hos-tile, okay?" Weldon protested. "I just thought the girl was cute and sweet. She'd be perfect for Ollie if she wasn't so much older. Then, too, there's her boyfriend."

"Shut up, Weldon," I finally responded.

I was tired of his picking.

He laughed for a half mile because he'd finally got a rise out of me. "You all right, junior lover boy," he snickered. "I admire a man that can handle older women."

"Reference my last statement, sideburns."

"See there, Rand," Weldon laughed. "I can't understand half he says. Other half don't matter."

It was so cold you could see your breath.

Rabbit Champion was busy telling everybody that he and his boys had measured off exactly a quarter-mile distance for this big race, put shoe polish on the starting line, and put a red railroad flare at the end—right at the bridge.

I wasn't paying much attention; I was busy searching the crowd for Evie. I got off by the lonely gas pump at the country store and tried to be inconspicuous. I climbed up on the cement island and nonchalantly examined the crowd. Not much extra curricular action going on. One of those drag-strip girls Weldon was talking about must have been busy in the back seat of a Mercury. Maybe back near the rear of the station at the edge of the woods. But nobody was paying the situation much attention. People seemed to be more aware of the Blue Mountain special and the boy driving it. He was way over six feet tall. I don't see how he drove the old car, but somebody said they welded him a special seat and he could work the pedals from way back. They called him "Tree."

I was only partially interested. My other eye was busy scanning the crowd of greasers and dragstrip girls. It was an unusually large crowd. The hangouts up town must've been empty because there was a covering of special cars by greasers wanting to check out the hemi setup. On most nights I'd been right there with them, but I guess you could say I'd discovered the first bite of young love, and I was eager to get a glimpse of the cause of it.

And I was full of uncertainly.

What was I to do if I saw her? She was a senior and I was still months shy of a drivers license. I couldn't even drive by her place and pick her up for a date—if she would even be seen outside of school with me. And, what car would I drive? Uncle Doug Thomas drove that sporty new Chevy, but it was Miss Jewel's car.

The crowd was still gathering. More cars came down from other counties and they were beginning to get a little edgy about the parking. Like that old Russian joke I'd heard one time. "The reason the Russians hated us was because we had all the cars and they had all the parking places."

Two or three shouting matches and one short fistfight broke out near the country store, but I'd seen blood on white skin before so I avoided the fisticuffs and got off from Rand and Weldon and scouted, fender to fender, for Preston's mother's Mercury.

My heart jumped for a second.

There was that very Mercury behind the store, its front fender protruding from the darkness into the yellow of the lot's overhead light. Evie, in a car with Preston, parked behind the store? Couldn't be! I had to investigate. Feeling like a fool in search of another one, I glanced in all directions, saw no familiar faces, no ties to home territory, and started my meandering gait toward the identified car. I thought of the boys with the Blue Branch girls. "Love on the seat covers," Weldon called it.

Not my Evie. I wanted her all to myself.

"Platonic relationship" aside. I was learning fast that there was no such thing as a platonic gig with a cool chick. If she ever touched your hair, or studied your face, looked for you in the middle of a crowded hallway, or wrote a poem that might suggest something of the young heart, well, maybe, just maybe, she had enough interest to not be hanging out at Silver Run as a drag-race girl. Surely not.

I got bumped several times by bigger, older kids hustling off toward the starting line. I didn't say anything. 'Just kept my eyes on that Mercury with its nose out of the shadows. A couple of cigarettes were flicked toward me and one gruff voice called me a name that more nearly described a yard dog, but I wasn't deterred. I was on a search-and-learn mission.

I stopped a minute and watched absently as two kids, my elders, swapped spit right in front of me. I was thinking of what I might do if I saw Evie in that old Mercury but the participating boy stopped his tongue wrestling and stepped toward me. "What you lookin' at, goober face?" he asked tersely.

I shrugged my shoulders and continued on toward the back of the store while he bent the girl over the hood of a car and trapped her between a metal part and a hard place.

"Oliver!" The voice stopped me just before I reached the corner of the store.

I stopped dead in my tracks and glanced around. "Aren't you Oliver? That shy boy from my English class?"

I had to respond. I looked until I saw a tall, attractive girl pointing toward me. She sat on the front row of Mrs. Murray's class and was a top student in homework, neat dresses, beautiful hair, cool eyes. If I hadn't been busy worshiping Evie, I might've wasted my nights dreaming of her. She was racing fuel for a love-starved heart. Her name was Gladys Sue.

I was totally shocked that she knew my name.

I managed a weak smile and looked at her with my eyes slightly shifty. I didn't know if I was supposed to speak back or just nod my head.

"What's a smart boy like you doing out here at the drag strip?" she asked.

"Well..."

"I'll bet you're here with your brother, aren't you? Billy Rand. That's your brother. He's cute."

"Well..."

"I like it when you read your essays in class," she said, smiling. So I studied her eyes some more, trying to figure out how to respond.

"Mrs. Finkle did you wrong in class the other day. Why was she accusing you of copying somebody else's work?"

"Well..."

"Where are you going? The race is over yonder."

"Well I..."

"You boys. Y'all got it lucky. You can go to the bathroom anywhere. Horace is out there in the bushes now. I'm waiting on him."

I smiled a parting smile, half-lifted a hand in a farewell gesture and was resuming my efforts to expose Evie and Preston when Gladys Sue spoke words I wish I could've recorded for future reference. "Meet me at my locker, Oliver," she said. "Monday morning. Before English. I want to show you something."

I should of had a heart attack on the spot. I should of just dropped over dead and been raked off in the bushes and forgotten. That's how she locked down my systems.

Before I could react, however, a heavy hand found my shoulder and a voice that'd make the devil pee in fright addressed me. "Why you talkin' to my girl, Jamback?"

It was Horace, fresh back from his relief in the undergrowth.

"We...we... got... E... English together..." I stuttered.

He laughed and used that singular grasp to rotate me back on the path I was walking before his girl stopped me.

"If I see you near Gladys at school," he warned, "I'll stomp a wet spot in your butt. You got me, creep?"

He let go and I dived between several cars beside the country store and crept up on the corner site like a crime-book sleuth.

The interior of the Mercury was totally dark. The rear of the business was unlit. There was no way to see much of anything. That's why the sport models came early, parked out back, and brought in the willing souls to make memories with. Memories that'd warm a cold winter night in the long future of adulthood.

I didn't want to stand out in silhouette by leering around the corner but I had no choice. Maybe they were down in the back seat, exploring the miracles of the night. Would I be any different from Weldon flashing his giant spotlight if I went browsing into their loving space?

What should I do?

Evie. Why'd you put me in this place? Was she cheating on me? Poor, defenseless Jamback boy—Oliver W. Holmes?

If she wasn't really my girl, was it really cheating? Was my claim sovereign? Can you be sovereign in a relationship?

I got some help when a light came on briefly in the car. I stopped dead again. It was a boy—and he was lighting a cigarette. Preston didn't smoke. Neither did Evie.

I couldn't make out the boy's features. I saw just a red dot as the cigarette gained oxygen to burn. I was caught in a snake pit. Scared to move and scared not to.

"And what are you doing over here, handsome boy?"

The voice came softly and sweetly to my ear and I almost wet my blue jeans because of the suddenness of it. I turned back around. Even in the shadows of the passive setting of the country store's shadows and dips of total darkness, I could tell who was addressing me. Evie, I knew, was smiling at me.

"Getting some relief," I said, swallowing a lump in my throat.

"Pardon me," she said quickly, turning around to leave.

"No, no," I said, moving toward her. "Not that kind of relief. I... I... was overcome by the mass of the crowd. I simply wanted to..."

She stopped, and I rounded the building I almost ran into Preston. He was standing near Evie like a misplaced fireplug. I thought of saying the "s" word, then corrected my course and headed back toward the starting line.

"Aren't you speaking, Oliver?" Evie called, firmly, almost angrily. "Come back here and talk to Preston and me!"

I looked around for Weldon. I didn't mind taking orders if the boys weren't around to hear them issued.

I wasn't sure what to say, but I would address Preston without shaking his hand or asking if he planned on kissing Evie, tonight, or if they were a steady item now. But I could be decent and speak. "Hey, Preston," I said.

"Hey, Oliver," he replied in his high voice.

What was that squeaky mouse doing at a drag race? Dating your girl, you idiot, I told myself.

If I hit him square in the mouth, he wouldn't get any sugar tonight. But then I wouldn't either. I'd simply be behaving like those other greasers. Blood on white skin.

"Who you riding with tonight, Oliver?" Evie asked.

"Weldon and Billy Rand."

"Oh, where are they? I didn't see them."

"They're over there checking out that 'hemi'."

"What exactly is a 'hemi'?" she asked.

I thought how to answer. "Hemispherical heads on a Chrysler motor. That just means the engine can get more air and gas mixture and it can make more horsepower. It should outrun everyone else."

"Why do they race then—if the hemi wins?"

"Well, there are lots of variables."

She shook her head. "Don't confuse me any more. Preston wanted to see the race so we left the valley and came here. Aren't you surprised to see us?"

I wanted to say, "Bet your sweet buns I am," but that would be a crude Shermanite response. I couldn't talk to Preston's date that way. Or my Evie. Why did I have to see them together? I was standing there all smooth and cool, but I actually wanted to get far, far away and hang with the boys or Eness Voit. Why talk to her? Didn't all my heart-wrenching discussions at school mean anything to her? How could she play nonchalant with Preston? How could the twins switch out with the boys? Were all women just heartless when a boy pitches his emotions into the ring? We had feelings, too.

Preston had not said anything else to me. I needed to address him, but what could I say? "Get off my dream?"

"Where are you parked, Preston?" I asked, politely.

He pointed toward a jumble of cars that must've included his momma's Mercury. I didn't see it.

"We got here late," he said, pleased that we were talking. Evie was right. He was a nice guy.

"You know Eness?" I asked. "Or the Blue Mountain boys?"

"Actually, I don't know any of the participants, but Mother informed me that the boy they address as "Tree" may be down the cousin line somewhere. Mother does not approve of late night, illicit drag racing, but I got special permission to leave the valley tonight so Genevieve and I drove over here to see the event. It should be a jovial time."

My Lord, I thought. Does he really talk like that? I'm a practicing poet and I usually talk like those other illiterates. Maybe Genevieve liked that kind of talking. Maybe I was just the biggest fool of assumption since that Johnson guy put it in the dictionary.

Preston reached over timidly to take Evie's hand, missed contact, and made another attempt and connected.

I said the 's' word, low and in disgust.

"What did you say, Ollie?" Evie asked.

"I said, 'shift' as in shifting gears. The racers must shift properly in order to win. One of those variables."

"Oh," she murmered and the two of them started toward the starting line holding hands.

I was more pissed than a Japanese Sumo wrestler, but I couldn't show it. I had to go see the cars, pretend to be interested in them, forget the "Wuthering Heights" couple, and get on about my business.

So if Eness Voit made the grand gesture again. If he invited me to climb into that race car and roar off down the makeshift strip at a hundred miles an hour with him, I would certainly do it. And I'd smell the roses over the gasoline fumes. Yeah, I'd do that. I'd ride in that homemade race car, and we'd outrun the hemi, and our names would be right there, again, with the Silver Run notoriety of outlaw racers. We would be valley stars in our own sphere and then, hopefully then, Evie would give me a nice smile and maybe a hand to hold. Maybe even a peck on the cheek.

Naw, man, I wanted full service on those full, sensuous lips. I wanted a hug in a dark area where my red face couldn't be seen or laughed at. I wanted to hold hands and sit in the dark with my girl. And if she kissed me, I'd never tell anybody, even if they tortured me and beat me with a stick and told lies on me.

After a while, Eness showed up in his car and the hemi worshipers changed gods and went off to swarm all over his new car. I figured I owed him a look since he had taken me with him on that ride on the golden rail of fame last time out. So I tried to get close to the black beast disguised as a '55 Chevy.

It took a while to get there, but I was glad I made the effort. It looked like a flat-out race car. The interior was gutted and the side windows were gone. Eness must've had to pick his side roads carefully on his way to Silver Run because that loud monster would've waked every sleepy cop in Bentonville and Oxanna.

Talk about loud. It wasn't two minutes into the examination of Voit's-machine when another snorting animal came down the north mountain and found its way through the cold winter night. I forgot about Eness and the hemi—and even Evie. If my stomach had gone queasy before over the thoughts of Saturday night hand-holding, it went to lower track distress when Moorefield parted the masses and stopped dead right on the ziggly starting line of Rabbit's shoe polish.

He didn't have to get out of the car. The masses came to him. He just sat there, solitary and defiant, while the drag-strip girls swooned and the greasers cussed. He was as welcome at Silver Run as a hooker at a Southern Baptist Convention.

Rabbit was the race organizer so he took his wormy self up close to the defiant one and offered advice. "This here's a one-race-only night, Moorefield," he said in his high, pitchy voice. He waved his bet-gathering clip board for effect.

"So," Moorefield finally responded as the crowd hushed and listened for his words. "I only need one race to beat you cotton pickers. Run the best you got up here to the line."

A burly man with a beard and the demeanor of a wild bear in the woods stepped out of the greasers and confronted Moorefield. "My name's Mannike. We ain't racing no convicts tonight," he said, loud and accusing. "Best you get your sorry butt back up the hill before I drag you outta that car and save the judge having to sentence you."

In the fanfare of the night, I'd not given a thought to Moorefield. I knew his dad had gotten him out of jail the same day as the arrest, but he hadn't been back to school. I heard they were moving out of the state. Of course, I had lived life happier with him out of our daily routine. And now this. The biggest night of Silver Run's esteemed history and up shows the Golden Boy to turn everything into chaos.

The big bearded guy wasn't yielding an inch, even though Tree was out in the far-side crowd, trying to hold him back. "You got nerve being seen, Moorefield," the big man was saying so loud that his voice boomed over the murmuring of the restless crowd. "Jeremiah was close to a lot of us here. We can even the score for him right now. Why don't you get outta your daddy's car, kid killer? I'll stomp your butt in the dirt!"

I tried to ease back out of the circle that had surrounded the red car. I didn't want to see any more violence. I had seen death up close and solemn and I didn't like the view.

If Moorefield got out of the car, I was sure the big man would've killed him on the spot with his bare hands. And then Eness spoke to the multitudes. "If Moorefield wants to race," he said waving his hand in the air and asserting his stance. "We'll race him."

"What right's he got to race?" Rabbit protested. "I ain't holding his money."

Eness pointed at the big man from Blue Mountain. "One of us needs to run this momma's boy and put him in his place before he goes off to prison. We'll beat his car and take his momma's money. Besides, Mannike, if you kill this boy tonight, you'll go off to prison yourself. Let's just race him and shut him up."

Mannike stepped past Tree's grasp and pointed at Moorefield as he addressed Eness. "I thought you knowed better, Eness. You been around some."

Eness looked puzzled. "This here boy's dangerous. He ain't playin' by no rules. He ain't here to win no money or to outrun neither one of us."

The crowd waited to see why Moorefield was present. I was especially interested.

Mannike continued, "He's here to cause trouble. He's here to hurt somebody. Don't you know anybody who'd knock a friend off a railroad tressel onto a freight train is a sick son of a... You race this boy and I guarantee something bad'll happen. Mark my words. Tell me how it works out, folks, because I'm loadin' up my car and goin' home. Y'all hang back and watch something bad happen if you want to."

The crowd was stunned.

Moorefield sat in his car and seemed to be half-grinning in the glow of his dash lights.

I knew Moorefield's evil first hand. The big bearded guy might have been a good old boy from Blue Mountain, but his observations were dead-on. I wished I was on my way out of there myself.

Rabbit was talking to Eness. "You run 'im, Eness. It's just you 'n him. I ain't takin' no bets. I ain't tellin' no tales. Big man spoke the truth. We all here'd like to see that rich boy get his dues. It's up to you."

Eness was quiet for a good while.

Somebody in the crowd started up a chant of "Race 'im! Race 'im!" and it caught hold and went around like a lynch mob getting energized.

Then Eness pointed at me and called for me to go with him, and despite my struggle to get back to Rand and Weldon's car, the greasers laid hands on me and forced me through the window of the race car. I *felt* the sounds in the tin acoustics of the car. Strong hands buckled me to my seat and a great cheer went up when the two cars roared to life and became vicious voices of the night. I closed my eyes and felt like Louis XVI riding the death cart. The sound was insane.

People fell back away as the black beast, under Eness' control, edged its way to the shoe polish on the blacktop. But they didn't go far. The crowd divided somehow and replenished itself on both sides of the narrow drag strip.

I didn't even look at Moorefield. I didn't want to see those eyes crossing past Eness and into my face. He commanded me without effort.

We needed a thousand feet of blacktop—straight line running—farm to market road. The usual dips and potholes. The trees, stark in winter, curiously hanging their heavy branches across the dark road, made a tunnel that could not hold the pervasive sounds. Ten or twelve seconds to the bridge. That's all my life required at this time. Mere seconds on the clock.

Then what?

My face went flush and my hands started to sweat. The force of the race car was overwhelming. I felt helpless. I could hardly breathe. The noise just got louder and louder.

A sudden surge of the car startled me. I felt the tremendous torque. The vibrations and sounds within the metal coffin rolled around until they were killing my ears. I wanted to put my hands over my ears as soon as I could resist the force that was pinning us to the seats. Would that chance come?

We hit another gear and the screaming filled my soul. The force was too great to fight. We were gathering speed like a mythical animal that defied the gods and rose to the heavens. I understood instantly about the flash of God's lightning—so quick and lethal that men cowered and sought shelter. Our metal enclosure was challenging the forces of nature. We were wrapped in a black tunnel that had no way out.

I could not feel Moorefield's presence beside us. Where was he? What had happened? Had he quit the race?

The pale yellow lights fought with the night in front of us. We were moving faster than the ability of the lights to show our way. All I saw was the speck of red straight ahead where the road allegedly met the bridge.

The shifting ceased. Now the engine was screaming in a flat tone like it needed more air but it wasn't available—as if it had spent itself in the dash of about ten seconds. Seconds that felt like endless time.

I felt, rather than saw, Moorefield's beast beside us. It was beginning to gain its breath. Its stronger motor was starting to cut into our lead. Within two or three seconds we would be crossing the bridge.

After those thoughts, I couldn't say exactly what happened. One instant we were dead on the victory point—the finish line. Next, we were moving laterally, the car swerving as it tried to go forward while something beside us seemed to be pushing it out of the desired path. I felt movement as if the tires were no longer locked to the earth. There was a feeling of moving without effort through a night that parted ways for us. We were helpless in the vapor of midnight, rising silently over the creek bank that reached to pull us from our flight.

Way off down the woods there was the mournful sound of a wolf calling. Calling like the world was lost and he was, too.

But then, just like your mind works when it comes back from a long, complete sleep, my mind began telling me that long, mournful sound was not the phantom of a wolf that Sherman and I had chased in our dreams. Rather, the sound was manmade and close by. I couldn't turn my head to ascertain the noise, but the moaning stopped, and in its place I could hear a crackling noise like I'd heard at Grandma Wilton's house when the fireplace was brimmed out with forest saplings and the flames were trying to catch hold to help drive off the winter cold. I decided to assess the damage that seemed to be all around us.

We had gained flight over the bridge, or somewhere near the bridge, because our black, screaming beast had somehow got itself airborne and I remembered floating through the night like a kite broke loose from its string, except we didn't tail-swagger backwards like a loose kite. We were more like a stray shot that loses its intended path and goes off straight arrow toward some unannounced target and ends up hitting whatever's in its way.

Crazy thoughts made themselves present in my mind. I wasn't sure if I was dreaming or what. The noise continued, joined by a great groaning of the beast like the metal was stretching itself out of a womb and growing forthright in its own ability—its own ability to make itself into something other than a rocket sled—a sled that fought with the night like the prowler that hunted through a great night and did what its instincts willed it to do. Except my instinct was to study this situation, but my vision was not clear. A light was growing near my left side and heat was beginning to work on my feet. There was something odd in it all. I couldn't shake my head to clear the vision or the thoughts because something strong was preventing me from moving and seeing.

I heard voices outside my metal cocoon, loud voices, cursing each other. One voice was high-pitched and excited while the other was steady and calm. They were close by, and soon after they were out past my ear. I couldn't hear anything except that struggling sound—bodies in conflict with each other and gasping for breath in their struggle to breathe. A determined shout from one combatant ended in a large air intake. Then I was aware of a slapping sound, like coughing and gasping, and heavy footsteps in the night, as if alone on the earth and not caring who heard them.

They were now way beyond my hearing. I picked back up on the light that was growing brighter off to my left. I could see just enough to make out a partial silhouette of a person next to me. I still couldn't move my head and my feet were getting warmer against the naked metal of the car's floorboard. I could move my hands a small degree but something had me pinned to my seat.

We had flown through the growth of the creek bank, but our flight failed when the nose came down and we hit something. We must have hit something because the headlights went out just before the senses in my head went out. I could slowly gather those senses again, as the night took tiny steps away from me.

The light was chasing the darkness. That's what it was. Wherever that light was coming from, it was about to bring full disclosure to me, trapped as a muffin in a baking pan feeling the heat working.

I thought I smelled something burning, too, like rubber or electrical parts, or something like that, because I realized for the first time that what was growing inside the crippled car was a fire. It was all over the person's side to my left—Eness! Eness was out cold. *He* had been making those animal-like sounds. And now it was the fire coming out of the engine area, licking past his door and reaching into the ruptured passenger seats—his and mine.

I had enough motivation in real time to start my struggle. Even though I couldn't move much, I could undo the super straps from navy surplus that had probably saved us in the initial crash. But now I couldn't force the riggings loose. The metal clips Eness had secured over my shoulders and lap were under such great stress that they failed to yield to my efforts.

I couldn't look down to ascertain their whereabouts because of the metal roof and the over-head rollbar. They were pressed together just enough to keep my head from moving laterally.

The flames were on my side as well, and the smoke was starting to fill the cockpit. I coughed and tried to find a fresh breath but the posture of the containing metal kept me upright and fastened to the bomber seat like wallpaper. I couldn't get free and Eness might not even be alive. Best I could determine, he was dead on the spot.

"Eness!" I shouted between coughs. "Eness! Wake up! We're bad off, man! That fire's coming up on us and I can't move! Eness! Don't you die, man! We need help!"

Eness never moved. He never heard me.

I felt cheated. All those years Momma had lectured us kids on staying away from bad influences and dangerous places and here I was about to die in a fireball of a race car with a greaser named Eness that Momma would never have approved of. All because of a stupid drag race with the embodiment of evil, soulless Moorefield—and at an outlaw drag strip at the midnight hour. In one fell swoop I'd violated all of Momma's terse terms of surviving adolescence. And I would be cheated of a long and altruistic life because I had shunned every single rule she'd laid out for us. I had cheated myself.

"Hold still, Ollie, I don't wanta cut ya!"

I didn't recognize the voice. Maybe it was the smoke filling up my lungs and eyes. Maybe I was just going into shock because I was pinned like a wrestler on the mat and the fire and smoke working together were about to overwhelm me. And then my head felt like it was being ripped out of a metal mold, but the good news was that I could feel fresh air before I could breathe it. I was on the cold ground and I was coughing and trying to regain my breath.

I was disoriented. 'Couldn't seem to get myself straightened out, couldn't shake the heavy smell of gasoline in my nostrils now that the smoke was clearing out of my system. I seemed to move in slow motion, trying to make out things around me.

I knew it was cold. The earth under me was wet and cold. My feet felt wet now that they were away from the hot metal of the car.

The car. I looked back toward the brightest part of the night. Surreal. It couldn't be real. The car was burning on both ends, a hulking shattered sleeve of twisted metal, half-deposited in the creek bank on its behemoth side, in the cold, shallow waters of the creek. My side of the car was tilted crazily toward the water. I could see someone working, reaching into the car like he was trying to do something.

My buddy Eness. Was he gone? Who was that at the car? He'd called my name. He knew me. I heard a low groan behind me. Someone was moving in agony in the half-shadows. They weren't exactly moving, just kinda rolling forward and slowly backwards like they had a pain they couldn't subdue couldn't control by any movement.

I crawled my way toward the dark form over the uneven earth lighted by the fire from the creek bank. As I got closer I could see the familiar clothing and form of my nemesis. Moorefield! What was he doing here? Why was he in agony?

As I got closer, his eyes opened and his audible groans subsided. He must have sensed my presence because his face grimaced in a grotesque show of hatred and anger. "Holmes! You. It's always you, Holmes! I always have to deal with you. Can I tell you how much I hate your sniveling, greasy little face? White trash Holmes..."

I didn't say anything. I still didn't understand why he was writhing in such pain. Why didn't he get up off the ground where he was soiling his expensive clothes, and assault me? Was he waiting for me to help him? How could I do that?

Then he reached a hand toward me and I could see it was dark and wet.

He hissed, “You did this, you little idiot. You and your family. Good for nothing. And I had to take the...” He doubled back over in pain and screamed out obscenities to the darkness away from me.

I sat down a distance from him and looked back toward the burning car. I saw someone pulling Eness from the same window that had given me escape, and the two bodies fell into the creek water as if exhausted. Finally, one thin form half-lifted the other and carried it military style, like a comrade carrying a wounded friend from the battlefield. They made it several yards from the burning gasoline before collapsing in one heap on the night earth. I stumbled over the uneven clay of the creek bank until I was close enough to make out who it was.

Eness was on his back, coughing and gasping for air. Doug Thomas was exhausted next to him. When I got close enough for Uncle Doug to see me, he grinned displaying his stained, yellow teeth.

As he caught his breath, he said, “Y’all win that there race, boys?”

17

"Look out how you use proud words"

—Carl Sandburg

Momma studied my bandages as I sat on the living room couch. She was more concerned than angry.

When Billy Rand brought me into the house and helped me down gingerly on the couch, she had examined my burns and the sticky salve, and held her mouth as tight as I'd ever seen it. Her usually inquisitive eyes were struggling with a deep sense of compassion.

My head hurt awful and my vision was still slightly blurred.

"Don't be hard on him," Rand was saying, being his usual magnanimous self. "It was my big idea to go to Silver Run. He was just following us. Me and Weldon."

"And what was he doing in that race car? The one that left the highway and plowed into a pasture, or creek, or bridge or any other place y'all can tell a lie about it."

Rand was quiet.

"We were doing fine," I tried to say, but my head hurt so much I closed my eyes and forgot what I wanted to say.

"Fine?" she responded. "One Momma's boy burnt all over and his head knocked in. Another boy with such burns he'll probably die—if he's not already gone. What exactly were you boys up to? I don't mean the race. I mean why couldn't you just go watch the other fools ripping and roaring up and down the highway? Why is it y'all had to participate?"

We were both quiet.

Mary Ellen and Ryder came into the room in their pajamas and stared at me without speaking. A knock at the door spared us an immediate execution. Momma looked up to see her little brother push the door open and enter into the half shadows of our living room.

"What are you grinning about?" Momma groused to Doug Thomas. "You about got yourself burned to a crisp, too, didn't you?"

Old Doug flashed an actual smile that followed him around. Always ready to perform. Always ready to charm his big sister.

"Now, Sis, don't go fussin' over me. That there boy is hurt worse'n me."

"Both of you are foolish," she barked. "Can one of you tell me a good story of what happened before I lose my temper and beat both of you with a stick of stove wood?"

Uncle Doug sat next to me on the tattered couch and leaned back comfortably. "Feels good to set my head back," he said. "That hospital took most of the night. Reckon the sun'll be up before I find my car and get back home."

Momma glared at her brother, waiting for the adult version of the night's events. Uncle Doug protested slightly. "Hold your horses, Sis. I don't want to tell this story but one time."

"So, tell it!"

"Wait till the law gets here."

"Why's the law coming?"

"Because I think I'm under arrest."

"Nothing new. What for this time?"

"I shot a dude."

Momma was really angry now. "That's a good one even for you, Doug Thomas! Shot someone? On purpose?"

"Well, if you'd calm down and wait, I'll get to the whole truth. In front of the law."

"And when's the law coming, little Brother?"

"Well, just about any minute now. That big highway patrolman was the one dropped me off and he was suppose to follow me in here... I don't know where he got off to. How can I...?"

Another light rap at the door and the big man himself into the room and nodded toward Momma. "Sorry to disturb you, Mrs. Holmes. Your brother wanted to come here before I take him to the county. He needs to tell us all about what happened tonight. But before he does, suppose one of you boys tell us what happened early on in the evening. We need the entire story before I write my report or put this old vet in the coot house."

He must have known Doug Thomas pretty well.

Momma sat on the rocker and the big captain sat on a straight chair from the dining room. He looked patiently at Billy Rand and seemed to quietly coax him into words.

Billy Rand looked at the floor, then made a face like he wished he'd never heard of Silver Run. " 'Bout every Saturday night, me and Weldon—and sometimes Ollie—go off to Silver Run's old county store where the kids hang out."

"Where those hotrodders drive like fools," Momma put in.

Billy Rand didn't look at her. Didn't agree or disagree.

"Some boys from Blue Mountain had a hot car they wanted to race," he started again, his eyes on the worn wooden floor. "The idea was for those boys and Eness Voit to race to see who had the fastest car. They were to race from the store to the bridge over Brimer's Creek. Somebody lit a railroad flare to mark the finish line and somebody was taking bets. I think they were anyway. I never pay attention to that. But before the cars got cranked up, this new Chevrolet came rolling into the crowd, pushing people aside and nearly running folks down. It was Moorefield—that boy I told you about. We all thought he'd skipped the country after Jeremiah got killed, but he came rolling in the store lot like he was coming to a church picnic. I have no idea where he came from."

Billy Rand looked at the captain. Captain Bishop indicated for him to continue.

"The talk got heated up and nobody'd race the Moorefield car except Eness. And he would only go if Ollie here rode shotgun. They had done that before. Anyhow, Ollie didn't want to have anything to do with all that business, but everybody kinda pushed him forward and Eness put him in through the window. Then Eness strapped him in like he was a navy test pilot. Anyway, the two cars got to the line—as loud as I'd ever heard anything. So loud my ears hurt and I got back off the line and stood by the gas pump.

"Well, somebody threw a flag on the ground and those two cars tore out like spooked deer. The black car was wild. Its front tires were off the ground and Eness was swapping gears. Anyway, best I could see, Eness was winning easy at first, but we could see down the straightaway where they were racing, and the Moorefield car got to catching up toward the end. All I know was Eness' black car went sideways and off the road. How and why I don't know. But it hit that creek bank head-on, and within a few seconds a little fire showed up out the side of the car. I thought Ollie was gonna get burned up so I tried to find Weldon to drive down there, but when the crazies saw the car wreck, they all tried to get away back toward town so the law couldn't question 'em. It was total chaos. People screaming. Cars bumping into each other. Everybody trying to get away at once. I took off running toward Ollie and Eness to get down there to the creek. By the time I got there, Ollie was already on the ground away from the wrecked car and I saw two people laying over near the water. Turns out, it was Doug Thomas and Eness. Eness was barely breathing.

He looked like the fire had burned him some, and he was knocked out from the impact, I guess.

"When I looked around, I saw Doug's car on the side of the road. I vaguely remember a car passing me, but I guess Doug didn't take time to pick me up. Moorefield's red car was parked near it. Some of the other kids came down to check on the wreck and one of 'em found Moorefield passed out on the ground. He had blood all over his shirt and sweater and he seemed about dead, too. I was scared for the whole business and I wanted to get Ollie to the hospital but the Talladega police and a State Patrol car came up about that time. Somebody mighta called from the country store's outdoor phone. I don't know. But the ambulances took Moorefield and Eness to Talladega and the Highway Patrolman drove Ollie to the Bentonville hospital. We stayed there waiting on him to be seen for hours. Weldon brought us home."

Rand stopped talking and the room got real quiet.

The girls had been standing behind the open wall that showed the dining room. They seemed interested in my wounds but they waited respectfully for the big man to speak.

"Where did you come in the picture, Doug Thomas?" Captain Bishop asked, looking dead at my uncle sitting next to me.

Uncle Doug rolled his head slowly on the back of the couch like he was looking for the right words to say. "I got in late," he finally spoke. "I'd heard about the race and I was just goin' down to check it out. By the time I got there, I seen Ollie being pushed in that winder of the black car and I done heard about that blonde kid that was pullin' up in the red car. I figured that blonde boy would win any way he could, so I pulled in close behind 'em on the road—just behind that mob of screaming kids.

"I was out of the car watching the race when they took off and got about halfway down the track. That Eness boy was smoking the red car pretty good but then Moorefield started catchin' up right before the bridge. He didn't quite make it to the other car's door, but I know what he done.

I seen it happen before on dirt track races and such. See, if the car behind wants to wreck the car ahead, all he's gotta do is give the front car a nudge in the rear quarter—kinda hit the side of the bumper or such and the lead car's got nowhere to go except out of the way. That's what happened. That snotty rich kid turned Eness sideways and off into that ditch. As soon as I seen it happen, I knew those boys'd need help gittin' outta the wreck—if they was still alive. They musta been doing a hundred miles an hour when they hit."

I looked over at Momma. She was shaking her head and holding her mouth tight as a sealed bottle.

"Where did the Moorefield shooting occur?" the Captain asked.

Shooting? I looked at Doug Thomas for his answer.

Typically, he grinned. Then he looked straight into Captain Bishop's eyes and started to talk. "I got to the wreck," he began. "Moorefield was already there ahead of me. He was walking toward the car where Ollie was."

Doug Thomas thought about his words awhile, a faint smile tattooed on his thin lips. We all waited quietly.

"That Moorefield boy," he finally resumed cautiously, looking serious now, studying the floor. "He had a gun. A shiny pistol. Stub nose .38, I think. I saw it in his hand while he was goin' toward the fire. I don't think he seen me comin' up behind him. He was starin' straight ahead like he had a job to do."

There was silence for a while, then Uncle Doug continued, "I think he was goin' over to shoot Ollie to get even. I seen his eyes that night in the store when him and that other boy tried to bully Ollie. They was goin' to hurt him and he ain't done nothin' to them.

"Ollie don't mess with them boys. He didn't deserve all that stuff they done to him. Even if he weren't my blood, he didn't deserve no shootin' in a wrecked car where he was all tied down and couldn't help hisself. How's 'at right?

"So I caught Moorefield from behind and we 'restled around some and I got the gun away from him. He wouldn't shut up, though. Called me crazy just like Ollie. And he said he'd have both of us killed before the night was over. He just kept on running that mouth so I figured he needed shootin'. Ain't nothin' to me to shoot a man 'at needs it."

"You mean," the captain interrupted, "you shot him in self-defense."

The room got real quiet again. Doug Thomas studied the floor some more and Momma got up and sent the girls back to their room. When she returned, Doug Thomas spoke again. "I swear before God, Captain. I pretty much just shot his butt. He needed it done to 'im and I did it. If he dies, lock me up. I ain't goin' nowhere."

Captain Bishop got up out of the chair and started for the front door.

I didn't know what to think.

Nobody else did either.

So nobody spoke except the Captain. "Why is it, Doug Thomas, that you're the most illogical person I ever met? And I've met a few."

Doug Thomas leaned forward on the couch. He was perplexed at the captain addressing him with his back turned to him. Doug shifted his hands slightly and tried to answer the rhetorical question. "What is it I done that makes you say such, Bishop?" he finally asked.

Silence filled the room as the captain turned slowly back to the present company. He seemed to be composing a speech that would cover all of our sins equally and completely. I was anxious to hear his response myself.

"I'm thinking, Doug, that you've got this exaggerated opinion of yourself. You're always quick to take up any guilt that'll make you a spot in the light of public opinion."

The captain did not smile, his face was as solemn as a drowning dog with a stone around his neck. I looked from face to face in the room, trying to read everybody's eyes. Nobody seemed clear on the words spoken.

"Remember the time when we were boys fishing and my doggone

cousin Cord fell in the water and went down a couple of times before you stripped off naked as a jay bird and pulled him out and saved his life?" Bishop asked quietly.

"I usually swum naked," Doug said seriously. "Weren't no girls around."

"And that time Blast got thrown off that stolen horse and you carried him down to Doc Harris, a couple miles away, to get seen about?"

"Listen, Bishop, I never stole that horse. Old Blast got that fancy idea in his head. I just happened by just as Blast got airborne. That fool couldn't ride a horse on a merry-go-round."

Bishop got quiet again and studied Doug's face carefully.

Doug was still mumbling about the reciting of sins past. "It ain't like you ain't never done nothing crooked yourself, Bishop. I could tell tales, too, you know."

"I know, Doug. But the point is, you had your share of lockups and glory to bask in. I'm taking this one away."

Doug Thomas was as near angry as I'd ever seen him. "Got to where a man can't shoot somebody no more, own up to it, and claim it as a sin before God and the law, and get his misdeed denied right in front of family and witnesses. It's easier to claim treason in this county than it is to get locked up over the truth! What kinda county you workin', Bishop? You big hypocrite."

"Watch it, Doug. I ain't past whipping that bony butt of yours, burned flesh and all."

Momma had been quiet all this while, listening to both men espousing the daily wickedness of life as he found it. I enjoyed the stories myself. I didn't know much about my uncle. Maybe that was just recreation for country boys during the Depression. Bishop seemed forgiving of their trespasses, but I wondered where he was going with all these past references.

"What you aiming at, Captain Bishop?" Momma asked.

Bishop didn't answer, but turned his back to us again. He didn't speak for a long while.

I was more confused than anybody in the room. Maybe they just had more information than I did. Maybe they already knew about the shooting. I don't know. I didn't know. My head was still throbbing and my vision was kinda askew. Did Moorefield deserve the shooting? He sure didn't know Uncle Doug Thomas. Nobody threatened a hardened veteran with a mental hangover from the depths of the world's worst war—nobody with good sense.

But Doug saw danger to the family much as Mr. Monte did. He couldn't prevent all the struggles in life, but he could face up to the ones that came to him.

Everybody waited on the captain. The investigation may have gone through too many ears, and he had to make sense of the tale that Doug Thomas laid out in front of us. His would be the final words on a night that would live at the front of our memories for a long while.

When Bishop turned back to us, there was no smile on his face. He was covered in a look of determination to end the inquisition and to set matters in the proper place. No one in the room would dare question whatever decision he made known to us.

"There's been a lot of hatred and just plain ruthlessness going on 'round this valley. Young folks don't need to have their innocence destroyed by ones that can do as they please—free of any moral character to guide them.

"My report will say Duncan Moorefield was accidentally shot while struggling with Doug Thomas. It will also say that Moorefield threatened the life of both Thomas and Oliver Holmes."

He paused before he said his last words. Nobody raised an eyebrow or an objection to his decision.

"I'll swear to the accuracy of this report in court," he said and left the room.

We all just sat there. Nobody said a word. Doug didn't seem to care about the jail thing one way or another. Just like he didn't care if he shot that boy or not. Me, I was confused. Maybe it had to do with the head getting rattled in the wreck. At fifteen years old, the world was one big challenge. Life would never be cut short regardless of what you did. It simply didn't work that way. Or did it? How about Jeremiah? But Momma knew how precious life was. She knew how close I had been standing to the end of it. She had experienced the world without leaving the confines of our long valley, and now she brought the world that was important to her back into focus. She sent Rand and me off to bed and offered the couch to Uncle Doug to sleep on.

I couldn't hear his response to the offer as we made our way toward the bedroom, but I remember finding him there passed out the next morning. But that night, as I got ready for a bed that called me fervently, I thought I heard Momma's voice soften as she discussed aspects of the night's race gone horribly wrong. And somewhere in that low rumbling of words that came through our thin walls like the final knell of night, she gave sincere thanks to her brother for saving me and Eness.

Ol' Doug must've already been asleep because I never heard another word.

18
Breezie Lane

We got up a trip to town and I didn't feel so bad about going now.

The word was out about Moorefield. I suppose I felt vindicated. At least I could feel right about being seen in daylight again.

Of course, Golden Boy had considerable explaining to do once he cleared surgery and recovery. I heard that they had him sequestered in that hospital room in Talladega. Apparently, the .38 bullet that lanced his stomach had done considerable damage. Someone said a surgeon from Birmingham was doing some work in the small town hospital that weekend and his quick, precise work probably saved Moorefield's life. I was relieved for Moorefield and for Uncle Doug.

Even though Captain Bishop was generous in his reporting on the case, I didn't want my uncle to feel any particular remorse over his action. I should have known better. Doug spoke freely to the family about what had happened. When news came down in a few weeks that the Moorefield kid was going to make it in the physical world for a while longer, Doug

Thomas expressed regret about the entire incident, but he was having trouble feeling remorse for Moorefield.

A few days later, Sherman T. and I were sitting behind the cab of Mr. Monte's truck. I didn't want to sit on the dirty bed but it was either sit there or squat for a long spell, so I just dropped down next to Sherm and felt the wind toss my hair around.

We'd stopped by the parsonage to pick up Raike but I didn't see Evie. I was somewhat disappointed. I'd already seen her at school, though. She had apologized about not looking after me at Silver Run, but her date had been one of the first ones to leave the troubled area when Eness and I went sailing through the night air.

And she sought me out at school the following week and was especially mindful of my scorched hair and bandages. I must have looked like a freak limping around the hallways, doing the best I could to ignore the laughter and finger pointing. For all my sensitivity, Evie paid the social ostracism business no mind. She walked me proudly to class and even sat with me at lunch while the other senior girls—and all the underclassmen—avoided me like I was a working apprentice for Jack the Ripper.

It was days later when all of the facts came out in the newspaper and gossip lines got to humming that I reached my vindication point. I went from local geek to the burnt-face freak. But when the bandages came off several days later, my red-marked skin made me look almost normal. I fell into my routine and enjoyed an almost celebratory existence.

When we went on into town, Mr. Monte found a parking spot, and he and Dad went down main street to see about a few items for the farm. We boys wandered over to the soda fountain at the drug store. Sherm was his usual self, trying to get a boob shot of the waitress, while Raike excused himself to go pick up something at the shoe repair shop.

The retarded waffer and I ordered cherry Cokes and slowly sipped the cool caramel while Saturday business circled all around us. Sherm saw a couple of city girls that smiled at him but when they had a good look at his muddy shoes and leering eye, they disappeared out the door and got lost in the heavy pedestrian traffic.

"This is a cool town," Sherm said, checking the aisle by the greeting cards for better targets, "but the girls spook easy. Guess they ain't used to seeing real men up close."

"Probably not. 'Glad I lost my bandages-and-slick-ointment look. That's a real downer with a city girl used to chocolate sundaes and crew cuts."

Sherm looked at my hair that was beginning to cover my ears and forehead without prompting.

"You do need a haircut. Want me to line up Margaret for you?"

Margaret was his mother. She didn't cut his hair. She sheared it. Sherman looked like a lamb on cut-for-market day.

"Thanks, but I'll pass," I said. "That sheared-wool cut ain't in with the woods babes I know."

He hooted his disbelief.

"What woods girls do you know, peasant dweller?"

"Lexie and Lydia. Lexie ran her fingers through my hair recently. Just minutes before she and Weldon pushed me out of the car and went off for a heavy breathing session. Lydia is a front seat kind of girl."

"Lotta good that does you. Besides, how can you tell Lyd from Lex? They about the same as the left side and the right side of a pecan."

"Weldon knows the difference."

"How's that?"

"One of 'em uses friendly persuasion different from the other."

"Meaning what?"

"He thinks they swap on him sometimes."

"How's he know?"

"He says they kiss differently."

Sherman liked that idea. His face lit up as he considered the obvious options of dating sisters. "Say, I could groove on that," he smiled. "Twice the sugar, half the price."

"Don't go running your mouth in front of anybody. That information was overheard during an almost adult conversion in his car. If word got out I was spraying his secrets around, the rides around town would get few and far between. And I like to ride."

Sherm made a soft whistle. "I'd like a ride, too. Look at that future momma that just came in the door."

Without expecting much in Sherman's limited range of attractions, I was surprised to see a young lady I knew come into the drug store. She paused briefly, seeming to collect her thoughts as to her shopping list before going for the merchandise. When she saw me, her face lit into a smile and she started toward me.

"Hello, Oliver," she said, extending a dainty hand.

"Hello, ma'am," I replied, then didn't know what to say.

But she was way too far ahead of me to let the rudder drag on a conversation.

"This," she said, pointing toward Sherm, "must be the erst-while mistaken Sherman Monte."

Sherm's face was as shocked as the first time he met the voluptuous Beatrice North.

"Say hello to Miss *Bentonville Times* reporter," I said.

We weren't properly introduced. "I'm Breezie Lane," she said and nodded toward Sherman.

With that stupid look on his face I knew why she didn't offer to shake his hand.

"Takes a while for conversation to sink in," I kidded. "His vocabulary is weak and his social skills are nonexistent."

Breezie chuckled.

Even if I was still testing the waters of puberty, her breeze was fine.

She wore a modest sweater that did an awful job hiding her blessings. Her hair was pulled back in a careless gathering that showed her dainty cheekbones and awesome blue eyes. The eyes must've fallen out of a summer sky and found a home just near her pert little nose. Her teeth were a match to pretty boy Moorefield's. If I'd been a few years older, I'd been on her doorstep every night of the week.

Sherm was still star-struck. He sat stock still.

"What are you fellows doing in town?" she asked innocently.

"We rode in with his dad," I replied. "Country boys like to see the bright lights every chance they can."

"You're not a country bumpkin," she retorted. "Not with that line of falsehood you string out for a girl. Last time I saw you, you were making pretty good conversation. Even with that bad head. How's the concussion?"

"Doing very well," I said. " 'Got rid of that one just in time to pick up another one."

"I heard your story," she said. "Captain Bishop gave me the scoop a few days back. We sold a lot of newspapers off of your adventures."

"Misadventures," I corrected. "But I'm all finished playing in fast cars with angry drivers. 'Bad combination."

She motioned toward a booth near our stools. "Would you fellows join me for a soda?" she asked, politely.

I was slightly bashful, but I'd rather be seen in public with Breezie than have ownership of a new Corvette. Well, almost.

Sherman remained nailed to the stool as if he couldn't believe a good-looking woman was actually talking to me. I was having a hard time, myself, realizing that my status as the valley weenie would be greatly depleted if only the senior boys in my gym class could see the star that was sitting comfortably across the table from me.

"I'm sorry I didn't get a chance to talk to you personally, Ollie," she said. "You were in poor shape for awhile, and I thought it would be insensitive on my part to come around banging on your door when the captain pretty much told the entire story. Were you pleased with the paper's account?"

I nodded as she ordered a Coke float from a soda jerk just slightly older than me. He had to close his mouth before taking Breezie's order. He was clearly under the same spell I was.

"I read everything I could find," I said, honestly. "Mr. Moon, the rural paper man, dropped off every paper that had my story in it. We usually can't afford the paper, so he gave us free copies. We were hot news for a while, weren't we?"

"You certainly were. What awful pressure you were under. I'm surprised you could hold up under such threats and physical assaults."

"The captain made me sound good," I said. "I'm a big weenie at school. But, you know, I felt like I could trust you from the first. I'm sorry I couldn't give you the story."

"Well," she said, those blue eyes starting surgery on that part of my brain that covered common sense. "There's still one little matter that needs seeing about."

"What's that?" I asked, my head empty of thoughts.

"The Snow Girl thing," she nearly whispered as if someone might hear.

Sherm glanced around.

Surgery ceased for a moment and my brain came back to me. What did she know? What had the captain told her? Should I put my two cents in?

"I heard there were photos," she said, acting like she was more interested in gathering a couple of napkins from the dispenser than she was in hearing about the pictures.

I didn't say anything. She paused her gathering and examined my face. "Did I speak inappropriately?" she asked.

I supposed she was being honest. I was afraid to agree or offer anything to the conversation.

"Do you know how they got the photographs?" she asked sweetly.

"I don't have anything to say," I mumbled. The previous feeling of being on the same page dissipated.

She examined my face further, almost pouting her lips toward me. "I have spoken out of turn," she said apologetically. "You must know something about those pictures that you have been sworn not to tell. If that's true, then I'm sorry. I wasn't being sly. I was simply making conversation."

Could I believe her?

I suddenly felt like a runaway truck had found me.

"Let's talk about something else," she offered. "Do you recollect your words to me at our meeting cautioning me to be alert around any vestige of the Klan members?"

When I nodded slightly, she nodded as well. So did Sherm.

"You were right. I've been getting threatening phone calls at home. Every night. This deep voice uses the worst language, telling me how they're going to dissuade me from writing any more stories about their secret society."

"They threaten you?" I asked.

"As I said, practically every night. This creepy voice comes over the phone and I keep thinking he'll set up a meeting or such, but he just starts this vulgar line of things."

"Can't you ignore the call? Not answer?" I asked.

"Well, he calls on the tenants' line at the boarding house. Someone always answers and calls me down. I've got this feeling about who it is each night, but I keep hoping he'll say something worth writing."

"Aren't you afraid?"

"Sometimes I am, but my editor wants me to continue to field the calls and eek out any information for a story."

"Sounds like dangerous work," I said.

"Mitchell says that's normal procedure. Lots of talk, very little action. Do you know my colleague Mitchell Rimple?"

I had to smile. "I know him."

"Why are you smiling? Did he put the squeeze on you? That weasel. I told him to leave you alone—that you'd had enough trouble from every direction lately."

"He didn't listen," I said, warming to her concern for me.

"He didn't come to your house, did he?"

"No. The school."

"The school? How unethical that sounds."

Was she being truthful or playing me like a cheap harp?

"I don't trust you newspaper people," I said. I wanted to see her reaction.

"You liked my predecessor," she said flatly. "Beatrice North."

"Emily Brubaker."

"Who told you? Oh, sounds like Mitchell. I understand he wanted to date Beatrice in college, but she pushed him away."

"She was my friend," I said. "She and I went through a war together."

"I know. I don't want to court warfare, but I could use a crumb of information on the poor Snow Girl. Is there a chance you know who she is? Just knowing that would open up a lot of things in this case."

I was silent again. Sherm seemed to sink into the booth.

My attempts at being clever usually backfired on me. Like holding a snake on the wrong end thinking you were safe.

"Why don't you talk to the captain?"

"I have. He won't answer anything. That's why I'm down to you. Mitch said to 'try interrogating the children—that's what Beatrice did.' "

She was taking straight aim on that shot.

"Beatrice didn't use me. She genuinely liked me," I objected quietly.

"Baby Doll Blue Eyes," she said, like she was explaining very elementary math. "Beatrice was just like me. Anything to get a story."

I didn't say a word, but I remembered the words Beatrice had spoken to me her last day in Bentonville. We were in front of the newspaper office, and in my mind and heart I knew her words were sincere.

I was not yet dialed in on this Breezie kid.

"Where did you get that name?" I asked. "Breezie?"

She sat back in the booth and looked around for our order. "My daddy liked unusual names. I can't tell you my real name. It's from the Bible but it's not particularly pretty."

"Does it begin with a 'B'?" I asked.

She smiled and nodded.

"Beulah?" I asked.

Her smile faded.

"How did you know?" she asked in disbelief.

"I belong to a Christian literary club with a senior girl. She picks out the books and we read them. They won't let me in the advanced classes at school, so she gives me her books and notes. Beulah appears in the allegory *The Pilgrim's Progress*."

Sherm glanced at me from the corner of his eye.

"You dear boy," she said, her attention starting to come back. "You're innocent and honest, aren't you? I thought no one could guess that name."

"I also have an aunt with that name. An old-timey Biblical name. But it doesn't fit you like Breezie does."

"Why can't you take advanced classes?" she asked. "What's special about that?"

"Only the smartest kids get to take those classes."

Sherm nodded.

"You're smart."

"Not like the folks from the richer families."

" 'Didn't know there were richer families around here."

"A few. Big farms. Cattle farms. Dairy farms."

Before she could ask anything further, her eyes changed focus and I saw that she was eyeing someone at the front of the drugstore. True to life, within a few seconds, the pompous and agitating reporter Rimple appeared at my side of the booth and he looked down with a smirk on his face.

"Last time I saw this person," he said, indicating me, "his principal threatened to reprimand my posterior for attempting to do my job. But look at you, Breezie, 'good copy' just sits in a public booth with you and gives you gems to register and report."

Breezie smiled. "Why don't you join us, Mitchell? Little Holmes, here, already knows who you are, and this is his friend Sherman. So maybe he'll connect with you outside the school environment."

My face said otherwise as the tall man motioned Breezie to slide the vinyl, and he dropped down across from me. I shuffled my feet to my side and looked cautiously at the smirk as wide as the Mississippi.

"How you doing, Holmes?" he asked immediately, ignoring Sherm.

"Fine. You?"

"I'm great. Just finished an article about the girl caught up in the last snowstorm."

Breezie smiled again. "Working on Saturday, too. Looking for that Pulitzer, Mitchell?"

He laughed. "Wouldn't it be ironic if I could win a Pulitz over this unfortunate incident without the assistance of the local people?" He looked right at me with a smile.

I looked away. " 'Deal with the faults of others as gently as with your own,' " I quoted, not meeting his eyes.

There was silence at the table for a moment, then the smirk again and his voice brought my eyes back to his. "What's that, Holmes? You waxing eloquent on me?"

"I read world literature," I said, barely masking my contempt. "That's a Chinese proverb."

Breezie was impressed. "Gee, Oliver, you are a smart kid. Where'd you find that if not in the advanced class?"

"My friend Evie," I said truthfully.

"How about this one, Holmes," Mitchell said, his mind obviously seeking to recall something to match my words. " 'A man thinks he knows, but a woman knows better.' That's Chinese, too."

I shrugged. I had one last shot that had stayed in my memory. " 'The tongue is a sharp sword which slays, though it draws no blood.' "

Further silence at the table. Smirk-face kept his sneer.

"Instead of brainy insults," Breezie said, "why don't we just agree to talk with civility?"

"I have nothing to say," I said.

Sherm, though no one asked, nodded too.

"You say that stuff, Holmes," Mitchell said, menacingly, "then you rattle off some proverbs like you're the smartest pup in the litter. Why don't you just answer decent questions without all this dodging and ducking? You got something to hide about this Snow Girl thing? Maybe if you'd cause one death from the train tightrope walk, you'd cause a little beauty to be left in the snow. You're not totally blameless of everything."

"Mitchell!" Breezie protested.

Sherm's head swiveled around.

"Well, look at the little wimp. I've seen demons with clearer consciences than he has. We don't know for sure how that Jeremiah died. All we have is this smart mouth's report. Maybe the girl was a visitor from out of town, come here to visit the family. Maybe sweet face did her in because of her rejection of his advances. What about that, Holmes?"

I'd said too much. I should have excused myself without trying to outduel the more experienced person. "A little knowledge is a deadly thing." I'd read that in a Herman Wouk novel. Now, I was in over my head and needed a way out.

I looked up to see Raike standing by the table. He smiled at the two reporters across from me and showed us his brown paper sack. "Shoes like new for half the price," he said. "You ready to go, Ollie? Sherm?"

"And who are you?" Breezie asked, sweetly.

"I'm Raike. My dad's pastor at the White Oaks Baptist Church in the valley. If you need a church home, come visit with us."

"Now isn't that kind? Thank you, young man. You take good care of little Holmes. Trouble follows him around, they say."

"Not only does it follow," Raike laughed, "But it catches him, too. Right, sport?"

"Oh," Breezie said. "Before you go, Oliver. If you change your mind about those photographs, call me at work or home." She began searching through her purse. "I have my card here somewhere."

I looked at Rimple as I prepared to depart. He had a shocked look on his face.

"What photographs, Breezie girl?" he asked, recovering nicely from fresh news.

"I told you earlier, Mitch," she said. "Ollie got the contents of the Snow Girl's purse from a couple of his classmates."

"You never told me that."

"Sure, I did," she said, occupied with her purse search, not facing the agitated Rimple. "We were touring the press room and the noise was exceedingly loud, but l told you that tidbit as we left the building."

"What idiot tries to talk during a press run?"

Breezie paused in her search and stared at the other reporter. "Mitchell," she said. "Why have you been so obnoxious lately? You snap at me and you make wild accusations toward a high-school student. Isn't that being a little insensitive?"

"How's it insensitive? He fails to cooperate with me or the law authorities and nobody pins him down or holds him accountable. I'm simply doing my job."

Raike decided to enter the discussion. "Why don't you practice your job elsewhere, mister, and I'll take my friend back to our ride home?"

Rimple looked pure hatred at me as I got up from the booth, but I knew my way out of a cave when I saw an opening. I put my last two coins in the world on the table and left without looking back. Sherman T. slid across the seat and followed.

19

"What can one do when there's no peace..."

—Ron Miller

Our gym class was all right.

I was skinnier than the sprinkling of juniors and seniors that bossed the class, but I had been blessed with quick feet and speed. Therefore, when the seniors tried to take advantage of me physically in whatever sport was in season, I didn't have much trouble putting distance from the threats. Any sophomores that got themselves caught in the grip of the older boys paid the penalty. The penalty was usually reprehensible. Not exactly fourth grade freeze tag.

I guess I say that because I was slacking during gym class one day, waiting for the afternoon dismissal bell. The sun was gone and the low clouds that had wandered into the valley off Cheaha looked like they were mad about something. The wind that blew them was purposefully blustery and cool, menacing the winter trees with enough force to challenge the weakest branches.

My face was sore from the heat but healing, and though my concussion was much better, the coach let me off from the touch football game going on down the short hill behind the gym. From then on, I was pretty much lone-wolfing it by the rear of the building. I should have known better than to be lonesome and careless at the same time when miscreants still roamed the earth. I must have nodded off when I sat down next to the building, or at least closed my eyes, because the dastardly duo came around the building and accosted me before I could react. Boother and Braska, God's fun loving children of the dark woods.

Boother grabbed my arms and pulled me up, pinning me to the wall, while Braska got close enough in my face to share his breath.

"I told ya, Boother," Braska was saying, his foul-smelling mouth kicking out his high woods venom. "He done took our stuff and run off with the money. I done told ya so. Ain't I told ya so?"

"Shut up, stupid," Boother said. "We ain't after 'I told you so,' we after that reward money."

Boother grabbed the front of my shirt, drawing me closer to *his* stinking teeth. "Where ya been, smart mouth?" he demanded.

"He been hidin' from us," Braska answered. " 'At's where he been at."

"Shut up, Braska. I told ya I'll do this here talkin'."

"Hit 'at red face a his with yore fist. Make 'at mouf bleed red."

"For the last time, Braska, shut up. I wanta talk to this here boy, not listen to yore tongue."

"Well, let me have a shot 'en. I wanna push that mouf in. Let 'im taste blood."

Boother was getting frustrated with his overactive brother so I guess he took his feelings out on me. He doubled a big hand into a fist and tried to tattoo my stomach to my backbone. I groaned and doubled over in pain.

"Let me git in a shot," Braska said, delighted his brother was doing something to get even with me. "Let me mash 'at mouth, Boother."

I tried to talk but couldn't think of anything to say that'd lessen the beating. All I could fall back on was that old principle of circumstances that said

"When in desperate situations, tell a lie."

"Hold up, boys," I gasped, staying bent over so I presented less of a target. "I got something from the sheriff that'll explain everything," I said.

"How ya plan stealin' our money?" Braska asked.

"Swear on my mother's Bible," I said. "That deputy sheriff gave me a receipt to show y'all that he got that evidence all nice and legal like and he put in for the reward in your names."

"How come we ain't heard from you in over two weeks?" Boother asked.

"Reckon you boys ain't heard. I got in a car wreck at a hundred miles an hour and 'bout got killed and got my head and face burned. You can see how red my skin is. That's the reason I'm up here by myself while those other boys are down yonder playing football. I got a head injury, too, but you can't see it."

"Can't see it!" Braska spit at me, pulling my head up by the hair. "You lyin' coon dog. Ain't nothin' wrong 'cept we caught yore lyin' butt."

"I done swore on my momma's Bible, boys. Ain't that sacred enough?"

"Show us 'at paper," Boother said.

"Ain't got it on me. It's home."

"Shore. We navy frogmen, too," Boother said.

"Honest to the Good Lord," I said. "If you boys were to give me just one afternoon to get home and get that receipt, it'd show you that the sheriff's doing right by the money. 'Course now, you know you gotta do a mite more to get the full amount."

"What full amount?" they asked in unison.

"Well, they said they'd reckon those pictures y'all gave me was worth about fifty dollars, but unless y'all could tell them more about who was in them pictures, then they ain't got nothing of value there. Don't you see?"

"What ya mean?" Boother asked, skeptical.

"Well, I don't know nothing 'bout them pictures. Whatever it was y'all gave me I put in that there paper sack and I gave it to the sheriff to look at. I never spied none of that stuff."

"Ya lyin' undertaker," Boother said.

"Honest to the Good Lord," I replied again. "They need to know exactly who that big fellow in the picture is, 'cause one a you boys done tore the face right off the film."

They both got quiet and both released me. I stood up straight and gently rubbed my midsection. Boother was a strong imbecile.

"Which one was it ruined that face and lost your five hundred dollars?" I asked accusingly.

Both were quiet some more, then Braska swore something that was native to his tribe only and punched his brother on the shoulder. "Thar ya go, Mr. Smartie. Ya done cost us more money," he said angrily.

"Shut up, Braska. I'm thinkin'. "

"Thinkin' what? How ya gonna lose us all that cash and this he'r boy don't git no beatin' he got comin'?"

"Shut up, Braska. I done thought of how I kin fix this here deal."

"How's 'at? Fess up yoreself like ya done the kiln'?"

I looked at Braska, then Boother. That was a new thought.

"You boys knew this girl?" I asked.

"Lard, no," Braska said emphatically. "Ain't never seen no girl 'at purty. But ole Boother here'd smooch the devil's girlfriend fer five hundred dollars."

"How's your deal work?" I asked Boother. "If y'all ain't happy with my news, then tell me something to take its place. This way with y'all beatin' my face in ain't meaning nothing."

"Makin' me feel a mite better," Braska said, "on ac'ount ya lied to us. I'm still gonna mash 'at mouf."

"Ya ain't doin' nothin'," Boother said. "I got this here deal covered. Lookie here, Holmes, how much ya reckon it's worth to know that hombre in 'at pitcher?"

"I told ya," I replied, trying to round out my speech to match theirs—an attempt to keep Boother's fist off my suffering face. "Pictures ain't no good unless you can tell who that boy was. I reckon that picture was complete and full when you got it. Right?"

Boother nodded slightly and his face seemed to tell of deep gears grinding behind his inbred eyes. Braska loosened his grip on my arms and I figured I'd be patient on Boother's thought waves, but I knew I needed to gain control of the situation.

"Ain't no big deal 'bout that boy in th' pitcher," Boother finally offered.

Braska leaned forward like he was receiving news, too.

"I seen 'im round the school lots times."

I thought of their absences from school.

"How's that?" I asked.

"Lots of days me and him ride the bus to school, but we don't go inside. Nobody don't never pay us no attention. Sometimes we go off down there in the woods and watch 'em girls gym classes where them girls come out in short thangs and run 'round all over the place."

"Y'all hide in the woods and watch the girls?" I asked, incredulous.

They both nodded and Braska grinned. "Gits me far'd up," he said, "see 'n all them legs."

I thought to reprimand them, then realized we boys in gym class did the same thing. Except we didn't hide and watch. We just gawked up close.

"What's that got to do with the pictures?" I asked.

"That boy there in them pitchers," Boother explained. "I swear I seen 'im on tha' schoolyard."

I thought a moment but nothing connected.

"How could that be?" I asked. "He looked too old to be a student from what I could make out."

"I ain't sayin' what he wuz doin', but he shur 'nuff come and go a few times."

"On the bus or drivin' a car?"

"Drivin'."

"What kinda car? Show me in the parking lot."

"Didn't see no car."

"How you know he wasn't on the bus?"

" 'Cause I was and he weren't."

I couldn't deny that logic.

"Describe him to me," I said.

"Huh?"

"Tell me what he looked like. Hair color, eyes..."

"Didn't see no eyes. I ain't funny."

"I know. I know. Tell me something."

"Well, he was 'bout tall as Braska."

Braska grinned and stood up straight.

"That's good. What else?"

"He didn' corn'r to where we wuz, so I never seen 'at face much."

"Who did he talk to? Any girls?"

They both shook their heads. "He looked 'round out back then he went off inside."

"Had blonde hair, lik' 'at Sno' Girl," Braska put in proudly, nodding his head. "I 'member 'at."

"Shut up, Braska, this here's my story."

They both went into thought like they were struggling with images and words of the past.

"Hey," Boother said, "can't ya jest go down th' shariff's office 'n look at 'em pitchers they got and pick 'im out."

"How'd ya know that?" I asked, surprised.

"I been round mor'n ya thank," Boother said proudly. "Thay took me for a ride once and took my pitcher fer this big book they had. Shariff said I was special—had my own page in 'at book."

I quietly agreed. Boother had been 'round all right.

“This deal of yours ain’t worth two cents, Boother,” I said. “You don’t know squat for me.”

They both drew back like they’d just lost a fortune at Las Vegas. They wanted the money.

“We still git somtin’,” Braska protested. “We done ar’ part up front.”

“Let me think a minute,” I said. “I gotta make this right with the sheriff and the captain. They signed off on you boys, but I want to see you get treated fair and square. Y’all done your part like you say, and I gave my word to be up front with you.”

Boother stepped up and patted me on the shoulder. He was looking past me toward the side of the gym. “We back in the hunt, Holmes,” he said, grinning like he’d just shot the biggest deer in the woods. “Look over yonder. There’s him right there.”

“You sure about that, Boother?” I asked after the shockwaves subsided and common sense set in. “If you ain’t sure, and I call the sheriff and we get the wrong person, then you and me are both behind the eight ball.”

Boother kept that stupid grin on his face like he couldn’t believe five hundred dollars just walked up on the schoolyard and started toward us.

Braska was slower than Boother. He scrunched up in the face, trying to figure out what his brother had seen that he hadn’t. Then, like summer lightning, a bolt of electricity ignited his feeble brain and he grabbed my arm again in excitement. “ ’At air’s him!” he exclaimed. “I seen that face a hunnert times. ’At’s ’im fer shur!”

I held up my hands like I was trying to slow a freight train down. “Before we take a step now, both you rascal...er, brothers are sure that’s the man in the photograph, right?”

They both kept grinning and nodding their heads like their neck springs were loose. I wondered at my own wisdom, taking two inbred girl-watchers-from-the-bushes types to I.D. a possible suspect in the Snow Girl case—the sarcastic, arrogant and snobbish news reporter, Mitchell Rimple.

I wasn't sure what to do. The mouth-of-the-South was displaying that ubiquitous smirk as he saw me and started toward me from about thirty or forty yards away. I didn't see where he came from, but he was on a mission. That ever-present notebook and the stubby pencil showed under his left cupped hand and he smoked a cigarette using the right hand. My knees went gitzo at the possibilities of the news flash, and my already crimson face must have made itself into a color DuPont was looking to match.

I turned to look at the shack dwellers, but curiously, they had disappeared like key witnesses to a Mafia murder trial. Maybe a good thing, I thought. Maybe a bad one.

Before Rimple reached me, however, there was another tug on my arm, this time softer and more hesitant. A female voice found my ear, and while I stood in awe of my discovery, courtesy of the dark-woods boys, Evie came within my side vision and spoke with the usual sweetness of an angel on loan from heaven. "What are you doing out here alone, Ollie?" she asked. "I thought you had gym class this period."

I shook my head, trying to refocus on Evie, but the Snow Girl suspect grew more prominent in my presence.

"I... I'm sorry, Evie," I stuttered in half shock and mostly fear. "I got off from the football game."

"Walk me up to the bus," she said, gesturing toward the yellow behemoths that were busy drooling their fluids on the gravely road in front of the school building.

"I... uh..." I stammered. "I can't. I'm waiting on him." I pointed in Rimple's direction. "I'm sorry."

I was hoping she would turn and go. Could she not see the suspected Snow Girl murderer coming toward me, ready to investigate my every thought? If Boother and Braska were right, even if he wasn't the murderer, it was ironic that he could write about the incident for the thousands of readers of the newspaper to wonder about, and all the time he'd known the Snow Girl and maybe something about her brutal death in the depths of the quiet snow, under the cover of darkness.

"Hey, little Holmes," the smirking reporter said, now coming close enough to converse. "What's the latest from Jamback?"

I stood in concrete and thought of planetary movements, Kepler's laws, and Pope's epithets. Anything but what he was saying. I was buzzed out. Evie saw my mental imprisonment, and with the adroitness of a person twice her age, she stepped in front of me and took the flak.

"I'm sorry, sir," she said kindly. "Poor Oliver has been suffering from a concussion lately and the affects of it are causing him temporary inability to focus. Don't think him rude. He's simply in one of those lapses where he can't think straight. I'll direct him up to the school bus. May I ask your name so I can relay your business later on when he's better?"

The smile on the Snow Girl's boyfriend died instantly. He frowned.

"Say, what kind of foolishness is this?" he asked. "Every time I get near this kid, somebody runs up and throws a lead shield in front of him. What am I, the bearer of evil? I have no bad intentions for him. I just got a few questions for the newspaper. Nothing life threatening. Who are you?"

Evie smiled while I kept my eyes on the ground. "I'm Ollie's friend," she said. "He and I belong to the same club in school. We write poetry."

"Bully for you, little girl. Why can't your boyfriend say something for himself?"

"Aren't you the person that barged into Mr. Gorman's office and tried to interview Ollie?"

"I saw him there, yes."

"I used the verb 'barged.' You barged in."

"Hey, you trying to get me mad?"

"No, sir. Just helping my friend."

"Maybe you two poets are more than friends."

Evie smiled at the reporter's coarse accusation.

"We have a platonic relationship, Ollie and I. At our maturity level, that's sufficient. We're Christian friends."

"Christian! That little fool? Why, he's been in more trouble than a gang of thieves. You seem like a sweet girl, but if I was your daddy, I'd select your company more carefully."

"My father allows me to select my own company, knowing I'm a friend to the world while being a child of God."

The reporter looked disgusted.

"Don't give me that Christian allocution—'Friend to the world.' Go put some makeup on your freckles, honey, and find you a stud football player. Be real worldly with the boys. You'll like that better than holding hands with this little wimp."

Evie stood her ground before I could say anything. "A Christian heart bears you no malice, sir, but please beware that our Father will forgive any sin save that of attacking His kingdom."

"What willie-wash is that, little sister? All I came to do was talk to this slug and I get a sermon on school grounds. Spare me the Bible recitation."

Evie kept her smile but started toward the school buses with me in tow.

"Services at 9:30 Sunday morning, sir. Bring your notebook or simply let your troubled heart be touched by the message. The White Oak Baptist Church—straight down 9. Good bye."

Thank goodness for Evie's perceptive powers.

She knew right away that there was an out-of-phase vibration from the tall reporter. Although she hadn't met him, she did have the benefit of having heard me detail his strangeness in Gorman's office that day and his rants the afternoon Sherm and I'd been visiting with Breezie at the drug store. So, when the big talker tried to get close to me in the schoolyard, she demonstrated a kind interference and Christian strength that he couldn't refute.

On the bus, I continued my evasive mood, held in an undercurrent of fear, knowing the brothers from Slow Mile Road were correct. Somehow, I could sense his fit with the rich family. But what could the beauty in the snow possibly have done to deserve to be placed at the foot of a dead, cold dam in the middle of darkness, with the betraying covering of a pure white snow hiding her rest upon the weeds? Had he no heart?

I shuddered in a cold fear. I had to notify the captain of the possibilities. I had felt enough uneasiness in the man's presence to at least garner a thorough investigation by the law. Would he continue to pursue me? And how could I contact the captain? We had no telephone at home.

"What's wrong?" Evie asked as I stood up beside her on the bus.

"I gotta talk to Sherman T."

"You can't," she said. "He had to stay after school for Mrs. Finkle. Cutting up in the hall. Can you imagine?"

I froze in place, swaying with the twisting bus.

"Does your dad have a telephone in his office?" I asked.

She laughed. "Sort of. Ours is not a well-to-do church. We have a party line. Do you know with whom we share a line?"

"Not 'No Nose'?"

She laughed again. "Bingo. You win a donut."

No Nose Tate was an enigma. An anomaly. No one in my generation knew what had happened to her face, but it was void of a nose. When I traveled past her house as a youngster, walking the dirt road with Rand, she'd sat on the front porch in her swing. When we got close enough to see her, Rand would take off running and I with him. No Nose would come to the edge of the porch and scream at us in an insane shriek, her hand covering her features from the eyes down, so we couldn't see the alleged hole in her face. As a youngster, my dreams were anointed in furious struggles of her image coming off the porch to chase me.

Now, she was simply a talker on the party line that two or three other families shared. Her time was usually allotted in such multiples that the other parties had scant moments to use the instrument of communication.

"What's the plan?" Evie asked.

"I need to contact Captain Bishop."

"Get off with me at the church and we'll try to use Dad's line."

I gratefully consented. If our call could not be made, I'd be stranded several miles from the house, and winter darkness set in quickly on these short afternoons. But what else could I do?

I asked Mrs. Steed to let me off at Evie's stop, convincing her that such an exit was necessary. Mrs. Steed ran her bus like Capone ran Chicago. Nobody tweaked the schedule without encountering a heavy dose of her particular red tape.

The church was dark already, nestled against the western hills that blotted out the sunshine that was barely finding its way through the grey clouds of mid-afternoon. With the exception of the bone-white steeple and towering cross on its roof, the church was already caving in to the shadows of winter's day. There were no lights on in the rear church office, and I was already conceding defeat as Evie twisted the lock on the office door and invited me inside.

"Daddy's at his other job," she explained. "We'll be the only people in the church. You scared, Oliver?"

"Cat got on climbing gear?"

"What?"

"Nothing. Where's the telephone?"

No Nose was on the line.

Evie listened quietly for a few minutes, then interrupted. "Excuse me, Mrs. Tate, this is Genevieve Creed. How are you today? No. Well, I'm sorry to hear that. Yes, ma'am. You're still on our prayer list. I put your name down in Sunday School just last week. Yes, ma'am, he does. He works that way. Well, we'll pray over that, too. Has your cat been feeling poorly long? That's pitiful. Yes, ma'am, I heard about that but Momma told me not to discuss that situation. That's mighty poor business, and... Yes, ma'am, I cannot discuss that either. Things like that happen.

"Mrs. Tate, I have an emergency call to make to the sheriff's office. Is it possible that I could borrow the line for five minutes? Yes, ma'am. I said the sheriff's office. Well, I'm not suppose to discuss this business. Yes, I understand you have such a right as a citizen, but if I don't call quickly... She did? Was she hurt badly? No, ma'am, you wouldn't know this person. Five minutes and then I promise I'll stop by your house after school tomorrow and tell you all about it. Well, yes, you have my sacred word of honor. Every detail. Five minutes and then you're back on. Don't pick up now. You'll break the connection. Please. Oh, thank you. Tomorrow for sure. Thank you. Bye."

Evie looked frustrated as she put her hand over the receiver. "That phony baloney," she said, disgusted. "Momma said there wasn't anything wrong with her that a good boost of the Holy Spirit wouldn't cure. She's got a minute to wind up her call. There she goes. Who do you want—the sheriff or the captain?"

"How about neither?" a voice asked before I could answer.

We both turned to see the silhouette in the office doorway.

There was just enough light from outside to overpower the dim illumination of the small desk lamp. But the visual was of minor consequence; I knew the voice and I knew Evie and I were probably in more trouble than either of us cared to imagine. Mitchell Rimple, the Pulitzer-aspiring writer, was there with us in the flesh.

I was tired of dancing with him. "Mr. Rimple, I presume," I said, covering the emotion that told me to clear out of this situation—to get clear of the Snow Girl suspect who was quickly cementing his position as a valid suspect with this tenacious pursuit of Evie and me.

"Are you stalking us? Is that how you get such great copy? Pursue the target until it acquiesces?"

"Target? Stalker?" he said, raising his voice. "Is that fair to be labeled as such by a pair of immature high school students? Labeled by two unlikely advocates of justice? Have I harmed or threatened to harm either of you little Christian converts? Could I not ask a few simple questions without the animosity?"

"If you have no objections," Evie said, "this little Christian girl will call for Captain Bishop to come sit in while you question us."

Rimple laughed. "Maybe we should have a lawyer present. Holmes is familiar with the legal profession. He recently caused the son of our most prominent practicing attorney to be incarcerated. He apparently has great persuasive powers with the law. Perhaps it is that persuasion that troubles me slightly, causes me to be tenacious as I seek answers from you two. Put the telephone down, freckle face."

His voice had dropped with effect as he got to the last sentence. Evie recognized the tone as well as I did. She laid the telephone close to the cradle, but not on it.

"Now, why would you two folks need to talk to Bishop or the jolly sheriff? Do you feel threatened in any way?" the reporter asked sarcastically.

"Why are you following us?" I asked. "You must have seen us get off the bus."

"Why are you two little miscreants hiding in the dark of the church? Perhaps a bit of good times without supervision? Ah ha, have we discovered the reason for your hideaway here in the church where no one seems to be around? Now I ask you, children, is that proper behavior in the house of your purported God?"

"Is it proper for a news reporter to stalk his story?" I asked, stepping a little forward of Evie.

"I don't stalk anyone. I don't stalk a story. I investigate unusual happenings—like bodies in the snow, Klan meetings at country shacks at midnight, lying little reprobates in downtown drugstores. Get my drift,

Bible thumper?"

"I get your drift. Do you get mine? How are you coming along on the Snow Girl mystery?" I asked. I figured I had nothing to lose.

I nudged Evie toward the door behind us. I had no idea where it lead but sooner than later we'd be needing it as a quick exit away from the man in front of us.

I couldn't see his face well in the dim light of the office lamp, but I could sense his erratic thinking from his tone and the inflection in his voice. He was an unpredictable person and a dangerous one.

"What do you mean?" he asked menacingly, referring to the Snow Girl.

"Did you see those two boys I was talking to back at the school?"

Rimple stood still and thought a minute. "I saw them," he said calmly. "Why do you ask?"

"They saw you, too."

"I imagine. What do you mean?"

"Those two backwoods brothers found something that belonged to the Snow Girl."

He remained in his spot just inside the door.

"What are you saying?"

"Her purse had a couple of pictures in it. Boother and Braska found it hanging from a limb over Owl's Creek. Guess what they did with it?"

Now he was totally cemented in place. If I could have seen his eyes , I could have measured our level of urgency in vacating the office. I nudged Evie toward the door again. She took a cautious step, eyeing our aggressor with intent.

"Why are you telling me this?" the reporter finally responded. "Do you have them?"

"They got passed along to the sheriff and Captain Bishop. Guess who was posed right next to our mysterious girl in the snow—smiling, with his arm around her shoulder?"

He seemed to smile in the half-light. "Are you baiting me, Holmes?

Are you pretending to know something you don't?"

"Pretending? Not really. I got a look at the photographs. If that's not you in the picture next to her, then you have an evil twin brother."

He still remained quiet.

I nudged Evie again. She took another small step.

"If there is such evidence against me, you little pimply-faced boy, why haven't the authorities descended upon me with Hell's purported fury?"

"Oh, they're ready to come get you, Rimple. They've been busy with other stuff, but they figured you weren't going anywhere."

"You're a lying little bit of white trash, aren't you?"

"Is that the best retort you have?" I asked, feigning bravery because I knew he was about to do something. I just didn't know what. "Why do you think I've been sidestepping you? I've known for a while about you. So does Captain Bishop. As soon as he gets his warrant, he'll be after you. And you know what else, prize winning reporter?"

Evie decided to put her two cents worth in. "God will forgive whatever sin you have committed, sir," she said. "Simply confess and ask forgiveness."

This time Rimple laughed out loud.

"You two little backwoods detectives have played a terrible hand, I'm afraid. The law has no more idea who left that young lady in the snow than I do. And I'm the investigator here. That's why I've been 'stalking' you, Holmes. I got word hereabouts that you know everything that goes on in this valley. I simply wanted to talk to you to get the full story. But, no, you have this paranoia about you that precludes my simple questions."

"Simple questions. All right, ask me a simple question."

He smiled and inched himself closer to the desk.

"Question one, Holmes. Where did you come up with the idea that there was a purse belonging to the unfortunate person in the snow?"

"Captain Bishop and the sheriff investigate, too," I said. "One of the sheriff's deputies traced the girl's boots and purse back to those two retards that live on Slow Mile Road."

"Retards? Slow Mile Road?"

"Yes. The boys I was talking to this afternoon at school. One of them waded Owl's Creek to get the purse off a branch of a tree. Wasn't it careless of you to leave such evidence at the scene of the crime?"

"What crime?"

"Whatever you did to her. She was alive at the dam, you know. If you had taken her to the hospital instead of hiding her in those bushes by the water, she might still be alive."

He was completely quiet for a moment.

"What evil tales you weave, little man."

"Let me know when I get close to the truth," I said, building to my theme. "I'm speculating a lot since I don't have all the details."

"Enlighten this poor reporter, Holmes. Tell me what you know."

"Speculation only, you understand," I said back to him. "She must have been someone you met at college, or soon after college, because she's younger than you are. She came from money so if you couldn't date Emily Brubaker—Miss North—you'd take a shot at another pretty lady. Except her daddy didn't want his daughter to date a nonachiever like you."

"Nonachiever?" he interrupted with a laugh.

"Not good enough for his daughter, at any rate."

He shrugged in the shadows and, though his voice was almost mocking in his response, I knew the danger remained. "Oh, we dated, Holmes. We were very good mates. She had money. I had brains. When she finished up at Ole Miss, she was coming here to be with me."

"What soured the deal then?" I wanted to know.

"Your little mind is seeking answers now. Why did we argue? Why did she run from the car barefooted? Why did I panic and leave her by the dam? You'd like to know those answers now, wouldn't you, smart mouth? You and your little literary mind, reading books too intricate for your understanding, using words too mature for your silly imagination, but showing that precociousness that shocks some people and causes others to detest your composed speech and your barnyard philosophy. Smart alecks like you make me want to shove their faces into a bucket of pig slop and hold it there until they quit talking. In your case, I'll delight in fixing your face permanently. You and your pretty, but equally sassy, girlfriend."

"You still haven't answered the motive question," I threw back at him. "Why did she run from the car? Did you hurt her?"

"No, smart butt, if you must know, I didn't lay a finger on her. We argued about motherhood as it affected her. She disagreed with my opinion of how she should approach that bit of news she came bearing. Ironically, although she disapproved of my solution for a permanent end to her approaching motherhood, she invoked the idea into action when she took off her boots and jumped out of the car onto the icy, snowy road."

"And then?" I asked.

"I'm innocent," he said, sadly, spreading his wide arms in surrender of the idea. "She slipped on the ice of the bridge and struck her head. When I went to her..." He dropped his arms and his head, and he seemed momentarily overcome with the tragedy he was forced to recall. He stood in silence for long moments of darkness, the shadows moving between us as the day lost ground to the impending darkness. I thought he may have released an emotional sob, but I wasn't sure. I knew he was less dangerous, but was capable of threatening two adolescents that were cautiously seeking an escape from the person who had brought the Snow Girl to our valley.

"But she was still alive when you put her down in the snow?" I said, brutally direct.

His head came up quickly, threateningly. "How do you know?"

"The captain told me. They did an autopsy."

He smiled, but in a sick way. "Leave it to your smart mouth to bring disheartening news."

"I said you could have saved her. You're the person who lost his sanity and put her down on the worst night of the year."

He paused again, his face confused in the shadows.

"Maybe I am insane, Holmes. This incident has raced through my consciousness a million times over the past few weeks. Going sleepless for long periods can cloud the brain and bring on thoughts. Different thoughts. Innocent thoughts that become ruined for all of us in this room."

He paused as if sorting out his thoughts. He looked into the darkness, then quickly back to me. "Sometimes people talk too much, say too much, act out too much. Theirs is an unpleasant perspective of the world that faces them. I believe that God of yours is testing me, asking me now what I'm going to do to relieve the pain that splits my heart into pieces over and over again. Over and over again. What can one do when there's no peace? When there are tears, no completeness to the wind. The wind can hear us. It can answer us. It heard me that night in the snow. It tried to whisper to me with that quiet insanity falling all around me, with the cold laying on me like a page from a Dickens novel, too thick to turn, too heavy to turn back. I can't go back over the pages. The book's too long. It requires reading forward. Books read forward only. Forward only. Like snow falling one way only. Only one way."

Evie punched me in the side. "Ollie," she whispered. "What are you doing?"

Rimple seemed to come slowly out of his trace and he became aware of our presence again.

"Yes, Holmes," he said, lowly, threateningly. "What are you doing?"

I shrugged with more bravado than I felt.

"This is no game," Evie said hoarsely. "Ollie, you're getting us into deeper trouble."

"How much trouble can you handle, Holmes?" the reporter asked, apparently hearing her request for me to ease up.

"You can't do anything to us, Rimple. We're under God's roof. He will protect us," I said.

He spread his arms in disbelief. "Where is your God, Holmes? I can't see Him. I don't feel his presence."

He chuckled as he stepped forward, almost to the front of the desk.

"God protects His own," Evie said firmly beside me. "We are His children and He has already won the battle against evil."

"Am I not also a child of God?" he asked with a laugh.

"You are His creation," Evie replied. "We are His children."

"You know, it's getting difficult for a good old atheist like me to carry on a conversation with converts like you folks. As violent and as passionate as you are down South here in cotton pickin' land, you still have this fascinating grasp of religion that startles me afresh every time you defend it, or embrace it, or call it your own—as if the rest of the world is simply wrong. Dead bone wrong. And you're always right."

He was coming around the desk now, and I saw him go into his jacket pocket and pull out something that glimmered in the occasional flicker of light. I pushed Evie toward the dark doorway just as the reporter's long arm, his hand clutching the knife, swung through the air toward me.

I quickly dodged his awkward lunge and followed Evie into the blackness of the hallway.

"Lock the door!" Evie screamed but I couldn't see anything, including the lock. Her hand grabbed mine and then she was stumbling and moving over the rough wooden floor as quickly as she could. I held her arm as tightly as possible, following her into a pithy darkness that promised no respite from the evil pursuit of our captor.

"Up these steps," she said, her breath coming short and fast as she began panting up the long staircase.

I looked up to see only a tight spot of light that seemed to beckon us. I had no idea where we were, having never seen this part of the church before.

"Follow me," Evie whispered. "This staircase leads to a high loft over the pulpit area."

It was an old church, built in the last century, so there were doors and passageways long closed off that were known only to the pastor's kids, I suppose. I only knew now that we made those steps with the help of the Good Lord because we had no idea where our pursuer was.

When we stopped on a landing at the top of the stairs, she looked confused in the pale light of some unknown source. I could see we were trapped between the man and the backside of the sanctuary ceiling.

"What now?" I panted.

"The wooden joists are so far apart we'll have trouble navigating them, but I've been up here before. Follow me. If we can get all the way to the front of the church," she said, "there's a window that opens to the roof. We can get through there."

We heard the running, stumbling steps of Rimple behind us, coming closer as we hesitated.

"Find that wooden area," I said. "Hurry! I'll follow you!"

Evie crouched, then jumped to a large piece of broken wood that offered support and a pathway to the front window, the source of the filtered light. Just as she landed, I felt something stir the air behind me and a strong hand had the collar of my jacket. Without thinking, I ducked low and shed the jacket in one swift movement, then I bolted the platform for the area where Evie waited. I made the jump, but the wood couldn't support both of us. With a loud splitting of ancient timber, the ceiling opened up below us and we both began sliding toward an enveloping hole.

Evie was not one to give up easily. Without a wimper, she reached for an old electrical cord that was hanging off the roof above us. The cord could not support our weight but we both got enough impetus to pull ourselves to the next joist, which groaned but did not collapse.

I risked a solitary look behind us and saw the dark form of Rimple crouched in fury, attempting to find a way to reach us.

Evie was making her way toward the next rough-hewed beam that offered a way to freedom, to safety, to the failing outside light. "Come on, Ollie," she said, her breath tight and short. "Try to make that next step."

I jumped the best I could from an unbalanced crouch and felt the flooring again giving way under me, but there was enough energy to get me to the next solid beam. Evie held out her hand for balance and tried to support her progress on the old church ceiling. The wooden expanse groaned in protest, but her weight was light enough to guarantee her passage forward.

With measured success, we began using the leap and pull procedure to work our way toward the window that represented hope. When I dared look back to ascertain Rimple's lot, I could see he was cautiously following us, staying just far enough away to spur his own advantage to the next step in the procedure.

When we got to about the middle of the church ceiling, Evie whispered, "He's gaining on us. Go ahead, Ollie," she said. "I'll find another way."

"We stick together."

"If we separate, Ollie, one of us has a chance."

I didn't know what to do. We needed another half dozen jumps to make the window. The planks seemed further apart and we could see no supportive target for our next jump. We were marooned on an island of desperation in the musty old attic and Rimple was fast approaching. "Evie, we've got to try to walk on the planking of the old ceiling," I said, anxiety effident in my voice. "We can't separate and we can't stay here. If we don't move, he'll have us."

As I said that, I looked back and saw that our stalker loomed larger than life. His movements seemed to foreshadow the pain and death his solitary blade would inflict upon us. I grabbed Evie's hands and pulled her out of Rimple's path. We rolled across the rickety planks, and Rimple's black form moved past us with a rush of stale air. The thrust of the weapon threw him into an awkward stance. He swayed back and forth unable to stabilize himself. Suddenly, he catapulted himself onto a large expanse of the century-old ceiling. For a second, he seemed suspended in air, and then the ceiling gave way completely. The scream of our attacker floated above his body as he disappeared into a hole he had created.

Captain Bishop arrived at the scene only minutes after Rimple's fall from grace. Mitchell Rimple had apparently not experienced God's grace. His bloody form on the altar of the White Oaks Baptist Church was as close to a sacred place as he had ever been.

20

"Call me Genevieve"

—Ron Miller

So it was ended.

All things became known in the community and a tranquil mood set in that let us get on with living without fear of every turn to the season.

Spring came around again to our valley and school activities took up a portion of our time. Evie and I were naturals for the junior-senior banquet and Momma used the reward money to send me off that night in enough style to satisfy everybody.

Weldon and Rand got all dressed up themselves and double-dated the Blue Branch twins for the crowning social affair of the school year.

I couldn't buddy with them so Uncle Doug let me borrow his Chevy. I was in heaven as I washed and polished the car that morning in the back-yard, anticipating the night ahead.

Genevieve, my friend and my girlfriend, broke tradition and put some makeup over her freckles and had her hair all dolled up at the beauty shop in town. She was the center of much attention as we danced on that old gym floor like we were on marble that our feet only touched when we descended from flight to go home.

When I took her to her front porch that night, she timidly looked at me from the shadows. With as much courage as I could muster, I kissed her full on the lips.

Sherman T. hadn't gone to the festivities but word got around that I had tasted sugar and he began badgering me immediately to tell him what it was like. I just grinned and never said a word. Uncle Doug Thomas slapped me on the back and told me to keep that token to myself. He understood how Evie and I were and he wanted me to savor all of life that I could with the innocence God intended.

But if I had to describe that singular moment to anyone, I'd say it was almost like the light kiss I'd received from Beatrice North when she left town and whispered a secret in my ear. Only this time, it was Evie who seemed to have plotted a different future for us as she ended our embrace with a touching of her own soft lips to my ear.

"Please call me 'Genevieve' from now on, Oliver," she whispered. And the night that had already turned magical for me extended itself into a realm of pure fantasy. Genevieve made me feel—*special.*

21
Doug Thomas' Passing

When Doug Thomas died the following autumn, a part of my youth died, too.

He had been working at a filling station, changing oil and doing light mechanical jobs. He and Miss Jewel had left Jamback and moved to Talladega so he could find that position, but he'd been there only a few months before he passed away. He had a heart attack at work and never recovered. He was forty-three years old.

I remember his funeral like it was yesterday: the bright, colorful American flag covering the coffin, the flowers, the family members I'd not seen since childhood—many aunts, uncles, cousins, and other kin I'd see that day and never again.

Grandmother Wilston was completely drained. Doug Thomas was her last born and the first to die. She sat broken-hearted by the coffin and cried and hugged everybody that came by to offer their prayers. Momma sat alone on the front pew and looked off into space, as if her passive love would lessen the pain.

I didn't know how to feel. It was my first family experience of losing someone close to me. I simply wanted to melt away from the bright autumn day. I wanted to be an apparition. I wanted to will myself invisible, get away to Cheaha Mountain so I could walk out on that Bald Rock Ledge where I could see more sky than earth. 'Cause I knew Doug's spirit was out there in that haze of the perfect fall afternoon. He was there, laughing, rolling a prickly cigarette in his skillful fingers, his eyes looking toward me as he told me not to worry about him. He was finally free.

I remembered where he was buried. Years later, as an adult, I would venture past his "swelling of the ground" on a Sunday afternoon after I'd driven through the autumn trees of Cheaha, having chased the sun down the Talladega ridge.

I would always laugh and say, "I've come to see you, Doug Thomas," and I'd remember how he used to whisper to me, "Let's get in out of the rain, Ollie. The night's cold and the storm is furious with us."

And in my mind, we two vagabonds would climb into the backseat of the car and he would laugh and hand me a stick of gum to chew on, or a candy bar to munch on, or he would simply grin so I'd have something to remember him by. Like he knew he'd go on way before I did and he wanted me to remember.

And I would.

For all my lifetime.

Other Books by the Author

A Broken Reed
Winner of Mayhaven's Award for Fiction
(Prequel to Jamback Road)

The Body-Doer

No Shirt, No Shoes, No Sting Ray